D1715603

LAST
DEADLY
LIE

LAST DEADLY LIE

by

CALEB PIRTLE III

Published by
McLennan House, Inc.
206 South Rogers
Waxahachie, Texas 75165

Copyright © 1986 by Caleb Pirtle III

Library of Congress Cataloging-in-Publication Data

Pirtle III, Caleb, 1941–
LAST DEADLY LIE
I. Title
ISBN 0–918865–11–5
Library of Congress Catalog Number: 87–60037
Manufactured in the United States of America
First Printing

For those newspapermen who let me write the way I wanted to. In order of appearance:

Neal Clark, *Gladewater Daily Mirror*
Jim Servatius, *Plainview Daily Herald*
Frank Friauf, *Fort Worth Star-Telegram*
Joe Titus, *Fort Worth Star-Telegram*
Lee Walburn, *Atlanta Journal/Constitution*
Chris Wohlwend, *Dallas Times Herald*
Mark Ivancik, *Dallas Times Herald*

Thank you.

Fret not thyself because of evil men, neither be thou envious at the wicked;

For there shall be no reward to the evil man; the candle of the wicked shall be put out.

—Proverbs 24:19–20

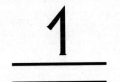

The sudden ringing of the telephone startled Alice in the darkness of an early July morning, but it was Birdie's flint-edged voice that jarred her awake.

"Max Gordon's missing," she said.

"What happened to him?" Alice brushed away a clump of blackened hair that had fallen over her eyes, and she sat up in bed, leaning back against the satin folds of her pillow.

"Nobody knows." Birdie stifled a hint of laughter. "He left home about nine o'clock last night, didn't tell Eunice goodbye or anything. Just drove away, and nobody's seen him since."

"Had he and Eunice been fighting?"

"Not that Eunice can remember."

"Who told you about Max leaving?"

"Eunice."

Alice shivered. "What does Eunice think?" she asked.

"Eunice thinks he's dead."

"Max is too busy to die."

Birdie softened her voice until it was almost a whisper. "I think he's run off with another woman."

"Then Eunice is right." It was all Alice could do to suppress the swell of excitement rising up within her. "If old Max has found himself another bed to whore in, he's as good as dead."

MAX Gordon's brains had been splattered against the bedroom wall, and to Nathan Locke the wet stain looked oddly enough like a weeping icon whose pleading eyes had been hollowed out by a shotgun blast. He frowned and straightened his silk tie, stepping out of the shadows that cowered in the musty corners of a cheap walkup hotel that catered mostly to drunks and drifters and girls of the night who gave away too cheaply what they could no longer sell. Nathan Locke suddenly felt very uneasy, almost oppressed by the surroundings. Silently he cursed the phone call, the strangely empty voice of Max Gordon, that had dragged him out of bed in the middle of the night. A chill wormed its way through his body, and a cold sweat dampened his forehead. Max Gordon had made a helluva mess of himself.

The aging banker lay across the bed, its yellowed sheets matted with his blood. A 12-gauge shotgun, a Christmas gift from his employees, was cradled in his arms. Max had often laughed about the gun. "It's beautiful, and somebody paid a lot of money for it," he would say. "But I'm not a hunter. I've never killed anything in my life. I don't know what the hell I'm gonna do with it."

Nathan Locke shuddered. Now he finally knew.

Max Gordon had his faults. But he was a gentle man who prided himself in always doing the right thing at the right time, saying the right words to the right people whether he meant them or not. He was a conservative—politically and otherwise—and he ran the bank's business by the book. Max Gordon never took a chance on himself or on anyone else. He was a civic leader, had served two terms as president of the Vicksburg Downtown Lion's Club, was an elder in the Basilwood Presbyterian Church, and had been, by far, the most effective fund raiser the YMCA ever had. Gordon had few close friends, but almost everyone in town knew his name and respected him. His picture was frequently published on the newspaper's society pages. He had no enemies, at least none that Nathan Locke knew about, and Nathan Locke made it a point to know everything he could about Max Gordon.

Gordon's ancestry dated back to the *Mayflower*. His mother had been a devout supporter and defender of the Daughters of the American Revolution. His grandfather swore allegiance to the Confederate gray that became his burial shroud two days after the sounds of gunfire had faded from the mud clay banks of Grand Gulf. He lived just long enough to witness the torching of his plantation home and hear the first whimpering cries of a baby son he would never hold to his inflamed chest. The ground that had held his cotton hid his fortune, back among the trees and vines that clotted together on the edge of the bayous in Blanchard Swamp. The slaves knew where it was. They had stuffed the landowner's money and silver in old crockery pots and buried them deep within the soggy earth. But the slaves didn't bother Marse Gordon's fortune. They simply waited until he was put away, then packed their ragged belongings and left, following the Yankee army's footsteps that finally led them north and beyond those vast fields of unpicked Mississippi cotton.

In time, Max Gordon himself became sole keeper of the old family money. He guarded it wisely, watched it grow, and let it buy for him the presidency of the suburban Basilwood National Bank. He wasn't miserly, just cautious. And no one, outside of Nathan Locke, had ever successfully tapped into any portion of the Gordon fortune.

"It's God's will," Locke had said.

"I'll stand up to any man," Max Gordon answered. "But I don't argue with God."

"It's for His work."

"He can depend on me."

"God bless you." Nathan Locke had pocketed the check without bothering to even look at it.

"He already has."

God wouldn't have to worry about Max Gordon anymore. Locke glanced down at him. The old man's skin was a harsh white beneath the single, naked light bulb that shone down from above him. A fly kept wading through the drying blood that seeped into the pillowcase. Locke stared at the banker's face. It had always been a kind face, a pleasant face. It was missing, replaced by a ragged hole where once there had been a smile.

The chill deepened in the room.

There were some people, Locke told himself, that he simply expected to live forever.

Max Gordon was one of them.

A banker. A husband. A father. Age sixty-two.

Now he was dead.

Why? *Why not?*

Max Gordon always did the right thing at the right time. That was his style, and he even bragged about it. He was so damn predictable. Why doubt him now?

On the last night of his life, Gordon had dressed in his finest gray, pinstripe suit, probably kissed his wife goodbye, told her not to worry, and walked out of his fine, two-story brick home in Basilwood Heights. His patent leather shoes were obviously newly shined, and his nails had been freshly manicured. Gordon was so meticulous, so well groomed in life, he wouldn't dream of meeting death any other way.

He had carefully pulled the flowered bed-covering back, lay down, and straightened the wrinkles from his suit. Max Gordon had placed his head on an old, foam rubber pillow, stuck the barrel of his shotgun into his mouth, took his final breath, and pulled the trigger with his thumb. It was, Locke reasoned, probably the first time Max Gordon had ever gone to bed in his life without first removing his shoes.

How long did he lay there?

Waiting.

Did he hear the shot that killed him?

Was there pain?

Or just sudden darkness?

What was Max Gordon's last thought in that frozen moment of time, wedged between the echo of the blast and eternity, when the old man must have suddenly realized that he could no longer prevent what he had done to himself.

Was there regret?

Shock?

Remorse?

Or satisfaction.

Nathan Locke took a deep breath and stepped toward the young policeman who had been kneeling beside Max Gordon's limp and waxen body, unaware that anyone else had come into the bedroom. The unexpected sound of footsteps startled him.

The officer looked up, his face strained, and asked, "Who the hell are you?"

"Nathan Locke." The voice was deep and incisive. "I received a telephone call from Mr. Gordon about an hour ago, asking me to meet him here." He paused and glanced again at the twisted body lying amongst the crumpled and faded flowers of the bedspread. It no longer looked human, just an odd assortment of arms and legs that had lost the brain it needed to guide them. "I'm Mr. Gordon's minister."

The policeman nodded. His eyes were tired and had a callous look. "I'm afraid you got here a little late."

"Could you please tell me what happened?"

"It's obvious. The old guy got tired of living and blew his brains out."

"Are you sure?"

The policeman stood, and a scowl darkened his face. "What does it look like to you?"

Locke shrugged. "Was there a note?" he asked.

"All typed out and lying neatly folded beside the phone."

That sounded like Max Gordon, Locke thought. He was so prim, so proper, such a fastidious businessman, he probably even had his secretary type out his own suicide note.

"May I see it?" the minister inquired. "Max called, but he didn't wait for me to get here. The note may have been meant for me."

The policeman shook his head. "The coroner has it. You can ask him when he's finished his investigation here." The young officer yawned and pulled a blanket from the closet, pitching it over the remains of Max Gordon.

Poor Max, Nathan Locke thought. What had possessed him to do such a deed? He was a successful businessman. He had a fine, though somewhat aggressive, son who worked in the bank with him. His wife was a pillar of Vicksburg society. He taught Sunday School. He made a lot of money, and he certainly didn't spend a lot of it foolishly. Max Gordon was financially set for life. But then, life could sometimes be unexpectedly and devastatingly short.

"When did it happen?" he asked.

"We got the call about two-thirty," the policeman answered, sitting down on the edge of the bed. "The manager of this place phoned in and said he had heard a shotgun blast. It woke him up. He tried to open the door to Gordon's room, but it was locked."

"Were you the first person here?"

"I kicked the door in." The officer glanced over his shoulder and saw the blood beginning to soak through the threadbare blue blanket. "It was messy," he said.

"Death always is."

Nathan Locke turned as a small, balding, puffy-faced man

with ashen eyes came through the doorway. His brown suit was wrinkled, and his tie was askew as though it were slung around his neck as an afterthought. He carried a black bag and stared at Locke through thick, horn rim glasses.

"That's the dead guy's pastor," the policeman said, his voice devoid of any emotion. "It seems like the deceased gave the Reverend Mister Locke a telephone call before he stuck the gun in his mouth."

The puffy-faced man frowned and arched an eyebrow. For a moment, he studied the minister before him, making mental notes as precise as any autopsy. Tall, probably an inch—maybe two—over six feet. A hundred eighty pounds, though a well-tailored suit usually made a man look thinner than he really was. Green eyes. A touch of gray in his black hair. Well tanned angular face, good-looking enough to be a prime-time television evangelist. And clean shaven. The puffy-faced man narrowed his eyes. He didn't trust anybody who was clean-shaven at three o'clock in the morning. He didn't recognize the odor of the cologne; no doubt imported and expensive, probably a gift from some well-meaning, doe-eyed sister in the preacher's congregation.

"I'm Doc Murray," he said as though bored with both his name and his job. "I'm the coroner. When there's a violent death around here, I'm the one they call to try and figure out how it happened. I seldom know who did it. I hardly ever know why it was done. There are some secrets that the dead insist on keeping to themselves." He paused, fumbled a moment with the black bag, then asked softly, "What time did Mr. Gordon call you?"

"At two–seventeen."

"You're sure about that."

"The clock sits right beside the telephone. It was the first thing I saw when I turned on the light."

Doc Murray nodded. "What did he say?"

"That he wanted to see me."

"When?"

"As soon as I could get here."

"Why?"

Nathan Locke paused and took a deep breath. "It had something to do about money."

Doc Murray rubbed his eyes and reached for his note pad. "Did Mr. Gordon owe you some money?"

"No."

"Did you owe Mr. Gordon some money?"

Nathan Locke forced a weak, almost apologetic, grin. "Mr. Gordon was a banker. Everybody owed him money."

Murray's chuckle was audible. His eyes darted quickly around the small room. The carpet was threadbare and stained with mud and cheap whiskey. The curtains were torn and smelled of dust. Dust strings and cobwebs decorated the lamp shade, and the sheets had been washed but never bleached. The mirror was badly cracked. The bedspread had cigarette burns. And a two-dollar, dime store Picasso print hung crookedly on the wall above the bed. The face of the man in the painting had been rearranged with an artist's brush. Max Gordon had rearranged his with a shotgun. The room must have been a sad and lonely place to die.

"Do you receive a lot of telephone calls at two–seventeen in the morning?" the medical examiner asked.

"More than I'd like." Nathan Locke suddenly wanted a

whiskey, and he felt a trickle of cold sweat inch down into the small of his back. "But people get depressed during the night, and that's when they want to talk to a minister. Listening to them is part of my job."

"Had Max Gordon been depressed?"

"He hadn't mentioned it to me."

"Did he make it a habit of calling you during the middle of the night?"

"Max was strictly a nine to five man."

"Why do you think he decided to call you tonight?"

Nathan Locke slowly shook his head and rubbed the back of his neck. A dull ache had settled into his temples, and a sharp pain seared his eyes. "I don't know," he answered. "Maybe he didn't really want to die. Maybe he wanted me to talk him out of it."

"He didn't wait on you."

"That's ironic, isn't it?" Locke said mostly to himself. "Max Gordon never made an appointment in his life that he didn't keep."

Doc Murray turned back to the blanket-wrapped body and jammed his notepad into the pocket of his coat. "Well, I've done what I came here to do," he said. "The ambulance boys should be here shortly to haul him away." He looked up at Nathan Locke and asked, "Do you want to say a prayer or something before we go?"

"It's a little late for that."

"That's what I thought. But some preachers are always looking for an excuse to pray, and death seems to be about as good as any excuse around."

"Max doesn't need our prayers anymore," Locke said, his

throat dry. "Wherever he's going, he's already there. Max just needs our sympathy." He nervously rubbed his hands together. "I understand he left a note."

Doc Murray looked surprised.

"I told him about it," the policeman said.

"There was a note," the medical examiner confirmed.

"May I see it?"

"Any particular reason?"

Nathan Locke's voice softened. "When a man takes his own life, if indeed Max did take his own life, it's an extremely difficult act for a family to understand and accept. Mr. Gordon's wife, I'm sure, will have a lot of questions. She no doubt will come to me for answers. I'd like to have a few for her."

"That makes sense."

Doc Murray reached into his coat pocket and withdrew a piece of letterhead stationery from the Basilwood National Bank and slowly unfolded it. Nathan Locke's voice, he thought, was suddenly full of warmth and compassion, and he wondered for a moment if aspiring young preachers took courses in warmth and compassion at seminary. Probably. His eyes quickly scanned the note, but he made no effort to hand it to the minister.

"Do you know a Martha Landers?" the medical examiner asked placidly.

Locke straightened his tie again. "No," he lied.

"Max Gordon did."

"Did she have something to do with his death?"

"She apparently had a lot to do with his life." Doc Murray

folded the note and put it back in his pocket. "I'm sorry," he said, "but for the time being, I think I'll just keep Max Gordon's last words to myself. If his wife needs any answers, just hold her hand and quote her something out of the Twenty-third Psalm."

Nathan Locke waited in pious silence for the mortuary attendants to come and take Max Gordon away. He watched as they wrapped him in a black body bag, loaded him on a stretcher, and bounced him down two flights of wooden stairs to the lobby of the Jefferson Davis Hotel.

The night manager grimaced as the corpse was wheeled past him. He didn't like for anything to ruin his shift, and Max Gordon had done a damn good job of it. Hell, he thought, he might never get the bloodstains out of a perfectly good sheet, and he might even wind up having to buy a new one out of his own paycheck. The thought gave him indigestion, and he took a red pill from his shirt pocket and knew he would feel like a million dollars before morning. A drunk lying on a hand-me-down sofa beside the door stopped snoring long enough to open one eye and belch.

Only the blonde sitting on the edge of her first-story window had any remorse for the dear and departed Max Gordon. She didn't know him. She had never seen him. But she knew she could have made his final hours a lot better than they had been—for a price, of course. Too bad . . . after the shot, she could have had it all. The blonde yawned and wondered where all the men had gone for the night.

Nathan Locke turned his car toward Basilwood Heights and felt his shoulders tighten. His headache had grown worse,

and there were, at times, spots exploding like flashbulbs before his eyes, dancing wildly amidst the neon that ran down
empty sidewalks like ragged, broken scars.

Before morning, he would have to tell Eunice Gordon that
she had suddenly become a widow.

He had no other choice.

Eunice would stand there in her satin robe, her face pale,
and stare at him with sleepy, disbelieving eyes. She would
probably utter something that sounded somewhat like a
scream, maybe even gasp for breath, grow angry, then bitter,
and finally waste the rest of the night wallowing in a bed of
self-pity. And all the time, she would be asking him, "Why?"

He didn't know why.

Only Max knew why.

And what the hell was he doing with Martha Landers?
Why in the hell did Max drag him out of bed in the middle
of the night, then go ahead and blow himself away among
strangers in a cheap hotel?

"I've got a problem," Max had said as calmly as if he had
been denying or approving a loan. "I need to talk to you."

"Good Lord, Max," Locke had answered groggily. "Do
you have any idea what time it is?"

"I know."

"Can't it wait until morning?"

"No."

"Where are you?"

Max had told him.

"What are you doing in a place like that?"

Max had hung up. He had hung up for good.

There were times when Nathan Locke wished he had

dropped out of seminary and gone into business like any other sane man would have done. This was one of those times.

He liked preaching.

He liked the prestige it gave him.

Privately, to himself, Locke even admitted that he liked the power it gave him.

But he couldn't stand it when people were slobbering all over him with their tears, expecting him to give a damn about their problems when he had trouble enough taking care of his own problems. They were parasites, always hanging on to him, never giving him room to live his own life, choking him with their stupid little afflictions until he sometimes could hardly breathe. The Reverend Locke's head pounded, and the July heat had plastered his shirt to his back with sweat.

What would he tell Eunice Gordon?

What did she want to hear?

The truth?

Probably not. Nobody ever wanted to hear the truth. *I am the way and the truth and the light.* The scripture kept running through his head, and it would not leave him alone. It haunted him. Okay. So God was truth. Nathan Locke could accept that. But everybody else he knew lived a lie.

Even Max Gordon.

Nathan Locke had plans of his own. But that didn't seem to ever matter. People expected him to be there when they needed him, and they always needed him. They wouldn't leave him alone. And he sometimes felt that hundreds of greedy, selfish hands were always reaching for him, grabbing him, tearing him apart, pulling him in every direction at once, dragging him down, sucking the very life from his veins. It was always something they needed. A prayer here. A scripture there. A song. A confession. Somebody was usually sick or on the verge of dying, about to fall in love or out of marriage. His time belonged to everyone but himself.

And now, Max Gordon had ruined a perfectly good weekend. There was a widow to comfort, a casket to close, a telephone call to Nashville that he dreaded to make. Someone was there waiting for him, someone soft and gentle, someone who loved him very much, and Nathan Locke would be tied up with a funeral. *Swing Low Sweet Chariot.*

He silently cursed his misfortune.

He cursed his fate.

Max Gordon didn't need the Twenty-third Psalm.

He did.

Max Gordon was a no-good, inconsiderate son of a bitch.

$$\underline{\underline{2}}$$

Alice couldn't believe what she was hearing.

"They found Max last night," Birdie was saying into the telephone.

"Who found him?"

"The police."

"Good Lord. What had Max been doing?"

"Max is dead."

Alice caught her breath and reached for a cigarette to steady her nerves.

"From what I hear," Birdie said confidentially, "Max stuck the barrel of his shotgun in his mouth and shot the top of his head clear off."

"Jesus Christ!"

"Splattered himself all over the room."

"My God, Birdie." Alice's voice was shaking. "Why would Max want to go and kill himself?"

"I think it had something to do with money."

"Max had a lot of money."

"If you ask me, I think Max got caught stealing from his own bank."

NATHAN Locke, from his vantage point behind the Bible, surveyed the eyes, hundreds of them, more like thousands of them, that had come to mourn the harsh and untimely passing of Max Gordon. Some had been crying. A few were closed in prayer. Maybe they were just asleep. And most were wide with unabashed curiosity. It seemed to Locke that the whole town of Vicksburg had crowded into the new rock sanctuary of the Basilwood Presbyterian Church to pay its last respects and pass on its latest rumors. The South, as he knew, took its deaths quite seriously, especially in its smaller cities, always when the deceased had been a man of power and wealth and there was the possibility of his being laid to rest amidst whispers of a dubious and tainted past. Human nature, Locke had known for a long time, was a fragile and contradictory thing. It abhorred the thought of dying. Yet, it treated death like a carnival sideshow and

19

couldn't wait to see how long it would take for the hurt and grieving widow to break down and maybe even collapse before their prying eyes. Human nature wanted tears and lots of them. A morbid kind of lust dwelt deep within its collective soul, and it liked standing close enough to hear the sound of a heart when it broke. It had no use at all for proud, stoic women who could put their men away with unbowed, unflinching faces.

Vicksburg should be satisfied with Eunice Gordon.

It was obvious she had been crying most of the night and all morning. Her shoulders trembled, and her face was buried in a lace handkerchief, no doubt federal expressed in for the occasion by Neiman-Marcus of Dallas. Eunice, pale in black, had leaned heavily on her son's arm as he led her into the church, and they were seated together in the front pew, their faces highlighted by the multicolored reflections of sunshine through stained glass. The crowd was straining to watch her every move, and many cried along with her. It was a time to cleanse the soul, and nothing was as effective as tears; the more the better.

Paul Gordon, the only son of the Vicksburg Gordon clan, stared straight ahead, his jaws clenched. But then, Paul's jaws were always clenched. He had grown up an angry young man, and the years had not subdued his anger. In college, he had worn long hair and faded jeans, and his father had thrown him out of the house. Paul had protested against the war, the president, the national debt, the plight of the blacks in Mississippi and South Africa, and the wanton killing of whales, Vietnam villagers, and any animal for sport. His hair was shorter now, styled once a month for $22.50, and his suits were tailor-made and never faded, seldom even wrinkled. He had come back home from California, traded in his degree for a vice-presidency at the bank, and was still protesting against the national debt, but nothing else. Paul was angry at his father for living off inherited wealth, and he was angry at himself for accepting it. He hated the money. He couldn't let go of it. It was his weakness. It was his passion. Paul Gordon wanted it all.

Nathan Locke's dark eyes scanned the scriptures he had prepared to comfort those who had come to be comforted and entertain those who had come for the show. A preacher's reputation depended on how well he could send some wretched soul on to its eternal reward. The rich old reprobates in Mississippi didn't care what anybody said about them as long as they were alive. They treated business as a good game of liar's poker, and they based their life on one basic homespun commandment: a man wasn't guilty unless he got caught, and those with enough money never got caught, much less convicted. Idle talk, no matter how malicious, never bothered them. But when the time came to lay it all down and give up the ghost, they wanted those final words spoken over them to be strong, powerful, and unforgettable. It was their last shot to have something akin to immortality etched in stone. Truth was not a prerequisite. Never had been. Never would be.

Nathan Locke smiled to himself. At the moment, he had everything he needed.

A rich and respected corpse.

An overflowing crowd.

A cooperative widow who knew how to sob loud enough and often enough to be heard on the back row.

And a sermon that would knock them dead.

Nashville suddenly didn't seem so important to him anymore. Nashville would always be there.

Nathan Locke quietly cleared his throat. Today, he would put Max Gordon's memory in touch with immortality. Old Max could indeed be proud that he had had enough guts to pull the damn trigger.

The stifled hush of the sanctuary was broken by the soft, mellow tones of the pipe organ, and by the rich baritone voice of John Madison, resplendent in his deep burgundy red robe, his bearded face aglow in the flickering light of a candle that not even the sunshine could dim. Nathan Locke could picture the scene behind him without bothering to turn around. John's head would be thrown back, his round face sweating, his hands clasped together tightly, and his eyes closed as if in meditation. He was singing, "How Great Thou Art," but Locke surmised that the young choir director's mind was on neither God nor Max Gordon. Hell, John Madison was singing about himself. His voice echoed throughout the sanctuary, and his words wavered slightly as though they were hanging in his throat by a single teardrop. Music was John's life. It was his ministry. He sang for churches, any denomination would do, at schools, civic clubs and banquets. If anybody wanted a song, John Madison had one, and he would sing all fourteen verses, if it had that many, and some of them twice. He read music. He wrote music. And he had a degree that said he read it and wrote it better than just about anybody else in Mississippi. He made old woman cry and young woman swoon. Personally, Nathan Locke didn't like the little bastard.

The minister shifted his weight in the high-backed chair

and casually stroked the black velvet armrest, gazing pensively out across the congregation. Most of the faces he recognized. The others, he guessed, were from out of town, probably men who had gambled with Max Gordon in the money game. No wonder they were looking so sad. Max didn't play unless he knew he could win.

Eunice Gordon was wiping her eyes, and she had bravely twisted a smile between the tearstains. Paul looked as sullen as ever. Locke hoped he would never have to tangle with Paul Gordon in a business deal. The young man was cold and calculating. He could be dangerous. But then, Max's son had always been more concerned about whales than his fellow man, with whom he had very little in common.

Birdie Castleberry was sitting just behind the immediate family, wringing her hands, because that's what she thought she was supposed to do, and trying to cry louder than Eunice Gordon so everyone would know she was there, up close, front and center. She had arrived at the church an hour early to make sure she got a good seat. Nobody enjoyed a juicy tragedy more than Birdie Castleberry. She thrived on grief and gossip. And if, perchance, no one happened to be suffering from any trial or tribulation, you could always count on Birdie to find a storm cloud behind every silver lining.

She was in Nathan Locke's office at least twice a day, always willing to share what she knew about everybody in town, and she didn't know anything good about anybody. Birdie was an obvious pain in the ass, but Locke didn't particularly mind. She was also his eyes and his ears in the church, and a preacher, like a politician, always needed to know who was for him and who was against him. Birdie Castleberry knew. Right or wrong, she knew. She was Clerk of the Session, the governing body of the Basilwood Presbyterian Church, and she loved the power it gave her. Nathan Locke gave her all the power she wanted, and Birdie told him everything he needed to hear. She functioned behind two basic philosophies: gossip repeated twice became Truth, and secrets weren't worth having unless someone else knew them, and she always made sure someone else did.

Alice Setzer, twice widowed, once divorced, sat shoulder to shoulder with Birdie Castleberry. She seldom found time to sleep at night, believed that the plots from most soap operas were based on her life, and she was Birdie's personal grapevine. One word to Alice, and telephones began ringing all over Vicksburg. AT&T, Nathan Locke sometimes thought, should have named her Woman Of The Year.

Alice was slim, almost petite, and she refused to grow old gracefully, not as long as there was a doctor in Jackson who could cut away the wrinkles beneath her eyes without leaving any scars. She had been married to the Mayor-Pro Tem of the city, but he gave her up for a twenty-six-year-old blonde who sometimes doubled as his secretary and spent more time massaging his back than gossiping on the telephone.

Alice Setzer was an embittered, martyred woman with piercing eyes and a pinched face who saw no reason why others should not suffer as badly as she had. Locke noticed that the flecks of gray were magically gone from her hair. He smiled to himself. Hairdressers in Vicksburg always did do a good business before the morning of a funeral.

Locke sorted out other faces in the crowd. Howard Daniels

had closed his print shop to come and say farewell to Max Gordon. It was the least he could do. Gordon had been loaning him money for the past decade or so, never complaining at all when the payment was a month or two late, and most of them were. Howard Daniels was a man Nathan Locke knew the church could depend on, sincere, hard-working, the salt of the earth. Daniels owned one suit, a dark green polyester, that he wore to church, and his appointment to the Board of Trustees, he had often said, was the most important thing that had ever happened to him. Daniels, at forty-seven, was overweight. His dark green suit fit too tight across his broad, sagging shoulders. His fingernails were stained permanently by grease and dried press ink. But it was good, honest dirt, and his eyes smiled even when he was sad. The eyes were now crying for Max Gordon.

Raymond Lynch, thin and wiry, wearing glasses much too big for his face, was the eighth-grade history and social studies teacher, an activist at heart who had come to Mississippi three years earlier from a private school in Massachusetts. He had simply grown tired of teaching about the moral values of civil rights to a classroom untainted by a black face. He had, at last, rebelled against his own hypocrisy, packed up, hit the road, took a wrong turn in Tuscaloosa, and wound up in Vicksburg, where he found a school that had all the black faces he wanted. The hubcaps on his '79 Pontiac were stolen during his first week in town. Raymond's pants and sport coat seldom matched, and his striped tie was at least two years out of date. His sandy hair was thinning, and he wore tennis shoes, regardless of the occasion. But Nathan Locke saw that Raymond had dug out his cleanest dirty sneak-

ers to honor Max Gordon. Raymond Lynch was a wild-eyed
liberal in a land that had no affection for wild-eyed liberals,
even those who had found some rational justification behind
the banker's decision to end his own life.

"It was a protest," he said to Locke as the two men strolled
together across the late-night darkness of the funeral home's
parking lot.

"I don't buy it."

"Why not?"

"Max wasn't the kind." The headlights of a passing car
flashed across Locke's face. "A man protests when he wants
something and can't get it. Max had everything."

"Not everything."

"What in God's name could the man want?"

"Freedom."

Raymond grinned. Nathan Locke frowned.

"Freedom from what?" the minister asked.

"How would you like to be married to Eunice Gordon?"

Locke felt like laughing. Maybe Raymond wasn't so wild-
eyed after all.

He closed his eyes and tried, for a moment, to imagine
Eunice Gordon, all hot and bothered in a black lace negligee,
lathered up in a fit of unbridled passion, then decided that
unbridled passion was probably against her religious upbring-
ing. So were black lace negligees. Prim. Proper. A fragile,
aging china doll. That's what Eunice Gordon was. Look—
but don't touch. Break it—and it's yours. Eunice Gordon
had never been broken. Nor bought. Nor owned. By anyone.

Max had kept her reasonably happy—at least his money
had. It kept her running in the right social circles and playing

bridge on Thursday mornings at the right country club. Most importantly, it kept her prominent in the social columns of the daily newspaper. Vicksburg might not know her. But Vicksburg certainly knew her name, and that was all Eunice Gordon really cared about.

She had one basic regret in life.

Max Gordon had loaned George Edward Basil the millions he needed to conceive and build the fashionable suburb in which she now lived. It was, she sincerely believed, a place strictly for those who happened to be rich and important and Presbyterian, and she was always afraid that Baptists and Methodists would run the neighborhood down, even if they drove Cadillacs, and those who lived in Basilwood Heights did.

Eunice hated the name of Basilwood Heights.

The community should have been called Gordon. Maybe Gordon Acres would have been nice. Or Gordon Gardens.

And she never let Max forget it, especially when he foreclosed on George Edward Basil and finished the second and final phase of the development himself.

Nathan Locke's intense, dark eyes sought out Katherine Basil in the crowd, and found her. It wasn't difficult. She was a portly woman, a proud woman who apparently gave up diets years ago and enjoyed every inch of her two hundred pound body. Her face was round, her hair red and piled up, as always, into a frivolous clump on top of her head, and her bosoms were a test for any fabric. Locke wondered if the lace bodice she was wearing would stand up to the immense strain and decided that it probably didn't make Katherine Basil much difference. She had always bragged, behind certain closed doors, that George liked his women big and often, and she had never disappointed him. George had died where he spent a great deal of his life.

The recession of the late seventies had been rough on those who gambled with somebody else's money, particularly if it belonged to the bank. George Basil went to sleep one April night a rich man, and he woke up bankrupt. Two weeks later, as he lay sprawled between his wife's enormous breasts, his heart gave out its last normal beat, then gave out for good. he coughed once, belched, and died with a hard-on.

Katherine Basil always blamed Max Gordon.

The day Max foreclosed on Basilwood Heights, she often said bitterly, was the day George began to die. He lost hope, then his faith, then his confidence in himself. He had built one fortune with his bare hands. But then, he was simply too old, too tired, and too demoralized to try it again. Max Gordon had been his friend. Max Gordon had stabbed him in the back. When a man has nothing to live for, you might as well go ahead and type up his obituary, Katherine Basil had told Locke when he came to comfort her, because he's going to need it. He's a dead man even before he draws his final breath.

Katherine Basil sat with her head held high and her arms folded in defiance.

Let Eunice Gordon cry for awhile.

Let her sleep alone when the nights grew cold.

Katherine Basil was wearing the only smile in the church.

All the faces were there that were supposed to be there. For some, funerals were social events, places where it was important to be seen. New dresses. New suits. New shoes.

New questions. No answers. And people had a tendency to talk about people who didn't come or were afraid to come or had some deep-seated reason not to come.

Tom Beecher, the retired state attorney general, had flown in from a weekend bass fishing trip on Florida's Lake Okeechobee. He was a crusty old maverick who preferred fish to people, but who had taken care of Max Gordon's legal affairs for years. If anyone knew Max's secrets, if anyone knew what insanity might have crept into the banker's brain, it would be Tom Beecher. His eyes were closed, and Locke suspected that the old barrister was snoring.

Wade Ferguson had cut short a fund-raising seminar in Jackson—it took an act of God to tear him away from making money. Short and rotund, Wade had been born with a perpetual smile and a natural gift for shaking hands, stroking the well-connected, and loosening up the grip they had on their collective bank accounts. If there happened to be a spare dollar anywhere that was earmarked for charity or politics, Wade Ferguson would figure out a way to get it.

Charles Page was probably wondering what would happen to his investments now that Max was no longer around to keep an eye on them and refinance the losses every year or so. Charles no longer knew how much money he had, nor did he care. When he reached the age of seventy-five, he simply turned all of his ideas and bookwork over to Max Gordon and said, "Send me a check every month until the funds run out." Max had diligently done what he was told. He also cut checks each month for Wade Ferguson, for the church, and, of course, for himself. Wade sat next to Charles, and before the service began, he had whispered, "Don't worry. I'll find you another good banker." Locke hoped they wouldn't forget the church.

Morris Adams, wearing his white carnation boutonniere, his trademark, was representing Presbytery. Years ago, he had been privileged to glimpse Max Gordon's will, so this was obviously one funeral he couldn't afford to miss. He had arrived late so that everyone would know he had come to share Eunice Gordon's sorrow. Now he settled comfortably into the velvet pew cushion and hoped that Nathan Locke wouldn't get carried away with his own words and preach all morning.

Susan and John Heatherley, newcomers who were still working hard to break into Vicksburg society, never turned down an invitation to a party. And as far as Susan was concerned, Max Gordon's funeral just might be the most important party of the year. She was only sorry that poor Max had not been considerate enough to take his life back in December, back when it would have been cold enough for her to wear her Russian sable jacket. When she had it on, Susan Heatherley had often told herself as she modeled it before her bedroom mirror, she just might be the most stunning woman in Vicksburg. She was certainly the most tempting, and she wasn't hesitant at all about showing off her beauty, particularly at cocktail parties, which was one reason why wives kept omitting her name from their invitation lists.

And, of course, there was Helen Jensen, her short hair frosted the color of sunshine, sitting alone, seething because her husband was in court instead of in church. Robert was always in court, an attorney who had an office on the outskirts of town and generally took care of blacks who stabbed, shot, vandalized or divorced each other. The Jensens drove ten miles every Sunday morning just so Helen could be a part of Basilwood Presbyterian Church. She found a measure of prestige mingling with those who had money, and she spent every extra dollar Robert earned shopping where they shopped and buying what they bought, whether the Jensens could afford it or not.

Nathan Locke sometimes felt uncomfortable, the way Helen would sit there during worship and stare at him as though he were standing naked before God and the church. Maybe to her, he was. He pitied her. Helen Jensen was so damn insecure, and she kept smiling at him, her eyes reaching out to him. If she lost ten or twenty pounds, she might even be a good-looking woman.

Locke looked closer and frowned. The faces that should be there weren't all there after all.

One was missing.

Where the hell was Martha Landers?

And *what* had Max Gordon written to her or about her the night he met his maker?

Martha Landers. Sweet. Lonely. Unwed. And unwanted. Or did Max know something about her that no one else had even suspected?

Locke tried to put her out of his mind. He couldn't be worried about Martha Landers now. That would come later. Maybe even tonight. First, he had a job to do, one full of pomp and circumstance and dignity.

That's what the good people of Vicksburg expected and demanded at their funerals, and, by God, that's what Nathan Locke would give them.

They wanted someone to find meaning in an abominable act that had no meaning.

Nathan Locke could see it in the eyes that burned with shame, especially among the wealthy, among those who had known Max Gordon best. Max, in death, had disgraced them all. The hotel had been a two-bit whorehouse. The room had smelled of cheap whiskey and stale cigarette butts. The bed on which the remains of Max Gordon lay had been broken in, then broken down, an hour at a time, by men with no last names and working women who were as broken in and broken down as the mattress itself. And Max, God forbid, had had the indecency to scatter his brains with a squirrel gun.

A man of his stature deserved better.

The time had come for Nathan Locke to right a wrong, to make sense of the senseless. He felt a sudden swell of excitement, a surge of power, rising up within him. The life and death of Max Gordon no longer mattered. All that Vicksburg cared about was what he—the Reverend Nathan Locke—had to say about the life and death of Max Gordon.

The crowd had not come to see Max Gordon.

Max was gone.

Ashes to ashes.

And dust to dust.

The crowd had come to see him.

And like a puppeteer, he knew how to pull and manipulate the strings attached to their emotions. He could touch their memories and make them smile. He could ease their pain, find a way to put their fears to rest, squeeze their hearts until they cried, then brush away the tears. It was an art. It was drama, Greek tragedy at its best. All the world's a stage, someone had written, and now he stood there upon it alone, and he held the trusting, fragile lives that flocked before him in the palm of his hand.

Gentle.

Compassionate.

They waited, and they hungered.

For a word.

A prayer.

A eulogy.

A reason for living and for dying.

The sanctuary became silent and expectant as the last notes of John Madison's singing voice hung for a moment among the exposed wooden rafters, then slowly faded away. Nathan Locke stepped forward, his black robe rustling slightly against the carpet, his face framed by the flowers that had been grouped ceremoniously around Max Gordon's silver casket, mostly roses and mostly red, blood red.

The Bible lay open in his hand, and Locke's gaze was so hypnotic, so forceful, that even the crying stopped. He stood there, looming out of the shadows, waiting until every eye was upon him, caught, then trapped, by the sunlight that reflected like fire off the gold cross hanging around his neck.

Nathan Locke clutched his Bible tightly and slowly raised it into the air. A tear dampened his eyes, and his voice was low, but rising like the rumble of summer thunder that boiled deep within a distant cloud.

Death, he knew, was unavoidable.

But suicide was unforgivable.

He could make them understand.

And accept.

He could make them forgive.

With a word.

And a prayer.

The blessed memory of Max Gordon—husband, father, and friend, age sixty-two—would live forever. Nathan Locke would make sure of it. Tears could wash away all shame from man and beast, and he would have every eye wet with tears before he was through.

It was God's will. It was God's way.

Nathan Locke allowed himself to smile amidst the teardrops. God, he loved a good funeral.

3

For Birdie and Alice, it was difficult to break themselves away from the silver casket that lay perched above a mound of red Mississippi clay. Max Gordon had too many secrets, and that troubled them.

They were the last to leave the cemetery.

"Eunice sure did take it hard," Alice said softly as they walked slowly back across the gentle hillside.

"If you ask me," Birdie snapped, "she took it a little too hard."

"What do you mean?"

"I think all of that crying and carrying on was strictly for show."

"Why would Eunice do something like that?"

Birdie paused and glanced back at the July heat waves bouncing off the hood of the black hearse. "I think Eunice is hiding something she doesn't want the rest of us to find out about."

"About Max?"

"About herself."

Alice's eyes brightened. "What do you think, Birdie?" she asked, her voice beginning to waver.

"I think Eunice has got herself another man."

HELEN Jensen felt like crying again, but there were no tears left. She felt like such a fool. She had cried for Max Gordon, and she hadn't even liked the man. She had cried for Eunice Gordon, and Eunice had always treated her like a little girl from the wrong side of the tracks who had ventured into a neighborhood where she didn't belong. She cried because she was mad, because she felt sorry for herself, because Robert had abandoned her again, and because Nathan Locke had told her to cry. Helen Jensen would do anything Nathan asked her to do and as often as he asked her to do it, if only he would ask.

Her minister was, she believed, the most magnificent man she had ever seen, everything that Robert was not: tall, slender, dynamic, proud of who he was and confident of what he could become. Nathan Locke's face was strong and forceful as though hand-chiseled out of marble by some master sculptor. His shoulders were broad, his eyes sensitive, his hands gentle when they touched her, if only they would touch her.

Nathan Locke was only the second man in her life who had ever made Helen Jensen blush. The first was her seventh grade math teacher, Mr. Rollins. She couldn't remember his first name. It no longer made any difference. He was the junior high football coach, young, cocky, his blond hair streaked by too many hours in a southern Mississippi sun. Mr. Rollins smiled a lot, winked more than he should, and she sometimes thought his bulging muscles would surely burst through the seams of his shortsleeved shirt. It was a time in Helen's life when muscles on a boy or man of any age were important to her. She could close her eyes at night in the security and darkness of her own bedroom, and if she tried hard enough, Helen could almost feel the warmth of Mr. Rollins's breath blowing soft against her skin. She could even smell the locker room sweat that clung to his body when the cold days of February melted into May. And Helen discovered that if she pictured his nakedness in her mind and massaged herself in the right places, the ache that burned deep within her would find peace and be calmed for the night.

She had been late leaving school one afternoon when she stumbled into Mr. Rollins walking out of the gym. He was wearing a white sweat shirt and blue shorts, and the tan on his muscular legs was as bronzed as his face. His smile was as broad as always.

"Hello, Helen," he had said innocently enough.

She blushed.

"You're hanging around school a little late today, aren't you?"

She blushed again.

"Studying or playing?"

"I had a student council meeting to attend," Helen mumbled, embarrassed at the attention Mr. Rollins was giving her.

"Sounds boring to me."

"It was."

He propped his foot up on a hallway chair and began dribbling his basketball, slowly, deliberately, up and down, and his grin widened.

"Care for a game?" Mr. Rollins asked.

"I've never played basketball." Helen lowered her eyes, and she could feel herself sweating under her arms.

"I wasn't talking about basketball."

"What kind of game did you want to play?"

The coach shrugged. "Whatever game you'd like. Just me and you. One on one."

Helen stepped back abruptly, her face crimson. Mr. Rollins kept staring at her, and his gaze cut deep, and it stirred her in a way she had never been stirred before. She was tall for her age, had long legs, and the baby fat that plagued most of the girls in the seventh grade had been trimmed away. Her body had hardened, and it was beginning to take shape, and Mr. Rollins had apparently noticed the slender curve of her hips. It pleased Helen. It scared her. She wanted to stay. She wanted to run.

"I've got to go home now," she stammered.

"How about tomorrow?"

"I don't know."

Mr. Rollins stopped dribbling and rolled his basketball aside. He reached out and gently stroked her long brown curls and pulled her slowly toward him. Helen grew rigid. Her pulse raced and she could hardly breathe. She smelled the locker room sweat that clung to his body and felt the warmth of his breath blow softly against her skin. Helen closed her eyes, and in her mind, Mr. Rollins was naked again. She thought he was going to kiss her. He didn't.

"I'll be waiting," was all he said.

She stood staring after him as he walked back into the gym, her knees weak, her heart pounding. Tomorrow, she thought. Tomorrow I'll find out what kind of game he wants to play and how to play it. Tomorrow I'll be with a man, and I'll know what it feels like to be a woman. Tomorrow her world would change. She shivered slightly. And the ache began to burn again deep within her. Tomorrow that ache would find peace and be calmed for good.

The next day, Helen left school an hour early and went straight home. She lay in the darkness of her room and cried for hours. For the last month of the semester, she avoided Mr. Rollins, refused to go near the boy's gym for any reason, and never forgave herself for being such a coward. Much to her relief and her regret, Mr. Rollins left that summer and took a job in another state, and she never saw him nor heard of him again. But Helen never stopped dreaming about him. For years, when Robert was late coming home, and he was always late coming home, the face, the smile, the tanned muscular legs, the nakedness of Mr. Rollins would cross her mind, and sometimes it would stay there all night, particularly when she massaged the right places to ease but never extinguish the burning ache that kept rising up within her.

Lately, however, the memories of her seventh grade math

teacher had been overshadowed by thoughts of Nathan
Locke. Mr. Rollins, she now recognized, had been merely
a boy crossing the threshold to manhood. Nathan Locke was
all man. The very mention of his name stirred her, and she
often sat in church during worship and wondered if he were
wearing anything beneath that long black robe, secretly hoping that he wasn't. There was a certain self-assurance in everything that Nathan Locke did. When he prayed, she knew
that God had no choice but to listen. And when he preached,
Nathan Locke acted as though he had gotten inside information on the scriptures from the good Lord himself. Perhaps
he had. And, Helen Jensen always thought, he would stand
there dramatically, his legs spread apart, his head cocked, a
confident little grin on his face, and look for all the world
like he had a dick ten feet long.

Robert didn't like Nathan Locke worth a damn.

But then, Robert didn't like any preacher worth a damn.
"They're all a bunch of fuckin' charlatans," he would say between sips of bourbon. "If you're rich enough, they'll preach
you into heaven. If you're poor, they'll condemn you to hell."

"Nathan's not like that," Helen argued.

"He's as bad as all the rest. He's just got a little more
polish than most of them. That's all."

"He cares about people."

"He cares about their money." Robert had laughed long
and loud. "He's not gonna get any of mine."

Thus far, he hadn't.

All Nathan Locke had gotten from the Jensens was Helen's
complete and undying devotion.

She would never forget that first time she had seen him

stride boldly across the podium, the Bible lying open in his
hand, a tenderness she did not quite understand flickering
like an eternal flame within the depths of his dark, piercing
eyes. It had been an Easter morning, and the sanctuary was
a garden of white lilies. Helen had driven across Vicksburg
alone, and she eased into a pew near the back, a stranger
in a church that had drawn her like a magnet to its Sunday
service. She was not a religious woman, certainly not Presbyterian, and she really had no idea why she had persuaded
herself to get out of bed early that morning and drive to
Basilwood.

Helen looked around her and suddenly felt very ill at ease
and out of place. She definitely did not belong in Basilwood.
Her dress was new, but among the Presbyterians around
her, it seemed drab and out of date. Basilwood smelled of
money, new and old, and the smell was almost suffocating.

Helen had decided to sneak out and leave, and then she
saw Nathan Locke come into the sanctuary. He was full of
dignity and grace, yet there was a touch of mystery behind
those hypnotic eyes that held her in their unwavering gaze.
Helen sat spellbound. She knew in her mind that the time
had come to stop running from God. He was alive. He was
here. He was in Basilwood. And his name was Nathan Locke.

Locke didn't preach about the cross that Easter Sunday.
He didn't talk of dying.

Or of eternity.

To Helen's relief, he didn't mention guilt or fear at all,
and he ignored devils and demons, hell and a lake of fire
where men who were dead could not die, where men would
cry out and still there would be no cool drop of water to

quench the thirst of their tormented tongues, now or forever more.

Nathan Locke talked of hope.

And faith.

And love.

Nathan Locke knew about love. Helen Jensen was sure of it.

Nathan Locke was love.

That Easter morning, without anyone asking, Helen Jensen bowed her head and gave her heart to God and her soul to Nathan Locke. It would be there whenever he wanted it. It would be there whether he wanted it or not. Anytime. Anywhere.

Now.

And forever more.

Amen.

That night, when she lay alone in bed, Helen closed her eyes and massaged herself in the right places. The body she saw in her mind was muscular and golden and smelled of locker room sweat. But the face belonged to Nathan Locke.

His tongue touched her.

And she screamed.

She awoke.

The ache that dwelt within her was a fire that could no longer be quenched. It burned hot, and it burned often, and Helen Jensen blushed everytime her minister took her hand in his and held it as she made her way out of the church.

Ten years of sitting down front and praying for peace had not dimmed the way she felt about Nathan Locke. But ten years had made a significant difference in her life. She and

Robert had never really been close, and now they were drifting even further apart. For the life of her, Helen couldn't
understand why they had even been foolish enough to get
married in the first place. In reality, it had been a simple
matter of obligation, consummated during a long, hot night
of lust and passion beneath the pines of Southern Mississippi
University.

Robert had his eye on a law degree someday.

Helen had merely been going to school because her father
wouldn't have it any other way. He was an educated man, a
Baptist minister. Her mother was a kindergarten teacher. A
college degree was not an option in Helen's family. It was a
requirement. So she studied the basics and hoped that her
hours would one day add up to a degree in something, in
anything. Helen didn't care. All she wanted to be was a wife.

And short, homely Robert Jensen was available.

He had squired Helen away from a fraternity dance one
night, and they drove without talking down a winding country
road that led into the pine thickets below the southern edge
of Hattiesburg. It was early June and stifling. The wind had
died away, and a ragged cloud fell across the moon as Robert
jerked his secondhand Ford to a stop in the darkness.

Helen felt his hand drop across her shoulder, and Robert
kissed her quickly and roughly on the lips.

"What do you think you're doing?" she asked, even though
she knew what he was doing but hadn't yet decided whether
she approved or not.

He didn't answer. Instead, he fumbled with the cap on a
half-filled bottle of bourbon, finally got it open, and took a
swig.

"You want a drink?" Robert asked.

Helen took the bottle, lifted it, and the bourbon touched her tongue hot and bitter. She shuddered.

"It's hot," she said, wiping her mouth.

"So am I."

"What's that supposed to mean?"

Robert opened his car door. "It's summer. It's a hundred and ten fuckin' degrees in the shade. And I'm sweatin' like a stuck pig," he said sharply. "That's what it means."

"Oh." Helen felt embarrassed.

She started to relax, then Robert kissed her again, and she felt his arm brush against her breast. Helen grew rigid. She was afraid he would do it again. She was afraid he wouldn't. Robert's lips parted, and his breath smelled like onions and stale whiskey. It came in short, quick bursts, and he squeezed her tightly, as though trying to feel her naked skin beneath the wrinkled skirt. Robert's hands grew bolder and for once Helen did not push them away. Sweat streaked down her back, and she could feel his chubby face, cold and clammy, against hers. It was suffocating. His glasses were smudged and fogged.

"Let's get out of the car," Helen whispered.

They stood together in silence and let the faint semblance of a summer breeze ruffle their hair. Helen took the bourbon bottle out of his hand and drank slowly, her head spinning slightly as the warm liquid burned against her throat.

Robert fumbled with the buttons on her blouse, then paused, waiting for her to say, "Don't."

She didn't.

Helen pitched the empty bottle into a bramble bush and

removed her blouse, then her bra, for him. Her skin was an alabaster white in the moonlight, her ripe, firm breasts hidden in the shadows of the pines.

"Jesus Christ," he muttered.

Helen lay back against the hood of the '62 Ford and let the heat of the metal work its way deep between her shoulder blades.

Robert stared. For a moment, he had quit breathing.

"Don't you want to kiss me?" she asked.

Helen felt his mouth smother her nipples, and a strange sensation swept through her body. She shivered and wondered if his teeth would leave marks or scars.

Daddy wouldn't approve, Helen thought.

Daddy always preached against sin.

Especially against lust.

And fornication.

But Daddy wasn't there.

She felt Robert's hand venture timidly under her skirt, then it was a claw, out of control, groping, pushing, probing.

Helen moaned.

Daddy would think she was a sinner, Helen thought.

He would make her feel guilty.

Condemn her to hell.

To a lake of fire.

Damn daddy.

Helen pushed Robert away and slipped her panties and stockings down around her ankles. She kicked them, along with her shoes into the pine straw.

"Jesus Christ," he mumbled, stepping back and beginning to unzip his pants.

"You said you were hot," Helen teased.

Her head was spinning, her bare bottom pressed against the heated metal, her skirt pushed up around her waist.

Suddenly she wanted to be home.

In her own bed.

Alone.

Daddy was right.

It was too late.

Robert was against her, breathing heavily, an animal groping and probing, frightened, excited, feeling good and feeling foolish and wondering why it was so hard trying to do what he had always wanted to do.

Helen braced herself against the car.

She felt like laughing.

And crying.

She closed her eyes and pictured Mr. Rollins, young and cocky, muscular and tan. Where was he now when she needed him most? Robert had begun to smell.

He penetrated her.

Damn, it hurt.

"Jesus Christ," he said.

He was out of control now, thrusting wildly, his fingernails cutting sharply into her shoulders.

Damn.

God, it hurt. Somebody had lied to her.

She wanted to scream, and she bit her lip until she tasted the salt from her own blood.

A hard thrust.

Then a harder one.

Helen felt Robert's body quiver and heard him groan once, and then it was over.

Somehow Helen hadn't expected it to end so suddenly,

so quickly. She had wanted Robert to be tender with her,
caring, loving, the way Mr. Rollins would have been. She
had wanted to soar with ecstasy, but apparently Robert had
soared alone.

He stepped back, and she opened her eyes.

Her head had quit spinning now.

And Robert was grinning.

Helen doubled up in pain. His grin faded. He looked down
and saw his penis smeared with blood and semen.

"Jesus Christ," he said.

The pain tore deep inside of her, and the tears came, slowly
at first, then she was sobbing uncontrollably, and a mournful
wail of anger and anguish tore from her throat.

"Are you a virgin?" Robert asked as though he could not
believe it.

Helen's eyes flashed darkly. "Hell, no," she wanted to
scream. "I was. But I'm not now, and I won't ever be a
virgin again, thanks to you, you little shit."

"Jesus Christ."

"I want to go home," Helen said softly, putting her blouse
back on. She knelt and rummaged through the pine straw
until she found her panties, stockings, and shoes. The bourbon had worn off.

God bless the bourbon, she thought.

She could always blame the bourbon.

"I didn't know you were a virgin," Robert said as he seated
himself behind the wheel of his Ford. He glanced at Helen.
She was staring straight ahead, her eyes dulled, her face
without expression.

"You could have stopped me," he continued.

Helen bit her lip again.

Robert waited for an answer.

Finally, when he realized there would be no answer, he started the car and drove in silence back out of the pine thicket.

"Don't blame me," Robert said sullenly. "It was your idea. I just did what you wanted me to do."

That hurt. Helen knew he was right.

But at the moment, she hated him, and she hated herself, and she knew she would never be able to face her father again, not as a fallen woman. He would look at her. His eyes would see right through her. And he would know.

He could read the sin that shone on her face.

And the wages of sin were death.

She wished she *could* die.

Robert parked in front of her dorm and tried to walk Helen to the door. She turned around, and her cold eyes cut through him.

"What can I say?" he asked.

"At least say something nice."

Robert shrugged and glanced away. "Thank you," was all he said.

"Jesus Christ," Helen yelled and slammed the front door behind her.

For three weeks they didn't speak to each other or to anyone else. Helen felt shame; Robert was stricken with guilt. She had let him take her most prized possession, and he had willingly taken it. She was a good-looking woman with great-looking legs, so Robert Jensen did the only honorable thing he could think of. He had been her first. He might as well be her only. He asked Helen to marry him. She cried all night, then accepted his offer. It was the only way Helen knew how to heal her wounded pride and clear her angry conscience. Two weeks after their weekend honeymoon in a seaside Biloxi motel, Robert rolled over in bed one night and said, for the first time, "I love you." Helen didn't believe him then. She still thought he was a lying sonovabitch.

Helen Jensen laughed quietly to herself. No, she and Robert had never been particularly close, but somehow their marriage had held together for seventeen years. Neither had ever mentioned that one hot night of lust and passion, disappointment and disgrace beneath the Hattiesburg pines. But she knew Robert had never forgotten. And she had never forgiven him. The lust she had felt that night now burned for someone else. The passion in their marriage had quickly died away. Robert still helped himself to her body whenever he got the urge, which wasn't often anymore. And, like the good wife she had promised to be, Helen never turned him down. She would simply lie there and wait until he was through. It seldom took him long. And the only time Helen ever felt the way she knew she was supposed to feel was when she closed her eyes, massaged the right places, and pictured the hypnotic face of Nathan Locke. It excited her most when she mentally fucked Mr. Rollins, then Nathan Locke, while Robert lay sleeping in the bed beside her. Robert had no idea what he was missing.

Helen wrapped her silk robe tighter around her, turned on the lamp that perched on an antique table in the corner, then slumped into a chair beside the oval mirror in her bedroom. She definitely did not like the looks of the woman staring with empty eyes back at her. The years had wasted her, or, perhaps, she had simply wasted the years God had given to her.

Her face was puffy, and there were faint signs of wrinkles forming beneath her eyes. Her long curls were long gone, and her hair had been shortened, then frosted. She had always thought that frosted hair made women look much younger, and she wondered where she had come up with such a stupid idea. Her skin was still soft and silky, but her body was no longer firm, and she could feel her bare breasts beginning to sag beneath the robe. Maybe surgery would help. She had read once that it would. Her long smooth legs had become thick, like her waistline, and Helen seriously promised herself that she would faithfully get back on her diet and back into shape before the summer was over. She could look as winsome, as slender as a schoolgirl again. It wasn't that hard. It was a promise she made to herself every time she looked in the mirror.

She hated that damn mirror. She hated the truth.

Helen knew that she shouldn't have let herself get so overweight, but Robert had never bothered to complain, so she kept right on eating, especially when she was bored, and Helen was always bored. Damn Robert. Robert probably hadn't even noticed. He never saw her anymore unless it was dark.

Helen heard a car door slam outside.

Maybe it was Robert.

Or Jeremy.

Robert had at least had the decency to call and say he was working late, whether he was or not. Jeremy would never bother to let her know where he was, how he was, or even if he were coming home. He seldom spoke to his mother anymore, and Jeremy detested his father. Man and boy were too much alike. Helen knew she had lost him for good to fast cars and some other mother's daughter. It worried her, but she could live with that. Lately, however, she had noticed that Jeremy's eyes were glazed most of the time, and he wore a crooked little smile day and night, and he laughed a lot even when nothing was funny. That scared her. He had quit going to class for two months before Helen even knew he had dropped out of school. Robert found him once sleeping in the doorway of an abandoned grocery store. Since then, Helen had no idea where or with whom Jeremy was sleeping.

She stood, glad to get away from the mirror, walked to the window and stared out into the night. Across the street, Raymond Lynch had parked his Pontiac beneath a streetlight and was walking briskly into the small red brick duplex he shared with Anna Fay Johnson who worked the night shift making greasy hamburgers down at the corner cafe.

There was obviously no reason to wait up for Jeremy. He was seventeen, insolent, on his own, and too stubborn to let her reach out and help him anymore. He was a rebel. He was adrift. Jeremy wouldn't be coming home again.

Robert, unfortunately, would.

Helen sighed.

Robert and Raymond had probably been out late together again, drinking too much whiskey and trading stories about the one common bond they had between them: their black brethern.

Raymond Lynch understood them, believed in them, and

fought for their rights every chance he got. Robert defended them when they strayed from the straight and narrow, which was often, especially on Saturday nights when the liquor flowed and a straight razor usually made all men equal in the sight of the Lord. Raymond loved the blacks. Robert hated them. Raymond took up their cause. Robert took their money when he could get it. And he spent his Saturdays out target shooting with a .38 caliber pistol to make sure he got it. Helen smiled to herself. It was dirty money, but it was enough to keep her among God's chosen few each Sunday at the Basilwood Presbyterian Church.

She lay down in an empty bed and planned to be asleep by the time Robert got home. She would have made it, too, if it hadn't been for the burning ache inside of her and the haunting face of Nathan Locke.

4

Morris Adams arched an eyebrow but made no response. He shifted the telephone to his left hand and reached for a pen. He was a man always in control of himself and the circumstances around him. He never registered any emotion even when his insides were churning, which they were now.

"Go on," he said to Katherine Basil, holding his white carnation up to the light, slowly twirling it in his fingers.

"It seems Max Gordon had gotten himself in deep financial trouble," she said, enjoying every word. "Bad investments, you know."

"Banks are having their problems these days," Morris admitted calmly.

"And bankers."

Morris Adams waited for her to continue.

Katherine Basil lowered her voice. "Then Max Gordon had to doctor the bank's books a little, just so he could come up with enough money to keep his reputation intact."

"What do you mean?"

Katherine cackled. "Somebody had seen him sneaking around at night with another woman. Max Gordon was being blackmailed."

"Are you sure?"

"Birdie Castleberry told me, and she knows everything that happens in Vicksburg and most of Mississippi."

Morris doubted it.

But he was not the kind of man to take any chances.

NANCY Locke had not gone to the funeral. She hadn't wanted to go. She hated grief and was oppressed by those who grieved, and Nancy Locke didn't need to see the tears of others in order to cry. She had done a lot of that lately, crying, but it hadn't made her feel any better. She did not believe that anything would ever make her feel better again.

Nathan was certainly no help.

He was a *compassionate* man.

Tender.

Understanding.

But only for others.

Nancy Locke suffered her long days of depression alone.

She had recently turned forty, a traumatic experience for any woman, she thought. But Nancy had worn her years well. She was still pretty by anyone's standards, small and petite, almost frail. Her hair was shoulder-length and auburn, but there were dark circles under her eyes, and Nancy's complexion had become pallid. That worried her. Everything worried Nancy Locke.

She had lost her youth, her enthusiasm for life. She had lost Nathan, and she didn't know why or to whom. She only knew that he was too busy for her anymore, and Nancy had no idea why a minister from Vicksburg, Mississippi, had to spend so much of his time in Nashville, Tennessee. She didn't want to know. Nathan had kept her in the dark for so long, and now she had grown accustomed to and comfortable with the darkness. It was the only friend she had.

In the beginning, Nancy Locke had been, it seemed to all who knew her, the perfect pastor's wife.

In the beginning.

God, that was such a long time ago.

Nancy rolled over in bed and turned away from the window and those sharp rays of July sunlight that flooded through the pink lace curtains. She glanced at the clock. It was ten o'clock.

God, it was late.

She didn't care.

Nancy seldom got out of bed anymore. It was her one place of refuge where no one would find her or bother her, and she could cry without offending anyone. Nancy never wanted to offend anyone, especially not Nathan. But she had disgraced him and become a burden for him, and Nancy, after staying awake all night again, came to realize that Max Gordon was the only intelligent being among them.

He had had a problem, whatever it was.

He didn't bother anyone with it.

He didn't offend anyone.

He simply ended it.

God, she wished she could be more like Max Gordon.

Nancy had first met Nathan Locke in seminary. He was young and dashing and the most beautiful man she had ever seen. He always said the right things at the right time, and his voice was powerful and persuasive. She loved to hear him preach, even when he was only practicing, but she could never recall what he said, only that he said it so forcefully and so well. At the time, Nancy had dreams of becoming a minister of Christian education. She loved children, especially the younger ones, and Nathan always said that they would make a great team. She had thought so, too. On the Saturday night after his graduation, they said their wedding vows, the perfect couple consummating a storybook romance, a marriage that must have been made in heaven. Everyone said it. Everyone believed it.

It became hell.

Nathan Locke took a small church near his home in Holly Springs, Mississippi. Nancy was still a year away from earning her degree.

"Don't worry," he assured her. "This is only temporary. You're young, and there'll be plenty of time for you to go back and finish seminary."

She never had.

It was a disappointment, but she could accept it. At least Nathan was happy.

Nancy had wanted children so badly. But two years after her marriage, she was told by a sad-eyed country doctor with a kind voice that she was infertile.

Barren.

A curse.

She cried for a week.

"Don't worry," Nathan assured her. "I love you anyway."

"How about adoption?"

"Out of the question."

"Why?"

"We can't afford kids." Nathan's reply had been cool, detached. "We're barely keeping our own mouths fed."

"What about someday?"

"Someday, we'll talk about it again."

"When?"

"When we can afford kids."

Now they could afford them. But Nathan had never mentioned children again, and neither had she.

For awhile, Nancy tried to fill the emptiness she felt inside her by teaching Church School on Sunday mornings. It didn't help. It only hurt. For an hour, she would be surrounded by bright, eager, loving, shining faces with chubby little squirming bodies, then she would stand in the church doorway and watch them all go home with someone else. And she would be left alone.

And lonely.

Nancy wanted so desperately to have a child of her own to cuddle and love and hold tightly in her arms at night.

But her arms were empty.

Nathan was not even there anymore.

He had hospitals to visit, meetings to attend, sermons to preach, bereaved to comfort, sick to heal, and souls to save. And at least twice a month, every month, the Lord would call him back to Nashville, she assumed, for personal consultation. He had time for everything and everyone but her.

So Nancy dutifully came to church each time the doors were open, sat on the front row, smiled a lot, never spoke a harsh word about anyone, knew her place and stayed there, kept her feelings to herself, and always agreed that, yes, her husband's words had indeed been touched by God Himself.

In Holly Springs, the choir director, right out of college, got herself pregnant and immediately left town without a husband. In Tupelo, there had been two divorces and two disappointed women, and Nancy had, for the first time, heard the whispers that said, *Poor Nancy, she doesn't know a thing.*

At the age of thirty-seven, she suffered her nervous breakdown. And Nathan was disgraced. Nancy could see it in his eyes, hear it in his voice. For a time, her every waking hour was lived in the smothering fear that Nathan would simply pack up one day and walk out on her without even pausing long enough to say goodbye.

But he hadn't.

He was a man with a growing church and an eye on the future. He was Presbytery's fair-haired boy in Mississippi, slowly building himself an empire, a power base among the wealthy and the influential who only wanted to be reminded every Sunday that God loved them and forgave them of their sins regardless of who they were or what they had done. They wanted an intellectual in the pulpit. They didn't mind if the sermon was over their heads as long as it didn't scare them to death. The Baptists had a monopoly on damnation, hellfire and brimstone, and by god, they could keep it.

Nathan Locke knew what they wanted.

And he knew they did not want a minister who would leave his wife in a time of her crisis and trouble. So he became the tender, loving, sympathetic, and long-suffering husband, strong enough to bear the burdens of the church, as well as those of his wife, bent but unbowed. To the congregation, he was her rock.

At home, he moved into a separate bedroom.

Nancy Locke dreaded the thought of facing another day. She looked at her hands, and they were trembling, and she felt that old, familiar fear clawing at her stomach. If she had any guts, Nancy knew that she would leave Nathan. But where would she go? There was no other place for her. Not now. Not after all these years. Nathan didn't respect her. He didn't love her. But he was all she had. Nancy was weak and a coward, and she hated herself for it.

She leaned over the edge of her bed and fumbled around inside the small cherrywood table until her hands found the glass neck of the bottle of gin she kept hidden there. She needed a drink to steady her nerves. That was all. She needed a drink to make her forget, to put her back to sleep again. Her hands were shaking so badly Nancy could barely unscrew the cap. She dropped it. Her eyes searched frantically for a glass, found none, so she drank from the bottle itself until it was empty, then felt it slide slowly from her fingers as the room slowly turned to lavender then faded away altogether. There was only one bad thing about going to sleep. She would have to wake up again.

Damn you, Nathan Locke, she said to herself.

What have you done to me?

What, in God's name, have I done to myself?

Nathan Locke was a disturbed man. The calm of his early morning had been shattered by a telephone call from Tom Beecher. It had awakened him, but the crusty old attorney's words had immediately cleared the cobwebs from his mind.

"Max Gordon had made out a new will before he died," Beecher said in his raspy voice. "I thought you would want to know."

"Jesus."

It was not a prayer.

"When?" Locke wanted to know.

"Just a few days before he shot himself."

The minister rubbed his tired eyes, and he felt the knot in his stomach growing larger with each breath he took.

"What kind of changes did he make?"

"He left just about everything to his wife."

"He didn't even love his wife."

"I questioned him about it," Beecher continued. "But he was adamant about the change. He told me it was his will, and he could do whatever he damn well wanted to do with it, and whatever the hell he did was none of my business."

"Does anybody else know about the new will?"

"Not that I know of. Not yet anyway."

Nathan Locke turned his black Cadillac toward the river and drove slowly along the worn red brick streets that would lead him into downtown Vicksburg. It was a balmy kind of day, typically July, and a searing sun cut through the gnarled and aging limbs of live oak trees, splintering its rays across

the sidewalk. The morning smelled of honeysuckle, delta
dust, and magnolias, and there were no clouds at all in the
sky to bring relief from the sweltering heat.

Locke adjusted his sunglasses and glanced at the architec-
tural antiquities that surrounded him. Vicksburg was a proud
old town, a defiant old town that found glory in its past. Its
present was its past, refurbished and restored, and many of
the oldtimers still looked askance at cars that came rolling
through with northern license plates. Vicksburg had fought
a war. Vicksburg had lost a war. Vicksburg was still pissed
off.

Nathan Locke grinned sardonically. It had been on a July
day in 1863, when Yankee General U.S. Grant had come
riding into town to officially accept and acknowledge the sur-
render of Vicksburg. The city was important to the South.
It was important to Abraham Lincoln, a river town that, some
even believed, held the ultimate key to Confederate commerce. Close the river, they argued, and the South will wither
away. Grant closed the Mississippi River after a forty-seven-
day siege and the loss of 17,000 of his own soldiers. He had
literally starved Vicksburg until the town fell to its knees
and begged for mercy or at least for a few scraps to eat.
Grant could have taken the city on July third. But he was
patriotic, or maybe drunk. He waited a day. And Vicksburg
never forgave him or his audacity. It wasn't until 1948, that
the town finally decided, against its better judgement, to
honor July Fourth again as a national holiday, a day of inde-
pendence. To Vicksburg, it had long been a day of infamy.
The wounds were deep and, for some with long memories,
they still had not healed. In the South, Nathan Locke knew,

hate could sometimes last forever, and it usually did. The South was interested only in life, liberty, and tradition, *especially* tradition.

Locke pulled sharply into a parking lot, pocketed his ticket, and walked briskly across the street to the two-story gray stone courthouse of Warren County. Its architecture was more like art deco, a product of the 1940s, and it looked completely out of place in antebellum Vicksburg. Locke shuddered. So much for tradition, he thought. He paused on the steps to straighten his tie and brush the sweat from a well-tanned forehead. The wrinkles had fallen from his tan suit, and the sun reflected gold off the cross he always wore around his neck. The cross was his calling card. It gave him prestige, a certain amount of dignity, and a reason—an excuse really—to go anywhere he wanted to go.

The minister removed his sunglasses and walked into the cool hallway of the courthouse. In a back corner, he found the small, cramped, cluttered office of Doc Murray. It looked pretty much the way he thought it would. Papers were scattered across an oak desk that must have occupied the same space since sometime before World War II. It was scratched and had probably never seen a coat of tung oil or furniture polish. On a table beneath an open window, Locke noticed a couple of legal books, a medical dictionary, and a dog-eared copy of *Field and Stream*. A man's office, he had learned long ago, was really nothing more than an extension of the man himself.

Doc Murray's pudgy body was wedged behind the desk, and he was sweating profusely. The sleeves on his white shirt had been rolled up, and the material was yellowed with age and plastered against the skin on his back. Locke barely recognized the coroner. It surprised him how little attention he had paid to Doc Murray that night when he walked into the hotel room and saw what was left of Max Gordon sprawled crookedly across the bed. He hadn't been able to take his eyes off the dead man. He had heard the coroner. That was all.

But that was the reason he now stood quietly, waiting to be acknowledged in the doorway of the coroner's office.

Doc Murray glanced up from the report he was writing and rubbed the back of his balding head. His hair had been cropped short, and the glass in his horn rim frames looked to be an inch thick. They distorted his eyes and were obviously smudged with his fingerprints.

"Can I help you?" Doc Murray's voice was flat.

"I'm Nathan Locke."

"I know who you are." The coroner frowned impatiently. "What I want to know is can I help you."

"I'd like to talk to you about Max Gordon."

Doc Murray shrugged and tossed his pen aside. His distorted eyes grew wary.

"Suicide."

Locke waited for him to continue.

Doc Murray had nothing else to say.

"Any reasons why Max would want to take his life?"

"A few."

"Good reasons?"

"Good enough to pull the trigger."

"May I sit down?"

Doc Murray nodded toward a cushioned chair in the corner. It was piled high with paper, too. "Throw the junk out of your way. It's not doing me any good anyhow." The coroner leaned forward and propped his elbows on the desk. "Why the hell are you so interested in Max Gordon?"

"I'm his pastor." Locke smiled apologetically. "At least I was his pastor."

"I thought all that pastors did was bury the dead and do the best they could to preach 'em on into Heaven," Doc Murray said dryly.

Locke tried to read the man but couldn't. He waited for the coroner to smile, then figured that Doc Murray had probably never smiled in his life. Coroners, he decided, did not have a lot to smile about.

"I did the best I could," he answered.

"So why are you here?"

"I'm looking for answers, I guess."

"What are the questions?"

Nathan Locke shrugged. "To be honest with you, sir, I have no idea," he said. "It's just that a man in my church, in my congregation, chose to kill himself. He was a good man, a decent man, my friend, and now he's dead, and I don't know why, and that troubles me a great deal." Locke lowered his voice until it was almost a whisper, gentle, yet harsh. "Maybe I could have helped Max if I had gotten there in time. I don't know. Maybe there was something I could have done if I had just paid more attention to the man."

"Are you looking for answers?" Doc Murray's face twisted with disdain. "Or are you trying to clear your own conscience."

The coroner's words struck a chord of anger deep inside

Nathan Locke, but the minister registered only a faint smile. Doc Murray had information he wanted. He might be able to talk the old man out of it, but not if there was an argument. Argue, and the coroner's mouth would shut like a steel trap. He couldn't afford to make Doc Murray mad or even suspicious.

"Maybe you're right," Locke said at last. "I hadn't thought about it. But maybe my conscience *is* troubling me."

Doc Murray relaxed.

"It shouldn't be," he said. "You can know a man like a brother and still never learn what really makes him tick. We're all like walking bombs. We can explode at any time. It's just that some of us have longer fuses than others. That's all."

"And Max?"

"His fuse had been burning for a long time."

Nathan Locke knew he must be careful now. He might be treading on holy ground.

"Was there an autopsy?" he asked softly.

"There always is when the death is violent, and Max Gordon's death was about as violent as you can get."

"Can I see the report?"

"I don't see what good it would do," Doc Murray told him thoughtfully. "But then again, I don't see what harm it would do either. I doubt if you can understand it anyway. It's written in all that legal and medical gibberish, which is how we get paid to write it."

For a moment, the coroner almost smiled.

He pulled a form out of his right-hand desk drawer, scanned it briefly, stood, and handed it to the minister.

"It's all here," he said.

"Thank you."

Locke had no real interest in the medical details of the autopsy report. Asking for it had only been a gambler's ploy. What Locke desperately wanted to see was that note Max had left behind. It intrigued him. No, Locke had to be honest with himself. It frightened him. He was hoping the report might make some reference to the note and its contents.

There was more to worry about than just Max Gordon's guilty soul. Two years earlier, the banker had written a will that left $2.6 million to the church, most of it to be spent at the pastor's discretion. Nathan Locke knew he could not afford to let that kind of money get away from him. It could be the opportunity of a lifetime. God had indeed been good to him, depending, of course, on what lay hidden in Max Gordon's note. If it mentioned anything at all about the new will, the note would obviously have to be discredited or destroyed.

The $2.6 million would give him the freedom, at last, to do everything he wanted to do in the ministry.

Radio . . . Television . . .

He was a communicator, and the world was waiting to hear the gospel according to Nathan Locke. He could mold lives. He could shape lives. He could not keep any of them waiting any longer. That was his destiny, and he could not escape it.

Radio . . . Television . . .

That's where the power was. That's where Nathan Locke wanted to be. That's where he was meant to be. It was God's will, and he knew it, even though he had never had a vision, seen God's face, nor heard a voice speaking to him from out of a burning bush.

But first, Locke had to make sure that Max Gordon, in some ungodly fit of passion, anger, self-pity or anguish, had not even hinted at changing his last will and testament in that final message he had left for all mankind to see.

But mankind hadn't seen it yet.

Doc Murray made sure of it.

At first glance, Nathan Locke was disappointed. Any information about the note had been purposely or accidentally omitted. And Locke realized that reading the autopsy report was about as close to Max Gordon as he was going to get.

It was close enough.

He read one line, stopped, then read it again. Locke fought to control his emotions and knew that his hands were shaking, and he couldn't make them quit. His throat went dry, and a cold shiver sliced in between his shoulder blades. He stole a glance at the coroner and saw that Doc Murray had gone back to writing his report. Nathan Locke's eyes widened, but his face was as dispassionate as ever.

Max Gordon had had a secret after all. Didn't they all?

And he had lived with it as long as he could, as long as he dared. Max Gordon had had his reputation, his family to think about. He was an honorable man.

His secret, if anyone found out about it, could have destroyed them.

He couldn't let that happen.

So he destroyed himself.

It was that simple.

With trembling hands, Nathan Locke carefully folded the

autopsy report and, without a word, laid it gently back on Doc Murray's desk.

The coroner looked up. "Did you see it?" he asked.

Locke nodded.

"I thought you might." Doc Murray's expression never changed. "I can't do a damn thing about it," he said. "Maybe you can."

"Maybe I can."

Nathan Locke walked quickly down the dimly-lit hallway and back out into the bright sunshine of a July morning. He suddenly felt as good as he had in a long time. Doc Murray still had Max Gordon's final note, and, by god, Doc Murray could just keep the damn thing.

Nathan Locke had no use for it anymore. He didn't care what Max Gordon had written or to whom. It no longer mattered.

$$\underline{\underline{5}}$$

Morris Adams had been staring at his telephone for hours, his mind troubled by what he had been told about the problems Max Gordon was facing on that lonely night he walked into a cheap hotel room and put himself out of his misery.

He didn't particularly like Birdie Castleberry. He had never trusted her. But he had learned long ago never to doubt her sources, whoever they might be.

By five–thirty, his office staff had left, and Morris Adams was alone. He picked up the phone, tossed his wilted white carnation into a wastebasket, and dialed Nathan Locke. It rang twice before he heard the preacher's strong, resonant voice.

"Nathan," he said without identifying himself, "I've just gotten word that Max was up to his ass in alligators."

"Who told you?"

"It doesn't matter."

"What'd you hear?"

"That Max had a girl friend, that he was being blackmailed, and that he had been stealing from the bank's funds to keep the blackmailer's mouth shut."

Locke sighed. "Morris," he said, "brace yourself."

"Why?"

"It's worse than that."

MARTHA Landers came alone to the fresh mound of dirt that had begun to sink into the gentle, sloping hillside. She had waited until the cars had all gone and the big wrought-iron gate was shut and the crowds had finally drifted away.

She hated crowds.

They always got in the way.

Max had never come to her side as long as there were crowds around.

He preferred the night.

The darkness.

Max never even took off his clothes until the lights were out.

Martha sat down beside the fresh mound of dirt and gingerly touched the temporary cemetery marker. Already the hand-scrawled words were beginning to fade, but still she could read them in the yellow glow of the moonlight:

MAX GORDON
Born June 4, 1924   *Died July 12, 1986*

Someone had handwritten beneath his name: *Devoted husband and father.*

Martha Landers' smile was sad. Bullshit, she thought.

Max Gordon was nothing more than a frustrated old man, afraid of growing older, afraid of dying before his time. He didn't have to be afraid anymore. Max Gordon had never been devoted to anything but the bank and his money.

He had tolerated his wife, but he didn't love her, or so he said, back when the nights had been colder and longer, and Max Gordon was reaching out to anyone who could make him laugh and keep him warm till morning.

And he had not understood his son.

That had frightened him, too.

Martha Landers seldom made him laugh. But she knew how to keep him warm, and he treated her like royalty. No one had ever done that for Martha Landers before.

She gently stroked the fresh mound of dirt, and a tear dampened her eyes. Martha had grown up in a shantytown on the outskirts of Vicksburg, but Max hadn't cared. Even the poor people had called her poor. Max had made her feel rich. She had always been too tall, too thin, with skin that would redden in the sun but never tan. In the softness of the moonlight, Martha looked her age, thirty-two. But the sunlight was harsh and unforgiving, and there was a hardness in her eyes that only the lonely and the wretched could understand. She had learned early in life that boys would date her only if she were willing to accommodate and satisfy their lust, one at a time, maybe more, and she was always willing, even in junior high school. She was a plaything.

Then.

And now.

Martha had grown to detest men. She couldn't do without them. For a night, for an hour, when she felt the roughness of their skin burn against hers, she could close her eyes and believe that she was beautiful. Martha had always wanted to be beautiful. In daylight, she knew that she had only been lying to herself, and she prayed again for darkness and the heat of another man, any man, any number of men. She found them in truck stops, in bars, in grocery stores, at ball parks, alongside the highway, hitchhiking to wherever she wanted to take them. They would rip her clothes from her fragile body, fondle her small breasts, find what they were looking for, kiss her goodbye, and vanish from her life.

No name.

No promises.

No attachments.

Martha Landers never felt pleasure nor pain nor love. She only felt beautiful.

Poor Max.

She lay her face upon the fresh mound of dirt and kissed it. The tears flowed more freely.

Poor Max.

He even thought she was beautiful. But then, Max Gordon was afraid to look at her in sunlight.

Yet, he didn't vanish from her life.

He kept coming back.

Again.

And again.

He had never been rough with her. He was so proper
and so polite. Max would bring her flowers, carefully remove
his pinstripe suit as soon as she turned out the light, hang
it up in the closet of the red-brick Magnolia Inn, take a
shower, always alone, then lay down upon the cool, white
sheets and wait patiently for her to make him feel like a
man again. Her face was too narrow. She knew that. Her
chin was weak, and her brown hair was limp, lifeless, and
her shoulders and hips were angular and bony. But Martha
Landers knew how to make Max Gordon regain his youth,
if only for a minute or two. For him, that had been enough.

Martha had found Max Gordon sitting in the back booth
of a bar where she had once danced for drinks and tips. It
was late, almost midnight, and a chilled rain pelted the brick
streets outside.

His glass was empty. So were his eyes. And Martha sat
down across from him, an inquisitive smile playing crookedly
across her mouth.

"Do you work here?" he asked.

"No."

"Do you want a drink?"

"No."

Martha's face was reflected in the soft red glow of a neon
light that underscored an advertisement for Stroh's beer. Her
eyes were hidden in the shadows, and her skin was pale,
almost ghostly, and the texture of fine silk.

"You don't look like you belong here," she said at last.

"Why not?"

"I don't see many men come into this place wearing pinstripe suits and satin ties."

The man only shrugged and glanced away. "It was raining outside," he explained quietly, "and I didn't want to go home. I drove by and saw the lights on in here. It seemed as good a place as any to get a drink."

"You look tired."

"It's been a long day."

Martha reached out and touched his cheek with her fingertips. "Do you need a friend?" she asked.

"Maybe."

"I need one."

Max Gordon took her hand, dropped a twenty dollar bill on the table, and together they walked out into the blowing December rain.

Martha Landers remembered that night and shivered.

Her tears mingled with the sweat that stained her face.

Poor Max.

He was so predictable. There would be a phone call on Tuesdays and Thursdays, and she would hear his voice giving her a time and a place, always the same time and the same place. Max wasn't in love with her. He couldn't afford to be in love with her. He was everything she would never be, wealthy, respected, a pillar of the community. He was, she believed, the only man who had ever slept with her who did not have dirt under his fingernails. Max was older, a lot older, and he was clumsy, but he was a millionaire. And when Martha was with him, even in the darkness, even for an hour, she knew that she was at last a part of the Vicksburg society that had always rejected her. The Daughters of the Confederacy be damned.

For awhile, Martha Landers even felt secure and smug

enough to attend the Basilwood Presbyterian Church and sing in the choir on Sunday mornings. She was, she decided, just as good as anybody and better than most. But that was a lie, too, and she knew it. She heard the laughter behind her back, and the ridicule stung, and she saw how nervous it made Max when she came walking down the aisle, her Bible in her hand, a serene, frosty smile upon her face. Their eyes never met, not even for a moment. His shame was his own condemnation.

No, Max was not in love with her.

He would never be.

But she was in love with him.

Now he again lay beneath her, beneath that mound of fresh dirt, and again there was no one to disturb them. Max would have liked it that way.

Martha Landers was his private woman.

His midnight woman.

His secret.

Poor Max.

Poor Martha.

Again she was reaching for him, her body sweating as it always did when Max was there and they were lying together arm-in-arm in a small motel room and the silence was interrupted only by his spasmodic breathing and the sounds of tugboats as they pushed their barges downriver toward New Orleans.

A damp wind matted her hair, and her lips tasted of salt. She kept reaching for him, her arms empty, her teeth clenched, a low moan ragged in her throat: digging, clawing, almost frantic, a prayer then a curse on her tongue, scratching and scraping her way down deep into the good earth, the unforgiving earth, down past the mold and worms until her broken fingernails touched the cold metallic surface of Max Gordon's silver casket.

6

Alice Setzer could still hear Susan Heatherly's breathing, and she knew that the silence at the other end of the telephone was either the result of shock or disbelief.

Probably both.

She waited.

When Susan finally broke the silence, she blurted out, "But I thought the police said it was suicide."

"They did at first."

"What happened?"

"Something's come up to change their minds."

Susan paused, then asked timidly, "Who would want to kill Max Gordon?"

"Who stands to gain the most by his death?"

Susan caught her breath. "Paul and his father never got along," she said.

"Paul hated his father."

"Could he have done it?"

"Your guess is as good as mine."

"Who knows about this?" Susan whispered.

"Just a couple of us, so keep it to yourself."

Alice hung up, glanced down her list of names, adjusted her glasses, and unhurriedly dialed another number.

NATHAN Locke was late. But then, he hardly ever got anywhere on time anymore. That, he guessed, was his fate or, perhaps, his curse. A pastor's schedule, it sometimes seemed, changed abruptly every time the phone rang, day or night, and his phone was always ringing.

He walked out of the church and into the late afternoon sun. The air was heavy, and he could see steam rising off the parking lot pavement as Helen Jensen pulled her Chevrolet back out into traffic. The humidity fogged his sunglasses, and, for a moment, Nathan Locke thought he caught the smell of distant rain. He hoped that the thunderhead, coiled in the west and becoming a deep purple, was not just another empty promise. He had grown weary of empty promises.

For the last three hours, he had sat with Helen Jensen in the dim solitude of his study and listened patiently as she wrung her hands and talked about how she and Robert had lost touch with their son. Helen was always looking for reasons to come into the sanctity of his study and wring her hands. She certainly had more than her share of troubles, some real and some manufactured. Robert drank too much. Jeremy, she feared, was on drugs. Robert stayed out too late. Jeremy no longer came home at all. Robert seldom spoke to her. Jeremy never spoke to her. Robert never made love to her anymore. She was afraid Jeremy would get some girl pregnant. Her marriage was crumbling, and she was a failure as a wife and a mother, and even God didn't like her anymore.

Nathan Locke felt more pity than sympathy for her.

But through her tears, she kept smiling at him, and those haunting eyes begged him to hold her, and when he took her arm, he could feel her tremble slightly beneath the touch of his fingertips.

Helen Jenson was a warm-blooded, lonely woman who, Locke told himself, needed a man as badly as she needed God. She wanted him—he didn't doubt it for a moment— and she struggled greatly to keep the ragged edges of her emotions under control.

"Jeremy's been gone for a week now," she said, barely able to hold her tears inside her.

"Why did he leave?"

"I don't know."

Locke sighed. He was always impatient with those who lied to him. "What happened on the night that Jeremy decided to walk out?" he asked, careful not to let Helen hear the irritation that had crept into his voice.

"He and Robert had been arguing." She smiled faintly. "But then, they are always arguing."

"What about?"

"What do fathers and sons argue about?"

"You tell me."

Helen shifted her position in the chair and leaned forward, placing her hands on top of the desk. Her yellow flowered sundress, trimmed with white lace, had a plunging neckline, and, even without straining, Locke could see where her tan abruptly ended and the whiteness of her skin began. Maybe, he thought, she had meant for him to see. Probably not, though. Helen wasn't blushing.

"Jeremy thought that Robert was treating him like a little kid, so he rebelled," she said. "And Robert refuses to admit to himself that his son is seventeen and almost grown."

"That's normal."

"So Robert wears three-piece suits. Jeremy wears old jeans and tee shirts, and he wears them for weeks at a time without bothering to wash them. It's as though those are the only clothes he's got."

Helen paused, then continued softly, "I washed a pair Monday a week ago, and Jeremy got so mad that he took a pair of scissors, cut them up, and stuffed them down the commode. He said he was tired of me trying to run his life for him."

"Are you?"

"What?"

"Trying to run his life for him."

Helen lowered her eyes, and her expression became faintly clouded. "Jeremy's not doing a very good job of running his own life. He dropped out of church. He dropped out of school. I'm afraid he's dropping out of life."

"What makes you say that?"

"Jeremy had rather live on the streets than at home. God only knows where he sleeps at night. He eats scraps and smokes anything he can get his hands on. He hasn't shaved in weeks, and his hair is long and stringy, and when I look into his face, I don't see the little boy that I raised anymore. Jeremy has the face of a stranger, and there's a hatred burning deep in his eyes that frightens me."

"Has he ever threatened you?"

"No."

"Has he and his father ever fought?"

"Verbally, they fight all the time. But they've never hit each other if that's what you mean."

"Are you afraid he's going to hurt you?"

"I sometimes think Jeremy has become a wild dog, running with a pack of wild dogs."

"And you want me to talk to him."

Helen choked back a sob. "Please, Nathan," she said. "I can't talk to him anymore. He doesn't listen to me. He hasn't listened to me for a long time."

Nathan Locke stood and walked to the window, staring out toward the memorial garden that decorated the south lawn of the church. The flowers had wilted, and their petals hung close to the ground, as if in shame.

He glanced at his watch. It was already a quarter past three. He had an appointment with Tom Beecher in fifteen minutes. He would never make it on time, so there was no reason to worry about it any longer. Locke whirled back around to face Helen Jensen, rocking back on his heels.

"Where does Jeremy hang out?" he asked.

"I don't know."

"Vicksburg's not that big," Locke said, seating himself on the edge of his mahogany desk. "But it's big enough to hide in if you don't want anybody to find you."

"Robert found him once sleeping in the doorway of an old grocery store."

"Where was that?"

"Down by the river."

"Does Jeremy have any friends?"

"None that he brings home."

"Any friends that he talks about?"

"I've heard him talk about somebody he calls Moon."

"Any last name?"

Helen shook her head. "Just Moon," she said.

"Boy or girl?"

"A boy, I guess. Or a man. Jeremy told his father that Moon was the toughest son of a bitch he had ever known." Helen suddenly blushed. "I'm sorry," she whispered.

Locke shrugged. "Don't be," he replied, his eyes smiling. "I know what tough sons of bitches are. I've dealt with a few of them myself."

For a moment, he thought Helen was going to laugh. Instead, she stood, shook the wrinkles from her dress, and stepped toward him. "You're the last hope I have," she said, timidly touching his shoulder. "If you can't talk some sense into Jeremy's head, I'm afraid no one can. I'm afraid I've lost him forever."

Locke took her hand and squeezed it.

Helen blushed again.

"I'll do what I can," he said.

There it was again.

Another empty promise.

Damn.

Nathan Locke felt rushed and tired and nauseous and disgusted with himself. He felt the pressure of her gaze upon him and wondered if his shoulders were broad enough and strong enough to hold all the problems that his congregation kept piling there. Too many expected him to be a miracle worker, and Nathan Locke no longer believed in miracles, not for himself nor for anybody else.

"Should I keep praying?" Helen asked, her voice tense, an awkward smile on her face.

"It wouldn't hurt." Locke squeezed her hand again. "God is a lot better at changing people's lives than I am."

Helen Jensen didn't believe him for a minute. She had made no effort to turn and leave until Nathan Locke released his grip on her hand.

Now he was in a hurry.

The afternoon, as it always did, had gotten away from him, and Locke wondered if Tom Beecher were still waiting. He slipped behind the wheel of his Cadillac as a faint glimmer of lightning cut a tattered seam in the thunderhead that had, at least for the time being, blotted out the sun. The rumble of thunder sounded more like a faraway growl, and an uneasy wind shuffled through the oaks that were scattered alongside Washington Street as he drove beneath their overhanging limbs.

Nathan Locke found Tom Beecher leaning against an old Civil War cannon that pointed toward the river. The old attorney met a lot of clients there. It was a quiet place and peaceful, a good place to talk about anything or anyone without being overheard. Tom Beecher was a suspicious man, and he had become a successful lawyer by assuming that all men and most women were guilty, and he never trusted any of them, especially those in serious enough trouble to hire him. He particularly didn't like preachers, salesmen, mad dogs, and other lawyers, saying on more than one occasion that the world would be a lot better off if they all dropped dead. But that might create something of a problem, Tom Beecher later confessed. He didn't like undertakers either. Beecher spit out those loose leaves of tobacco that had collected on his lips, folded his arms, and watched Nathan Locke walk briskly to the top of the bluff, unloosening his tie.

"You're late," he said.

"I apologize, Tom." Locke stopped to catch his breath as the sun crept out from behind the thunderhead again. "But my appointment with Helen Jensen ran a little longer than I had planned.

"Did you fuck her?"

Locke was suddenly speechless, and his eyes registered surprise, then amusement. Tom Beecher was incorrigible. He had made a living for almost fifty years knowing how to shock a witness or a judge or a jury and just when to do it.

"I'm afraid not, Tom," was all Nathan Locke could say.

"Then there's no reason for you being late."

There was also no reason for Locke to argue. He studied Tom Beecher closely. The old attorney's shoulders were slumped, but there was, as always, fire in his eyes. His glasses, held together with Scotch tape, sagged down low on his nose, propped just above an unruly walrus mustache, speckled with gray. His baggy trousers were held up by navy blue and red suspenders that clashed dramatically with his yellow and green checked shortsleeved shirt. Beecher wore a clip-on tie, complete with gravy stains, a fedora with a droopy brim, and shoes that he never bothered to polish. He was an easy man to overlook or take for granted.

The common folk who tended the land of rural Mississippi, however, related to him, and they kept electing Tom Beecher Attorney General until he got roaring drunk one night while celebrating his sixty-eighth birthday and decided that, by God, he didn't want to be Attorney General anymore. He went back to the courtroom, where he belonged, and made a small fortune in big-dollar trials by soundly whipping young out-of-town lawyers who always made the mistake of underestimating the old man with the funny hat and the gravel voice. They laughed loudest. Tom Beecher laughed last. He liked it that way.

He always preferred the river to his office.

"I might as well," he would say. "It's the only damn thing around here that's older than I am."

Nathan Locke squinted into the sun and felt the sweat clotting up on his forehead again. The wind was warm against his face, and the ominous, almost-forgotten sound of summer thunder was growing louder and nearer.

"You think we have a chance for rain?" he asked.

"Maybe. Probably not." Tom Beecher had removed his blue, wrinkled coat and pitched it across the dusty barrel of the cannon. Behind him, Locke could see the traffic beginning to stack up on the Mississippi River bridge that led back into the cotton lands of Louisiana.

"It's certainly threatening."

"The sky can be as fuckin' stubborn as a cross-eyed mule. It ain't gonna give us any rain, even if it's got some to give, which it ain't."

"The ground could sure use a little moisture."

Tom Beecher scratched his chin and frowned. "I don't think you called me out here to listen to my limited opinion on the goddam weather," he said, his gray eyes watchful and as suspicious as always.

"No, Tom, I didn't."

"Then what the hell you got on your mind?"

"Max Gordon."

"We might as well forget Max Gordon. What he did, he did. I ain't gonna defend the man. I ain't gonna judge him."

Nathan Locke removed his coat and slung it across his shoulder. He knew he could outsmart some people. He could outtalk others. He had to level with Tom Beecher. There was no other choice.

"You handled Max's affairs, didn't you?" Locke asked.

"His legal ones."

"And you drew up his will."

Beecher nodded. "I did the first one," he said slowly. "It seems that Max decided to write the second one himself."

Nathan Locke went cold, and his throat was suddenly dry. Fear gnawed at his innards, but his face remained calm, placid, and he wrapped his fingers around the spokes of the cannon's wheels to keep his hands from visibly shaking.

Damn.

"I was surprised when you told me that Max had a second will," he said. "I wasn't aware he had one."

"Max probably did a lot of things we weren't aware of."

"When did he write it?"

"I don't rightly know, Nathan. I got it in the mail the day
before he killed himself."

"Is it legal?"

"He wrote it. He signed it. It's in his handwriting. There's
no court in the country that'll rule against it."

Damn.

Tom Beecher shoved his hands into the pockets of his baggy
trousers and glanced away. He had wondered what had been
troubling the Right Reverend Nathan Locke. Now he knew.
His mouth twisted into a cynical smile.

"You're not worried about the weather, Nathan," the old
attorney drawled. "And I doubt if you give much of a damn
about where poor old Max is spendin' eternity—that is if
he's spendin' it anywhere at all. What the hell you're interested in is findin' out just how much money poor old Max
left you in his will."

"I'm concerned about what he left to the church."

"Bullshit."

Sometimes Nathan Locke regretted that he had not yet
had the opportunity nor the pleasure of preaching Tom
Beecher's funeral. The old attorney, in his own words, could
be slicker than fresh cowshit, and he loved to play mind
games, and he seldom lost. When the time came, at last, to
stand before the judgement bar of God, Nathan Locke,
though he hated to admit it, knew he would feel a lot better
if Tom Beecher were there giving the closing arguments for
his soul. Anger replaced the fear that had been building up
within him. It steadied Locke. He was no longer apprehen-
sive. Now he could face reality, whatever it might be, on
its own terms.

He smiled.

"Max had always been a faithful contributor while he was alive," the minister said calmly. "The church was an integral part of his life. The church was important to him. Max had helped fund it, and he had helped build it. Whenever the church needed anything at all, all we ever had to do was knock on Max Gordon's door."

Tom Beecher spit a stream of tobacco juice into the dust that was swirling around his shoes. "I'm afraid Max ain't gonna hear your knockin' anymore," he said.

Locke shrugged and continued, "A couple of years ago, he gave me a copy of his will. In it, he made provisions to leave the church a rather generous bequest."

"Two point six million, as I remember."

"You remember correctly."

"I hope you ain't spent it all, Nathan."

The afternoon grew suddenly darker. Thunder pounded at the sky above Nathan Locke's head, and the limbs on a nearby oak began to creak and roll with the wind.

To Locke, Tom Beecher's words had been a direct slap in the face, and he didn't like it. "I don't believe I quite understand," he said warily.

"Max cut you out," the old attorney answered, the wind tugging at the brim of his hat. "He didn't leave the goddam church a pot to piss in."

"What did Eunice do, talk him into leaving it all to her?" Locke spoke too quickly, too sharply.

Beecher shook his head. "She didn't get it all either."

Contempt clouded Nathan Locke's eyes. He stepped back and waited for Tom Beecher to laugh. The thunder was like a cannon shot, and lightning danced above the treetops.

"Tear it up." Locke's voice had turned cold and brittle.

Beecher arched an eyebrow. "Tear what up?"

"The handwritten will."

Beecher shrugged apologetically. "You know I can't do that, Nathan," he said. "I've got the law to uphold. I've got to shoulder the burden of a good and decent man's trust. He empowered me to make sure that his last wishes, those in his last will and testament, would be carried out just as he wanted them to be carried out. That's an awesome responsibility, Nathan."

Now it was Locke's turn.

"Bullshit," he said. He turned his back against the wind and felt the anger dying away. His smile was again one of self-assurance.

"Did you question Max about why he would be so foolish as to write his own will when he had the smartest lawyer in Mississippi working for him?"

"You bein' facetious?"

"I'm serious as hell." Locke began pacing the ground, and he raised his voice, choosing his words carefully. "A man who serves as his own attorney has a fool for a client, or so I've been told," he said. "Max knew that as well as anyone. He was a businessman, a cautious man, a conservative man. He never made a rash decision in his life. He never signed his name to anything unless he got sound advice from people he could trust. I knew Max Gordon as well as you did, Tom. And he was definitely not the kind of man who would do something as nonsensical and absurd as write his own will."

Tom Beecher bowed and quietly clasped his hands together in mock applause. "That was a helluva sermon, reverend."

"I'm surprised you didn't talk to him about it. That's all."

"I intended to, Nathan. God knows I intended to." A strange sadness fell across the old attorney's face. "But I'm just too doggone old to get in a hurry anymore. And I thought I had plenty of time to talk to Max. That's the trouble with all of us, Nathan. We all think we've got plenty of time that we don't have anymore."

Locke shrugged. He couldn't blame Tom Beecher for that. He had been just as guilty. About a lot of things.

"Who knows about it?" His voice was softer now.

"What?"

"The handwritten will."

"Just me and you, I guess."

Nathan Locke waited for the echo of a tugboat's horn blast to fade away downriver before he said, "You know it won't fly in court."

Tom Beecher's face was stoic. "It's like I told you, Nathan," he said. "I'm just any old country attorney. I'm not the judge."

"You know it won't fly," Locke repeated.

"Probably not if Eunice decides to fight it." His words weren't a concession, just a simple statement of facts.

"Does Eunice know she's sharing Max's money with somebody else?"

"Not yet."

"Max had been out sewing a few wild oats in the twilight of his life, hadn't he, Tom?"

"Maybe. He was only a man. Maybe he thought he was in love again."

"Martha Landers must be a hell of a woman."

The look on Tom Beecher's face soured. "Martha Landers is a fuckin' tramp."

"I thought you were just an old country lawyer, Tom, not a judge." Locke's barb cut deep.

"Go to hell, preacher." The fire had gone out of Tom Beecher's voice. He was suddenly tired of playing this mental and verbal chess game, and his shoulders began to sag. After a long pause, he asked, "How the hell did you know about Martha Landers?"

"We preachers have our connections."

"From above?"

Locke grinned. "From all over." Then he added, "You know there's no way in hell that Eunice is going to sit back and be willing to share Max's money with some other woman. She'll fight for every last nickel."

"Like a bulldog with the fuckin' smell of blood in his nostrils."

"It'll be messy."

Beecher nodded.

"It'll be a lot messier than even you realize."

"What do you mean?"

Nathan Locke sighed. He played the one hole card he had been saving, even though he didn't really think he needed it anymore.

"I know why Max Gordon killed himself."

Tom Beecher's eyes widened in surprise. "I'm waiting. You've apparently got much better sources than I do."

"Max Gordon was a southerner and a gentleman. He was a proud man. He believed in his own dignity. His reputation was the most important thing in the world to him. He could live with everything but shame and disgrace. He could not face anything that might taint his good family name." Locke paused. "Max Gordon had herpes," he said.

"Blessed Mary mother of God." It was as though the old attorney had suddenly and unexpectedly been kicked in the stomach. He turned away in disgust and walked to the edge of the bluff, sadly shaking his head, disbelief then anger settling into his tired, ashen-gray eyes. "Are you sure?" he yelled back against the wind.

"I'm sure. I saw the report."

"Herpes aren't something I would recommend for my fellow man," Tom Beecher snorted. "But they sure as hell aren't the end of the world."

"They were for Max Gordon."

Without a word, Tom Beecher pulled a sheet of yellowed, wrinkled paper from his hip pocket, unfolded it, and stared for one final time at Max Gordon's last will and testament. Then he slowly tore it apart and watched the wind scatter the ragged pieces down the clay bluff and on toward the muddy waters of the Mississippi.

Locke couldn't be sure, but he thought for a moment that Tom Beecher might be crying.

$$\underline{\underline{7}}$$

*Birdie Castleberry slowly stirred the ice in her crystal whis-
key sour glass as she and Eunice sat together on the white-
column verandah of the old Gordon homeplace. For awhile,
she thought it would rain, but now the thunder had moved
on eastward, and there was a faint streak of sunshine on
the western edge of the clouds again.*

A sardonic smile crossed her face.

*"Alice was telling me about running across Susan Heatherly
yesterday," Birdie said.*

"Susan's a sweet girl."

"Susan doesn't believe Max's death was a suicide."

Eunice's eyes darkened. "What does she mean by that?"

"According to Alice, Susan thinks somebody killed Max."

"Who would want to do a thing like that?"

*Birdie shrugged and paused for a moment to sip her drink.
"The way I hear it," she whispered, "Susan is going around
saying that Paul had something to do with it."*

"That's ridiculous," Eunice snapped.

"That's what I thought."

"Susan's a little bitch."

*Birdie nodded in agreement and reached again for the
imported crystal cooler that held their afternoon supply of
whiskey sour. For some reason, she thought, it seemed a
little sweeter than usual.*

L OVE.

That's what the Reverend Nathan Locke preached on that Sunday morning, standing tall and straight in his black robe, those dark eyes firm and as hypnotic as always. His smile was broad and sincere, and he made it a point to shake as many hands as he could before the morning worship service began. He was what God had wanted him to be.

Love.

And *grace.*

That's what life was all about. That's what God was all about. Nathan Locke was proud to be alive at such a great and wonderful time on earth, and he was even prouder to have the footsteps of a Nazarene called Jesus to follow.

Thank God.

And *Amen.*

But no hallelujahs, not in a good and honorable presbyterian church anyway.

There was a hush, and every eye was on him, and Locke kept pricking at their emotions with the inflections of his voice, sometimes sharp, sometimes gentle, sometimes loud and sometimes soft, sometimes barely a whisper.

Love.

And *grace.*

And *faith.*

It was what they all needed. It was what God had meant for them all to have.

Love.

And *grace.*

Faith.

And *charity.*

"And the greatest of these is charity," he said softly, quoting from Corinthians Thirteen.

Those who heard him went home saying that it may have been the finest sermon Nathan Locke—or anyone else for that matter—had ever preached.

Two days later, the last will and testament of Max Gordon was officially probated. Eunice cried, as widows are supposed to do, but she went home happy. Paul, still an angry young man, but an angry and wealthy young man, went back to his president's office at the Basilwood National Bank.

And on Wednesday morning, Nathan Locke formally announced the construction of the Max Gordon Memorial Communications Center at Basilwood Presbyterian Church.

8

Eunice Gordon had purposely arrived at the garden club meeting early. She was standing beside the front door of the antebellum home, waiting, watching while Susan Heatherly, her face aglow, her smile radiant, paraded up the sidewalk toward her.

"My, but don't you look lovely today," Eunice said cheerfully.

Susan's smile broadened.

"Why thank you," she answered, her face beaming.

The older woman, the matriarch of Vicksburg society, gently placed an arm around Susan's shoulder and asked softly, "How long have you and John been living here now?"

"It'll be four years in September." Susan's voice was light and musical.

"Do you like it here?"

"Oh, yes. Vicksburg just has to be the most beautiful, most charming place we've ever seen."

Eunice felt her smile turn into a twisted frown. "Well," she snapped, "if you want to keep living here, young lady, and if you know what's good for you, you'll learn to keep your bitchy little gossip and opinions to yourself."

She turned, marched into the home, and slammed the screen door behind her. Susan stared after her in shock. Her face was flushed, and she had no idea what in the world Eunice Gordon was talking about.

THE nights were what Nancy Locke dreaded most. That's when Nathan was home, and those were the loneliest times of all. She could hear him in the study, sometimes pacing the floor, sometimes flipping through the pages of a book, writing a letter, perhaps, or a new sermon, doing whatever it was he had to do at night behind closed doors, always behind closed doors, and always alone.

His congregation didn't really understand Nathan Locke, Nancy told herself. He was a very private person, one who preferred to keep to himself. He was basically insecure and a loner, gratified by the admiration that people heaped upon him but uncomfortable with it. He lived amongst the crowds. He preferred the solitude of a mountaintop.

That was the real Nathan Locke, but no one would ever believe it. No one ever had. They all saw him as outgoing, maybe even flamboyant, a man who loved to surround himself with humanity. His laughter came easy and often. Yet he knew how to cry when those around him were sad and hurting. He had never cried for her, and that was why Nancy Locke spent so many nights sad and hurting.

She stepped out of her robe and into the shower, letting the stream of hot water pound relentlessly against her face. Steam rose up and wrapped itself around her, and Nancy sometimes dreamed of simply standing there, massaging her slender body with soap, until she finally washed herself away.

She might as well, she thought.

No one would miss her.

Nathan probably wouldn't even realize that she was gone.

She closed her eyes and waited. Her skin tingled, and the water burned. She kept waiting. Finally her skin quit tingling, and the water didn't seem so hot anymore. She opened her eyes, looked down, and saw that she was still there.

Depressed, she stepped back out of the shower and towel-dried her auburn hair. It fell loose upon her shoulders, and Nancy remembered how Nathan, his face twisted into a grimace of pleasure, used to grab her hair with both hands and hold on tightly when she made love to him at night. Her body shivered. That was such a long time ago. She wanted him again so badly. She could find other men who would be glad for the privilege of bedding her down. Nancy didn't doubt it for a moment. She wasn't that old. She was still trim, and her stomach muscles were as firm and flat as they had been the day Nathan married her. He couldn't get enough of her then. She had even teased him about editing the word fornication out of the Bible. Nancy's sigh was forlorn and full of self-pity. Nathan Locke had apparently gotten enough of her. He might think she was used up, but other men wouldn't.

Nancy reached for her satin gown and felt it soft and sensuous against her skin.

She smiled.

Other men would find her attractive. Other men would be glad to wipe away her tears and hold her close and hold her tight and hold her often, whenever she needed them.

Other men would be there waiting for her when the lights went out on a summer night and she came to them like a shadow, naked in the moonlight, her lips moist, and only a gentle, tantalizing breeze to separate their warm and eager bodies.

But damn.

The smile faded.

She didn't want other men.

She only wanted Nathan.

Nancy added just enough rouge to give her cheeks a slight blush and caressed her long, slender neck with the fragrance of Shalimar. God, she wished she could hide those blue veins that lay just under the thin surface of her pallid skin. And she shuddered when she glanced in the mirror and caught a quick glimpse of those dark circles that looked more like purple bruises beneath her eyes. God, she needed a drink. Nancy hadn't had one all day.

When she first discovered gin, Nathan had constantly and harshly criticized her drinking habit, at first in the privacy of their home and later to anyone who would listen to him.

It was a weakness he could not accept. He preached to her, then he cursed her, then he began to ignore her. He never mentioned her passion for gin anymore. He never mentioned anything to her anymore.

Maybe it had been the gin that drove them apart, Nancy decided that morning as she lay alone in her bedroom.

Gin.

It was the devil's own brew. At least that's what Nathan had said it was, and Nathan was never wrong.

Nancy had pulled herself out of bed as the room spun around her. It hurt too bad to open her eyes. She was too sick to raise her head.

Gin. It had to be the gin.

She didn't need it. Not really. She could whip it. This time Nathan was wrong. Dead wrong. Gin wasn't a crutch. It had only been a convenience.

Damn.

For a moment, Nancy had been afraid she was going to pass out. Then she hoped she would, and she could almost feel herself floating again somewhere in a black, cold abyss where she was free, and she belonged to eternity, and the problems of life had lost their grip on her, and she was no longer sad.

The room stopped spinning.

Nancy had tried to open her eyes and found they were already open.

Gin was a curse, she told herself.

She could do without it.

She loved Nathan Locke.

Not gin.

She would give up one to get the other, to keep the other. Whatever it took, she would keep Nathan Locke. She couldn't let him go. Not now. She needed him too much.

Nancy had called out his name.

No answer.

She called again. Her voice was trembling.

The house was empty.

Damn.

The house was always empty.

The last thing Nancy Locke did before she threw up all over the bedroom floor was promise herself that she would never take another drop of gin again. It was a sacred vow, made just as the black abyss reached up to take her into the unholy sanctity of its bosom again.

When she awoke, the vomit had already dried upon her face, and her fingernails had clawed a ragged hole in the stain that was seeping through the sheets and ruining her satin pillows.

Nancy Locke paused in the darkened hallway. Her throat was dry, and her tongue longed to taste just one last drop of gin. She looked toward her bedroom door. It was closed. She had closed it to keep herself out, to keep herself away from the nightstand where the gin, cool and tempting, was waiting for her.

Nancy heard Nathan's heavy footsteps carrying him again into his study.

She braced herself.

For a moment, she forgot the gin. She was thinking only of her husband, the stranger who sometimes occupied her house. Her hands were shaking so badly that Nancy could barely tie the tassled belt that held her gown in place. It was white, almost transluscent, and trimmed with lace, the kind of gown women wore to bed with special men when they had no intentions of sleeping in it.

On this night, Nancy Locke had no intentions of sleeping at all. She and Nathan could begin anew. Surely she was woman enough to rekindle the old spark that had once flamed so brightly between them. All she needed was a chance. Nathan could not turn her away. She had never turned him away, not even during their honeymoon when she ached so badly and was so tired she could hardly move. Tonight belonged to her and Nathan, and she would do things for him she had never dared do before. She gingerly turned the brass knob and pushed the study door open.

Locke was bending over his desk, concern etched deeply in the rugged lines of his tanned face. Shadows crouched low in the darkness behind him, and he was using a pencil to trace off the backstreets of Vicksburg on an old Chamber of Commerce map that he kept folded in his Bible. He was wearing jeans and a faded Levi jacket over a black shirt with pearl buttons. For a minute, Locke did not realize that he was no longer by himself in the room. He had not heard Nancy enter, walking lightly on her bare feet.

Locke looked up, stunned, his face devoid of expression. Nancy smiled.

He had not seen her smile like that for a long time.

She waited for him to speak.

"That's a pretty gown," he said at last, not really knowing what to say.

The smile moved to her eyes.

"Thank you." Hers was the voice of a little girl. Locke almost thought he heard a childish giggle catch in her throat. "I bought it just for you."

Nathan Locke straightened, folded the map, and put it into the pocket of his jacket.

His face was stern, his eyes caught the flash of Nancy's thigh as she began walking slowly toward him. The gown was clinging to her skin, and he could see her nipples, hard and proud, straining beneath the satin.

A wave of uneasiness crept through his body.

Nancy slowly moistened her lips with her tongue. They glistened red in the dim light that spilled out from the small lamp on the study desk. There was a hungry look in her eyes.

There was no doubt what Nancy had on her mind.

Locke just couldn't figure out why.

For Nancy, for so long, sex had been a waste of time. For Locke, sex with Nancy had been simply a waste. He was man enough to know that lust wouldn't last forever. But he had been foolish enough to believe that love would. For Nathan Locke, any semblance of love had died away even while he still felt a flicker of lust stirring within him. Nancy was pretty enough, he guessed. But she bored him, both mentally and physically. He had grown. His vision about the world around him and his place in that world had expanded. Nancy was still a farm girl from the delta who couldn't cope with the pressure, the demands of being a preacher's wife. Locke used to think Nancy was petite, but now she looked skinny and angular, particularly around the hips. And it had been the gin that aged her, not the years. Her face was puffy, her eyes sunken. Locke could almost feel the heat from her body as she neared him. Their eyes met.

She reached out and touched his face with her fingertips. Her hand was trembling.

"I don't want to spend tonight alone," she whispered.

"My God," he answered, his voice harsh and raspy, "are you drunk?"

Nancy's hand fell from his face.

Her smile was gone.

"No." Locke could barely hear her. Nancy turned away and lowered her eyes, no longer able to face him. "It's been a long time since we've made love, Nathan."

He tried to answer but couldn't.

"And I am your wife."

Nancy waited for her husband to say that at least he was sorry. That shouldn't be difficult, not even for Nathan. There was no response. She looked up at him again and saw that his eyes were cold and distant.

"Am I that ugly to you?" She felt the tears begin to burn. "It's not easy for me to come to you and beg, Nathan." She was sobbing and her words were running together. "But I'm begging. Don't just stand there like a stone. Say *something*. Say anything. I love you, Nathan. And I want you. Don't just ignore me any longer, Nathan. I can't stand being ignored and thrown out of your life. I can't stand being lonely another day. Say you love me, or say you hate me, but, dammit, say something."

"I've got work to do," was all he said.

Nancy sagged to the floor, and Locke walked quickly around her. He hated any kind of face-to-face confrontation with his wife. They always seemed to begin this way and end with Nancy screaming at him.

"Nathan!" It was a scream.

He stopped in the doorway and looked back at her, so small, so fragile, so much like a rag doll slumped against the desk. The satin gown had fallen away from her bare legs, and her skin was sallow and bloodless in the harsh glare of the lamplight. Nancy's auburn hair hung limp where it had tumbled across her face. Her sunken eyes were staring at him, questioning him, accusing him.

"Who is she, Nathan?" Nancy asked in a strangled voice.

He gave her a cold stare and silently cursed the day he had ever met her. "I don't know what you mean," he answered, buttoning his jacket.

"Who is the woman you're sneaking out to see?"

Nathan Locke tried to grin, but it came out all wrong. "I'm not sneaking out anywhere," he said with a shrug.

Nancy's laugh was hollow. "Oh, no," she taunted. "You're a fancy preacher man now, Nathan. You're a man of the cloth, above all sin, annointed by God Himself. You're the chosen one. You don't have to sneak out anywhere anymore. Not you, Nathan. You just go wherever you're needed to heal the sick and save the lost and drive the demons from the widows' beds. It doesn't make any difference what you do, Nathan. You just do it in the name of the Lord, and that makes it all right in the sight of God and man and everybody. You're the forgiven one. Thank God for grace, Nathan. You better be glad that God has it. I don't. Not now. Not anymore."

"I have work to do," Locke repeated calmly.

Nancy turned her face away from him. It was as though he had not heard a word she said. Disappointment, then disdain lingered in Nancy's eyes.

"It's late." The hostility was gone from her voice, replaced by despair. "Almost eleven o'clock."

Locke ran a hand impatiently through his hair. "I must be going now."

"When will you be home?"

"I don't know."

"Surely your meeting won't last all night."

"It might."

"Who is she, Nathan?"

Without bothering to reply, Nathan Locke closed the study door behind him and, in doing so, shut Nancy out of his life as he had done so many times before. Right now he was on top. He had what he wanted. He had within his grasp the power that only radio and television could give a preacher. He was good. He knew he was good. Soon the whole world would know it as well. And he did not want

Nancy dragging him down as low as the depths into which she had fallen. There was no longer any room in his life for her or her silly, drunken tantrums. His wife definitely had to learn her place, stay there, and keep the hell out of his way. Nathan Locke was going places, and he didn't want any stumbling blocks around to slow him down or keep him from getting there.

The fresh air was a welcome relief, and the night winds blew cool against his face. The neighborhood was quiet as always, a collection of two-story brick homes with mansard roofs, dormer windows, and an occasional bay window looking out over the oak-lined cul-de-sacs. A security guard's patrol car was the only vehicle on the street. Locke slipped in behind the wheel of his Cadillac, took one last quick look at the map of Vicksburg, then drove away.

He knew the city. He knew it well.

But where he was going, he had never been before. He had preached about it. He had preached against it. But, until now, Locke had had no reason to go there. Maybe even now it was a waste of time.

Nathan Locke knew all about the dark side of big city streets. They had beckoned to him early in life, back when he was growing up on a Mississippi farm, hoeing cotton, chopping cotton, picking cotton, always longing to know just what lay beyond the far edge of the fields. During the summer after his graduation from high school, Locke simply dropped his cotton sack at the end of a row late one afternoon and began walking as fast as he could down that long, winding country road that led to Memphis, Tennessee. He never looked back. For six years, Nathan Locke didn't go back.

He felt as though he were a slave who had just broken his own chains and set himself free.

Jeremiah Locke had been a hard man, the kind of father who devoutly believed that God had given him a child solely for the purpose of the working the farm, and he worked Nathan from sunup to sundown, from can till can't. He was a big man, strong with broad shoulders, and he had never backed down from a fight in his life. He read the Bible to condemn his soul and drank whiskey to save it. His laughter was harsh, his eyes unforgiving, and he lost his cotton crop the year Nathan walked away to Memphis.

Nathan Locke had never really known his mother. She had died with a fever the year he was three, a fragile woman who lived her whole life in fear of the man who ruled their home. On the morning she drew her last breath, Amanda Locke slipped a gold, heart-shaped locket from around her neck and pressed it into Nathan's grubby little hand.

"Keep it," she had whispered, her voice fading. "It's something you can always have to remember your mother by."

A week later, Jeremiah Locke found the locket beneath his son's pillow, took it to downtown Holly Springs, and pawned it for enough money to buy a bottle of good whiskey.

Nathan never knew what had happened to the last and only gift his mother ever gave him. He only blamed himself for losing or misplacing it, and it gave him nightmares. He awoke most mornings, his eyes red from crying in his sleep. As the years passed, the blame turned to pity, then hatred. He stayed away from every girl who reminded him of his mother, and Nathan Locke saw a little bit of his mother in them all.

In Memphis, he got a job on the docks. The work was hard, but the pay made it all worthwhile. Gloria Taylor, who lived in one small room above a pool hall, took his money and shared her bed, but gave her love to another. She was warm and soft with blonde hair and a painted smile. She taught him the benefits of being a man. She made him glad that she was a woman. She made him forget that he had ever even had a mother. Gloria kicked Nathan Locke back out on the streets the day before her wedding. A week later, she was back down on the docks looking for him.

"I made a terrible mistake," she moaned.

Locke hadn't answered her.

"George promised we'd have a house of our own."

Locke's face was impassive.

"Now George has moved in with me." A playful smile tugged at the corners of Gloria's mouth. She wrapped her warm, soft arms around Nathan's waist, pressed her face against his bare chest and whispered, "I want you back."

"What about George?"

"I'll kick him out."

Nathan slapped her. He had never hit a woman before. He would never hit one again. It was just that Gloria was too damn good at kicking people out of her life. He laughed and sauntered away, leaving her to wipe away the blood that was clotting on her lips.

That night at eight–forty-seven, Nathan Locke became a changed man. He would never forget the time. He had been walking across the edge of Overton Park when he heard the powerful, seductive voice of the Reverend Chester Hardin. Beneath the trees, Nathan saw a big, striped gospel tent,

crammed with people, some weeping, some praying, some
stricken unconscious by the mighty power of God. That's
what Chester Hardin called it, and Nathan didn't doubt it
for a moment. The atmosphere was charged with an electricity
that chilled him to the bone.

He stood in the shadows of the tent, captivated by the
spell that the evangelist had cast upon all those within the
sound of his voice. He was a puppeteer, manipulating their
emotions with every word that passed through his lips. He
spoke, and they listened. He told them what to do, and they
obeyed. When it was time to cry, they cried. When it was
time to shout, they shouted. When it was time to fall to
their knees, they fell. Nathan Locke studied Chester Hardin's
face. It was carved from granite, stern, sincere. His eyes
were like burning coals, piercing, frightening. Nathan had
never realized before that one man could have so much power
over so many people. It surprised him. It amazed him.

Chester Hardin wasn't just a preacher.

He was a hypnotist, an illusionist.

At that moment, Nathan Locke heard the voice of God
call to him. At last, he knew what he had been placed on
earth to do. He had seen power. He wanted power, even if
it belonged to God. Nathan looked at his watch. It was eight–
forty-seven.

He had walked out of the cotton fields of Mississippi. Now
he turned his back on the bars, the strip joints, the neon
glitter of Memphis and walked out of the dark side of town.
He had not been born again, perhaps. But Nathan Locke
had definitely seen the light. There was a calm, a curious
peace within him that he had never found in a bottle of

whiskey or in Gloria Taylor's bed. He couldn't explain it, but he understood it, and Nathan Locke would never be the same again.

He took his last thirty-six dollars, bought a secondhand suit, and enrolled in seminary. Nathan wrangled a scholarship to pay his first year's tuition, then he found a night job to pay for the rest. His sermons were radical, a little too emotional for those who preferred the cold, formal rituals of the Presbyterian faith. But he could be spellbinding. His professors said privately that he should have been a Baptist.

Nathan Locke, even before graduation, had been tapped as a rising star, a young man for Presbytery to keep its eyes on. He was a leader, good-looking in a rugged sort of way, full of charm and charisma, a man who could take new churches and build a strong foundation beneath them.

He quickly outgrew one church in Waterford. Nathan only took it to be near his father again. Jeremiah Locke never once came the ten miles to hear him preach.

He built another church in Cleveland.

Then he carefully laid the groundwork he needed for an empire on the outskirts of Vicksburg, surrounded by the financial and social elite of Basilwood Heights.

Nathan Locke had been careful. He did not make mistakes. Save one. He married too quickly simply because he thought a good preacher needed a good wife. She would be important to his career. Soon, like his mother, she had been forgotten.

There were simply too many other concerns to worry about.

Tonight was no different.

Nathan Locke eased his black Cadillac alongside the curb and switched off its headlights. He sat there in the darkness

for a few minutes, collecting his thoughts, then, with a sigh
of disgust, joined the parade of sin and degradation that was
knotted together amongst the fierce, garrish reds and purples
of an angry neon night. Music blasted its way down the street
and spilled out over the river, but it had no tune and no
words that Locke could understand, just the rutting, grunting
sounds of animals in heat or in pain or both, sometimes shrill
and sometimes breathless but always pulsating and in synch
with the neon that flirted with the darkness and distorted
the shadows in the alleyways.

Locke was mesmerized by the faces that gathered around
him: young and old, male and female, though it was sometimes difficult to discern the difference between them. The
faces were gaunt and haunting, bearded and scarred, reeking
with the smell of cheap wine, beer, and dog manure. They
were sightless. They had seen too much already. Their eyes
were dull and lifeless, sometimes glazed, unable at times to
recognize the reflections of their own faces in the stained
and broken glass windows of the bars and juke joints that
had been wedged in between a hash house, a chili parlor,
and an adult picture show, places where men and women
with dull, sightless eyes of their own made a mockery of
love.

Teenagers with long, stringy hair, pimpled faces, torn shirts
and patched jeans stumbled down a cracked sidewalk, headed
for nowhere and in a hurry to get there. They shared their
wine with old, grizzled, soggy-faced men who had already
found it and never left. They were the lost, the damned.

Nathan Locke shuddered. He felt a chill even in the midst
of a stifled July night. *May God have mercy on their wayward,
drifting souls.* The sight of them sickened him.

A young girl, probably not yet sixteen, caught his eye and winked. Her blonde hair had come from a bottle, and she obviously hadn't been able to afford a new bottle for a long time. Her vinyl skirt was much too short, revealing a pair of shapely legs in black stockings that had a crooked seam. Her face was oval, the glow of the neon softened her skin, and she had the smile of an angel. She licked her painted lips and swayed slightly as she walked toward him.

"My name's Minette," she said.

"You don't look French."

"I can be anything you want." Minette licked her lips again. "What's your name?"

"It doesn't matter."

"What are you looking for?"

"A young man."

Minette frowned and leaned against Nathan Locke's shoulder. "You could have more fun with a young girl," she said.

"I'm looking for Jeremy Jensen." Locke pulled a high school photograph of the teenager from his pocket and handed it to the girl. She squinted at the picture in the dim neon light.

"Why do you want to find Jeremy?" Minette asked.

"I'm a friend of his."

She laughed ruefully. "You could be a friend of mine, too." Minette rubbed her body against his, and Locke could smell the odor of stale gin on her breath. The face of Nancy flashed into mind, but he quickly shoved it aside. He pulled a twenty-dollar bill out of his pocket and waved it in front of Minette. The dullness vanished from her eyes, and the smile of an angel became devilish.

"Do you know Jeremy?"

"Yes."

"Where can I find him?"

"He's usually hanging around Moon."

"Where can I find Moon?"

"Eating chili."

"Thank you." Locke placed the twenty-dollar bill in Minette's hand and turned to walk away.

"Hey, mister," she said.

He drew a deep breath and looked back at her.

"Is that all you want?"

"That's all."

Minette shrugged as she folded the bill twice and placed it in the sole of her right shoe. "Hell," she said with disappointment creeping into her voice, "for twenty dollars you could have had a blow job."

Nathan Locke found Jeremy Jensen slumped in a wooden chair, leaning against the back wall of the Silver Dollar Chili Parlor. His hair was unkempt, and a week's growth of stubble was scattered randomly across his face. His jeans were stained with motorcycle grease, and Jeremy was wearing a black faded tee-shirt advertising the last coast to coast tour of Motley Crew. Nathan Locke glanced around the dimly-lit little hole-in-the-wall cafe and decided that the name of the band on the shirt definitely fit in nicely with the regular clientele of the Silver Dollar. Cigarette smoke hung like a deadly haze above the wooden tables, and a jukebox throbbed out the blues. Shadows danced in the flickering candlelight. Sawdust littered the floor, and the acrid smell of rotting onions and oregano battled with the sweat and the smoke for Nathan Locke's attention. His eyes burned, and the stench was nauseous. He walked straight to the back table.

"Hello, Jeremy," he said.

The young man looked up, a perpetual sneer on his face. "Hello, preacher man," he answered. "I didn't expect to see you anywhere. It ain't even Sunday." He took a long, slow drink from a pitcher of lukewarm beer then set it heavily on the table and shoved it toward Locke. "Want a drink?"

The minister shook his head. "You're a little under age to be drinking, aren't you?"

Jeremy laughed. It was almost a cackle. "Around here, nobody gives a damn what you do or how old you are when you do it," he said.

"Is that why you hang out around here?"

"Maybe."

Locke leaned against the wall and folded his arms. He would have sat down, but he preferred standing, staring down on Jeremy with eyes as piercing as those of the Almighty Himself. It gave him the edge. Jeremy talked tough. He acted tough. But beneath that hard-boiled veneer beat the heart of a little boy. He could be intimidated, and Nathan Locke, when necessary, could be a master of intimidation.

"Your mother wants you to come home," he said, his voice soft but strong.

"My mother can go to hell."

"She's worried about you."

"She doesn't even know where the hell I am."

"That's what worries her."

Jeremy reached for the pitcher again. "So she sent you down here to try and sweet talk me with all of that high-fallutin' preacher talk of yours into going back home. Is that it?" He raised the pitcher to his lips.

"No."

Jeremy looked surprised.

Locke leaned over and placed the palms of both hands flat on the tabletop. He was virtually eyeball to eyeball with Jeremy Jensen, and his face had become as hard as stone. "I didn't come here to talk you into going home, son." His lips peeled back into a sinister grin. "I came here to haul your little ass home."

Jeremy's bravado began to fade. His chin quivered, and he spilled the beer down the front of his shirt.

"You sure you're a preacher?" he asked nervously.

"I'm a preacher."

"You sure as hell don't talk like one."

Nathan Locke didn't move. His eyes cut deep. "On Sunday mornings, I stand in the pulpit and talk about God's love," he said. Each word was like a pistol shot. "Tonight, I'm here to teach you about God's wrath."

"Don't give me none of that hellfire and brimstone shit," Jeremy said, his eyes darting uneasily around the room.

Locke's ominous grin widened. "Oh, I'll do better than that, Jeremy. If necessary, I'll beat the living hell out of you, but, like it or not, I'm taking you out of this dump."

"You can't."

"Think you're man enough to stop me?"

A shadow fell over Nathan Locke's face. The candlelight wavered, and the flame almost went out.

"By god," came a voice, "I'm man enough to stop you."

To Locke, it sounded like the voice of doom, uttered by Lucifer himself, deep and metallic and foreboding. Even the jukebox didn't nearly sound so loud anymore. There was no reason for Locke to look up. "You must be the man they call Moon," he said.

"I'm Moon."

Nathan Locke slowly turned his head. The man beside him stood well over six feet, and he looked annoyed, as though the minister had intruded into his private domain and interfered with one of his personal playthings. Moon was thick and beefy, his face hidden behind a black beard that, apparently, had not been trimmed in years. On one bulging arm, he wore the tatoo of a half moon, dripping in blood, although the years had turned it from blood red to pink. The sleeves on his shirt were torn out, and Moon had tried to cram his jeans down into the tops of his secondhand snakeskin boots. At the moment, he was digging grease out from beneath his fingernails with a pocketknife that, to Locke, looked as big as a Southern Mississippi frog sticker.

"I don't believe I have any business with you," the minister said dryly. "I came here to talk to Jeremy."

"If you got business with Jeremy, you sure as hell got business with me."

Locke felt his jaws clench. "I'm taking him out of here."

"He don't want to go."

"Jeremy doesn't have a choice."

Moon stabbed the knife into the wooden tabletop beside Locke's outstretched hand. It was the only noise in the room. "I don't want him to go," he growled.

Nathan Locke suddenly reflected a terrible inner dread on his face. He could feel a silent rage boiling up within him. His eyes became narrow slits. He knew what he had to do. God had no place for weak men. God had a place for Nathan Locke.

With one motion, he grabbed the burning candle, wheeled abruptly, and rammed the flame into Moon's satanic face.

The man screamed.

Molten wax poured into his eyes. He clawed desperately at his face. His beard smouldered.

He screamed again.

And Locke kicked him in the groin. Moon staggered backwards. Locke kicked him again, harder this time. And Moon went down to his knees, rocking back and forth. Locke splintered a chair over the man's head, and Moon lay in a heap on the floor, blood and sawdust matting his unruly hair. He groaned once, tried to rise, then was still. Locke hoped he was still breathing.

Without a word, he grabbed Jeremy Jensen by the back of his neck, jerked him out of his chair, and dragged him kicking and screaming across the floor, out the door, and down the cracked sidewalk.

No one really noticed.

The wayward, the drifting, the sightless merely looked the other way.

Jeremy did not quit kicking and screaming until Locke opened the trunk of his Cadillac, crammed him down in between the tool box and spare tire, and slammed the lid shut.

Helen Jensen wanted him to talk to her son.

Well, by god, he would talk to him.

And Jeremy would listen. He had no choice.

Nathan Locke drove to the Beechwood Motel where no one knew him, asked for and received a room at the far end of the parking lot. He paid in advance and signed his name as Leonard Parker. No one asked to see his driver's license or a credit card.

Locke parked his Cadillac between two eighteen-wheelers,

threw open the trunk lid, and led a sullen, subdued Jeremy Jensen into room twenty-seven.

"This is kidnapping," the boy muttered.

"Bullshit."

"Then what do you call it?"

Locke's face had lost its violence. His eyes were again full of sympathy and concern.

"It's time somebody sat you down and pounded some sense in your head," he said.

"Literally?" Jeremy asked with scorn.

"If necessary."

"Is that what my mother wanted you to do?"

"Let's just say that she's not opposed to the idea."

"She can't run my life anymore."

"No, she can't."

"And neither can you."

Locke unbuttoned his jacket, sat down in an overstuffed chair, and propped his feet up on the edge of the bed. Until now, he hadn't realized just how tired he really was.

"I don't want to run your life," he told the boy. "I just hate to see you throw it away."

"It's mine. I can do what I want to with it."

"Not as long as I'm around." Locke paused. Jeremy was watching him with eyes as cold and empty as a dead fish. "If someone were trying to kill you, Jeremy, I couldn't just stand idly by and watch you die. I'd fight like hell to save you." He paused again to give his words a chance to soak in. "Well, right now, you're trying to kill yourself, and I'm not gonna let you. I'll fight you as hard as I would fight anyone else to save your life. If that means talking to you,

I'll talk. If it means praying for you, I'll pray. If it means
knocking the shit out of you, I'll do that, too. Whatever it
takes, Jeremy. I don't care. That's ultimately up to you. But
whatever it takes, I'm gonna do it, so you might as well get
used to it. Whenever you look over your shoulder, I'm gonna
be there, either talking or praying or kicking. It makes me
no difference, Jeremy. I'm pretty damned efficient at all three
of them."

A strange calm spread over Jeremy's face. He sat down
on the bed, and the hard edge left his voice. "You're not
bullshittin' me, are you?"

"God doesn't have any use for bullshitters." Locke nodded
toward the bathroom. "Now get in there and get cleaned
up."

"Why?"

"You stink."

Jeremy slowly shook his head. "I don't understand you,"
he said.

"When a man becomes a man," Locke answered, "he puts
away his childish things, and there's nothing more childish
than running around dirty, looking like you've been laying
in the mud with a bunch of pigs. That's gonna change, Jeremy,
and it's gonna start changing right now. It's time you became
a man, thought like a man, and acted like a man."

"But I don't want to go home." It was a plea.

"You can stay here until you're ready to face your mother
and father. I won't tell them where you are, but at least
they won't have to worry about you being out on the streets
at night." Locke grinned. "You certainly can't depend on
Moon to protect you."

"I can't afford to stay in a motel."

"I'll pay for it."

"That ain't right."

Locke shrugged and felt the fatigue dig deep into his shoulder muscles. His body was tense, and there was a dull ache probing, pounding behind his eyes. "Don't worry about it," he said matter-of-factly. "I'll take the money out of the church's benevolency fund or something. We've got funds for more causes than we've got causes. Now get in there and take your shower. When you get cleaned up, we'll talk awhile, and you can tell me why you don't like any of us over forty anymore."

Nathan Locke sat back, rubbed his temples, and waited. The sound of running water was so peaceful, so comforting. The tenseness began to melt out of his body, and he felt himself slipping away, and he fought hard to stay awake.

So much of his life had been based on promises.

To himself.

To others.

Even to Nancy.

Promises kept. And forgotten.

So many of them had been empty promises. But not this one. He told Helen Jensen he would help her, and he had.

The sky was already creased by the first, faint rays of the morning sun when Nathan Locke got home. He found Nancy lying crumpled in the hallway floor, asleep, an empty gin bottle pressed against her breasts. He picked her up and gently placed her in bed, wishing that he still loved her, sorry that he didn't, and not knowing what to do about it.

9

On the last Saturday night in July, Birdie Castleberry held her annual midsummer formal gala at the Basilwood Country Club. Everybody who was somebody in the Vicksburg area received an invitation. Everybody who wanted to be somebody prayed that the invitation would come. It was, without doubt, society's uppercrust party of the year.

Eunice Gordon had talked to Alice Setzer, and Alice had talked to Birdie, and Susan Heatherly eagerly awaited an invitation that never came.

She fretted.

Then she fumed.

On Saturday afternoon, Susan called Birdie and said sweetly, "I'm so sorry, but my invitation apparently got lost in the mail. You know how it is with the postal service these days. I'm just calling to let you know that John and I are looking forward to the party, and we'll be there tonight."

Promptly at eight o'clock, while Birdie Castleberry watched with a pinched face and incensed eyes, Susan Heatherly made her appearance, wearing a new black, low-cut Dior gown that John could obviously not afford. It was the talk, if not the envy, of the party, and she danced at least one dance with every man who was there.

R AYMOND Lynch stepped back out into the late afternoon sunshine that splashed across E. T. Breithaupt's Old
Country Store at Lorman. His face was shaded by the row
of handsewn bonnets, all bunched together, a collection of
red, white, and blue checks, hanging loosely on a piece of
baling wire that had been stretched across the big, wide,
rundown front porch. Raymond wiped the sweat from his
face with a cold bottle of Coke and leaned casually against a
knotted post, nodding at Uncle George, an elderly black man
who spent his days sitting on a log bench beside the store
when he wasn't working, and Uncle George swore he was
just too damned old to work anymore.

"I see you're taking it easy again, George," Raymond said,
rolling up the sleeves on his denim shirt.

"No, suh." The old man frowned. His overalls were faded
and frayed, his straw hat tattered, and there were holes in

135

the soles of his brogans. "I been workin' hard just chasin' the shade from one side of this building to the other. The Lord must not think too kindly of ol' Uncle George or he would keep the shade in the same place all day."

He laughed—it was more like a wheeze—and Raymond laughed with him.

"It's been a hot summer," the schoolteacher said, glad to have the chance to talk with someone who had lived for so long upon native soil.

"The summers around here are always hot." Uncle George leaned forward, took off his straw hat, and began slowly fanning himself. "Why last week, it was so doggone hot I saw a dog chasin' a rabbit, and they was both walkin'."

He wheezed again.

"How long have you lived around here, George?"

"Since I was born."

"And when was that?"

"I don't rightly know, boss." Uncle George sadly shook his head. "I was just a little bitty boy then and too doggone young to tell time."

Raymond sat down beside him and propped his white sneakers up on the edge of the porch. "They tell me your father was a slave," he said softly.

"He shore was. He worked for Mister Jacobs and picked a lot of cotton in his life and never got paid for none of it. He got old in a hurry and stayed that way for a long time."

"And what about you?"

"Ol' Uncle George picked himself a lot of cotton, too."

"Did you get paid for the cotton you picked?"

"Yes, suh."

"How much?"

"A penny a pound."

"That's not much."

"No, suh." George shrugged his tired shoulders. "But it's a helluva lot better than gettin' nothin' a pound."

Raymond Lynch couldn't argue with that. He patted the old man gently and got to his feet. "I'd love to sit here and talk to you awhile, George," he said, "but I've got to get on back to Vicksburg."

"What do you do back in the Vicksburg?"

"I teach."

"You teach them kids to read and write?"

Raymond grinned. "Sometimes," he answered.

"Ol' Uncle George never learned to read and write."

"I'm sorry."

"That's all right." George's face suddenly glistened in the sunlight. He had lost his shade again. "Ol' Uncle George never needed to read or write." He paused, then added, "But I could flat figure that cotton at a penny a pound."

"I bet you could." Raymond started to walk away, but George's words stopped him.

"Say, boss."

Raymond turned.

"You gonna finish all that Coke by yourself. Ol' Uncle George could sure help you keep it from goin' to waste."

Raymond smiled and handed the bottle to the old man. "Why don't you just take the rest of it, George. I'm already as full as a june bug."

"That's tick."

"Huh?"

"Down here we say 'full as a tick.'"

Raymond shook his head. He sometimes didn't think he would ever understand the Southern vernacular, much less be able to talk it. "Well, George," he said, "whatever it is, that's what I am."

He walked across the dirt parking lot, got into his car, and drove away as the long shadows of the pines fell across the pavement in front of him.

Raymond Lynch had always been fascinated with the history of the South. Perhaps, he sometimes thought, that's why he had given up a good teaching job in a Massachusetts private school and come to Mississippi. At least, that was the lie he told himself. After three years in Vicksburg, it had become easier for even him to believe.

In reality, Raymond had never been able to figure out why such a backward, rural part of the United States could be so proud, even defiant, about a war it had fought and lost. Few in Mississippi ever called it the Civil War. Hell, one old-timer told him, there wasn't anything *civil* about it. Another referred to it, with anger in his voice, as the war of Northern Aggression. And an aging blue-haired matriarch of society had simply told him, "In my home, the war is never mentioned at all. But I do recall my mother telling us something about the Late Unpleasantness."

"How unpleasant was it?" Raymond had asked.

The matron's eyes narrowed, but the magnolia-soft inflection in her voice never changed. "Our homes were burned," she said. "Our crops were destroyed. Our men were killed. Our children went hungry. Our clothes became rags. Our land was stolen, our slaves taken away from us."

"It must have been rough."

"We survived," the matron said proudly.

"From what I've read, though," Raymond ventured, "Vicksburg did not even want to secede from the Union."

"We didn't. Vicksburg voted against secession."

"What happened?"

"The Yankees came anyway."

"And?"

"The bastards shot at us," she said sweetly.

Raymond Lynch had learned long ago that authentic history, the kind he liked to teach, was seldom found in a textbook. For the last three summers, he had done his research on the backroads of Mississippi, talking to anyone and everyone who would sit and chat with him for awhile. He rummaged through old ghost towns, trekked across the silent hills of deserted and sometimes forgotten battlefields, and was a familiar figure kneeling in country cemeteries at the close of the day.

Raymond found much of his southern history distorted by bitterness and hatred, pride and contradictions. Prejudice, he decided, was a way of life. A man could argue against it until he was blue in the face, but he couldn't change the way another man thought, not after all these years anyway. In Mississippi, prejudice was never judged, just accepted. Back home in Massachusetts, the injustice was just as severe, he knew, but it was generally practiced behind closed doors. There, when Raymond tried to ignore it, it was easy. He seldom saw it. But, try as he might, he never forgot the night poor Jimmy Gerald Washington had been dragged out of a pool hall and hauled down to the Blackstone River by three white men who had come, they said, to teach "a goddam nigger liar a lesson he would never forget."

The boy's mother had frantically awakened him about midnight, pounding on his door, screaming and pleading for someone to help her son.

"They're gonna kill him," she sobbed.

"They won't hurt him," Raymond had said, wrapping an arm around her, "This is Massachusetts." It was, he recalled later, a ludicrous thing to say.

Jimmy Gerald had always been bright-eyed and eager, but he was backward and bashful, slow to learn, and the children made fun of him in school. For years, he simply laughed when they laughed. He didn't know any better. He was in the seventh grade before he ever realized that no one liked him, that he didn't have any friends, that the others were laughing at him. From that day on, Jimmy Gerald seldom smiled. A week later he had dropped out of school.

The boy did odd jobs around town and, during one summer, Raymond Lynch taught him how to read the simple words in an old-fashioned *Dick and Jane* primer. Jimmy Gerald carried it, torn and wrinkled, everywhere he went, and he followed Raymond like a puppy dog. Raymond Lynch would talk to him man to man. Raymond Lynch had never laughed at him.

He had looked into the pained face of Jimmy Gerald's mother that night and asked calmly, "Where did they take him?"

"Down to the river."

"Why, for God's sakes."

"They gonna kill him if you don't stop 'em, mister Lynch. They gonna kill my boy."

For Raymond, the thought was simply too ridiculous to comprehend. The races, black and white, had always gotten along within reason. At least there had never been any open conflict.

Why now?

What had Jimmy Gerald done?

Raymond had called the sheriff's dispatcher. She would send a patrol car down to the river as quickly as possible, she said. But, like Raymond, the dispatcher didn't seem to be particularly concerned. This was Braxton, Massachusetts, population 4,218. People got drunk and were a little rowdy from time to time. Wives killed their husbands or vice versa, and they usually had pretty good reasons for doing it. Cars had been stolen, and kids occasionally broke into Jack Hardesty's hardware store. But nothing of any consequence ever happened in Braxton, certainly not between black and white. It was a civilized place, nonviolent and proud of it.

Raymond Lynch found Jimmy Gerald Washington ankle-deep in mud on the banks of the Blackstone. The harsh glare of a flashlight outlined his face, and it was frozen and twisted with fear. A rope had been tied around his neck, and his eyes were wide and bulging. Jimmy Gerald clawed at the knot under his chin, and he could hardly breath. Charles Lawson held the other end of the rope, hate embedded deep in his eyes. His suit was wrinkled, his tie askew, the veins in his neck were bulging with anger. Two members of his construction crew stood behind him, young and muscular and committed to doing anything their boss told them to do. Raymond Lynch didn't know their names. He would never forget their faces, cool, self-assured, free of any guilt or remorse.

"Turn him loose," Raymond had ordered.

Charles Lawson's laugh was that of a hyena. He pulled the knot tighter around the boy's throat. Jimmy Gerald was gagging now, spittle running down the corners of his mouth.

"You don't have any reason to hurt the boy." Raymond's voice was calm, his stomach churning.

"I got every reason to silence him."

"What's he done bad enough to make you start acting like an animal, Charles?"

"He's been goin' around town braggin' about fuckin' a white girl."

Raymond sighed sadly. "Jimmy Gerald's just a poor, semi-retarded boy who'll say anything to get people to listen to him. He's all talk, nothing else."

The knot was squeezed tighter.

"He's been showin' pictures."

Raymond shrugged his shoulders as if to say, "So what?"

"They were pictures of my daughter."

Suddenly, before Raymond could even move, Lawson yanked on the rope and jerked Jimmy Gerald to his knees, twisting the boy backwards and thrusting his head beneath the cold, rushing waters of the Blackstone River.

Raymond Lynch stood, his eyes in a trance, his muscles unable to work. Only ten feet away, the black boy was kicking and thrashing at the water, fighting, scratching, his hands waving wildly in the in the swaying glare of the flashlight, throwing odd-shaped shadows across the ground that spilled in agony into the black and murky water.

Raymond screamed.

His legs would not move.

He watched, his eyes horrified.

Not ten feet away a boy was dying.

He screamed again.

The water was alive, a swirling mass of anger and confusion, boiling and churning, a storm, a rage seething within the muddy depths of the Blackstone.

A boy was dying.

And a river would keep his secret.

His plea for mercy died with him.

Jimmy Gerald's arms stopped waving. They strained and stretched upward, every tendon trembling, his hands quivering. Then they fell. And the river was quiet.

Only Charles Lawson's voice broke the silence, "He ain't gonna tell no more lies about my baby," he said.

A week later, on the day the local newspaper ran a two paragraph story on the back page about the accidental drowning of Jimmy Gerald Washington, Raymond Lynch quit his teaching job, packed his car, and headed south. He was appalled at the nightmare he had witnessed on the river. He was appalled at himself for simply standing there and screaming, never once lifting a hand to try and save a young boy's life. He had been a coward even with Jimmy Gerald's eyes begging him to do something, anything to help him. Raymond Lynch was his friend. Raymond Lynch was his last hope. Raymond Lynch had stood his ground, saying little, doing nothing, watching a boy drown, watching him dragged beneath a brown and angry foam.

Charles Lawson had stood before him, the smell of hate on his breath, slowly wrapping the loose ends of a wet rope around his big hands. He said simply, "You ain't been here, and you didn't see nothin'."

Raymond left Jimmy Gerald in the Blackstone. His broken

body was found six days later and four miles downstream, wedged between the rocks. His face had been battered until it was barely recognizable. His eyes were open. They would haunt Raymond for the rest of his life, just as a mother's red eyes had looked at him accusingly when he stopped by the funeral home on his way out of Braxton. She didn't say a word, but she knew. She knew everything. Her boy was murdered, and the one man she thought she could depend on was running away.

As he drove that night through Alabama, and turned toward Mississippi, Raymond Lynch made up his mind. If the time ever came to fight again, he would not simply turn his back and walk away as he had done beside the Blackstone. For that, there would be no forgiveness on earth or in heaven. He tried to shake himself loose from the thoughts of Jimmy Gerald, but they never left him alone nor gave him any peace.

He did not approve of the prejudices he had found in Mississippi. But at least men were honest about them. If they didn't like you or the color of your skin, they let you know it. Back in Massachusetts, hatred and bitterness burned just as deeply, but everyone lied about it. Even he had lied about it, and that was the greatest sin of all.

Yet, man's injustices toward man weighed heavily on Raymond Lynch's conscience. They frustrated him. They tormented him. And he could see them everywhere he went: the rich taking advantage of the poor, the strong running roughshod over the weak, those who devoutly believed that God created all men equal as long as they were white and had a job.

Raymond shuddered. Mississippi had its troubles, and most

of them, he knew, were self-inflicted. Mississippi was no different from where he had come. Three years had passed, and still Raymond Lynch, when he closed his eyes on a steamy summer night, could hear Jimmy Gerald Washington gagging as the rope tore the skin around his skinny neck.

In Vicksburg, he knew he didn't belong. He would always be on the outside of society looking in, but Raymond didn't really mind. He understood tradition and knew that a person had to be a genuine fourth-generation sonofabitch with Confederate gray in his bloodlines to be socially acceptable.

He loved the story Tom Beecher had told him about a young man who left his southern home and ventured north to Chicago, seeking a job. The prospective employer, a CPA with a major accounting firm, called one of his references, a banker, and asked, "What can you tell me about Tom Johnson's credentials?"

The banker thought for a moment then answered, "He is a young man of unimpeachable character and impeccable bloodlines. His grandfather on his mother's side was a Lee and his grandfather on his father's side was a Beauregard."

"Hell," snapped the CPA, "I wanted him for a clerk, not for breeding purposes."

It made sense in Vicksburg. For Raymond Lynch, very little else made sense in Vicksburg. More times than not, he felt like the outsider he was. No one ever asked him about his bloodlines. No one wanted to know. He was simply a transplanted yankee, and that meant he was about as welcome in some circles as the chicken pox. At school, the students had accepted him quicker than the other teachers. He was dour, iconoclastic and sometimes irreverent, and his

classes appreciated his honesty. It troubled others. He didn't
glorify war. His heroes had warts and flaws; their failures
were just as important as their successes, and that made them
almost human. As Raymond Lynch kept telling his students,
a hero in history was nothing more than an ordinary man or
woman who, because of extraordinary circumstances, was able
to do extraordinary things, in spite of the odds. More than
once he quoted Will Rogers, saying, "God must have loved
the common folk more than anyone else because he made
so many of us." It was the one truism in life that he sincerely
believed.

The congregation at Basilwood Presbyterian looked upon
Raymond Lynch as something of a free-thinking maverick,
but a man who would roll up his sleeves and work as hard
as he could whenever the church needed him. He was, some
said privately, their one common man in an uncommon congregation, always wearing jeans, and sneakers, even on Sunday. Nathan Locke thought of him as a perplexing study in
contrasts.

"You're a puzzle I can't figure out," the pastor told him
one Sunday while they sat together in the church library.
"You're never exactly what you seem to be."

Raymond had laughed. "I'm just a simple man with simple
tastes," he answered.

"I don't mean to be personal," Locke said, carefully choosing his words, "but I've been told that you are a devout
supporter of the blacks and their quest for equality."

"That's a fair statement."

"You speak up for the blacks every chance you get."

Raymond nodded.

"You fight for their place in society."

Again Raymond nodded.

"Yet you are a member of Basilwood Presbyterian, and I don't believe that we have ever had a black walk through our front door." Locke scrutinized Raymond's face while he talked, searching for some clue to the secrets that were kept bottled up within the man. "It's not that I'm suggesting for you to go elsewhere, God forbid, but a lot of people I've talked to wonder why you don't attend a black church."

"I probably should."

"There are certainly plenty of them around."

"But I can't."

"Why not?"

Raymond's grin was full of mischief and contagious. "The blacks around here aren't presbyterian," he said. "And I'm afraid that I don't have a baptist bone in my body." He grew serious. "My politics may be a little outrageous and unruly sometimes," he continued, "but I want my religion full of pomp and ceremony on Sunday morning. I want my church dignified and its government orderly. I want to know where I stand with God, and I want to be able to go to sleep at night without the smell of brimstone burning in my nostrils."

"Are you running from guilt?"

"Aren't we all?"

Nathan Locke shrugged. He glanced at the cross in the stained glass window, ablaze in the glow of the afternoon sun. Its refracted colors danced wildly across Raymond's thin face and splattered across the far wall behind him. The minister abhorred hypocrisy. And there was nothing hypocritical at all about Raymond Lynch. The schoolteacher was frank and straightforward, a man who gave you his word then stood behind it. Locke might not agree with everything Raymond had to say, but he admired the man's courage to say it. He would definitely be an asset to the church. There was no doubt about it.

A year later, Nathan Locke sat down with his nominating committee and suggested that Raymond Lynch just might make a good, solid addition to the session. His suggestion was met with cold stares, disbelief. Locke leaned back, closed his eyes, and waited for the protests that he knew would come.

"You know Raymond's a goddam nigger lover, don't you?"

"He's not like the rest of us."

"He's a Yankee, Nathan. He doesn't understand the way we do things down here."

"He doesn't even wear a suit and tie on Sunday."

"Have you seen the old car he drives?"

Nathan Locke grinned to himself. When the last objection had died away, he sat suddenly upright, folded his hands together, and said simply, "Raymond's a good man. He's got good ideas and he's not afraid to express them."

"He can be a pain in the ass, Nathan."

Locke arched an eyebrow. "Sometimes we're all a pain in the ass."

"It's a mistake, Nathan."

"Maybe. But I want him. He's a good man to have on our side, and I want to keep him there." Locke chuckled. "We presbyterians have been fitting square pegs into round holes for a long time."

Tom Beecher nodded. It was as good as done. What Nathan
Locke wanted, Nathan Locke got. It was an unwritten, unspo-
ken rule that had not been broken in years.

Raymond Lynch walked into the session room, the last,
as usual, to arrive, and every eye was on him. He smiled
and nodded his greetings without saying a word, looking, as
always, out of place. His thinning hair, cut a little too long,
was windblown and bleached by too many hours in a relent-
less July sun. His face had been blistered and was peeling,
the curse of having fair skin in the deep south. The armpits
in his blue denim shirt were sweated down, and his jeans
were dusty from climbing around the steep banks of the
Grand Gulf Battlefield. He should have worn his checked
sport coat, Raymond thought, but, hell, it was too hot and
too late to try to impress anybody. He dropped his lanky
frame into a wooden chair, picked up the minutes from the
session's last meeting and quickly scanned them. For Raymond Lynch, it was merely a formality and generally a waste
of time. He seldom remembered what had happened at the
last meeting, and the minutes only recorded what Nathan
Locke wanted written down for posterity anyway.

The session, as it had been pointed out to him, had the
awesome responsibility of running the church. Maybe that's
what the Book of Order said. But as far as Raymond could
see the session only got together once a month to rubber
stamp whatever it was that Nathan Locke wanted to do. He
was the minister, the pastor, the high priest, the father supe-
rior, the dictator of Basilwood Presbyterian. He controlled

the money. He controlled the books. His word was law. But, Raymond figured, that's probably the way it should be. That's probably the way it was in most denominations.

The preacher knew what he needed. The session didn't. The preacher was out in the trenches and on the firing line everyday of his life. Let him take whatever ammunition he needed to do the job that needed to be done. As long as it was orderly, as long as it was legal, Raymond really didn't care what Nathan Locke did. Lately, though, he had an uneasy, almost frightening feeling that the minister might just be overstepping his bounds somewhat and operating outside of proper Presbyterian procedures. And that troubled him.

First, he had fired his secretary, and her dismissal should have been left up to the session. And there were rumors afloat that John Madison's days as choir director were growing shorter. Again Locke was making preparations to do what he wanted to do without even seeking session approval. Late one night over a beer at Tuminello's, Robert Jensen had even told him about a slush fund Nathan Locke had allegedly established for himself.

"Where'd he get the money?" Raymond had asked.

"He siphoned it off the pledges that had been collected for the building program."

"How'd he do that?"

"The man's smart."

Raymond had leaned across the table. "Where did you find out about such a slush fund?"

"Tom Beecher's taking care of it for him." Robert laughed aloud. "He's a lawyer. I'm a lawyer. Let me tell you, friend, there ain't no secrets in the courthouse. It's got a lot of walls, and they all talk."

Raymond frowned. Nothing nettled him like unfounded gossip. "Nathan already makes a lot of money," he said. "And I understand that he's even made a couple of investments that have paid off rather handsomely. He's got a new home and a new Cadillac, and the church is paying for both of them. Why the hell does he need a slush fund?"

"Greed." Robert Jensen swallowed hard and ordered another beer, a Bud in a frozen mug. "Those that get a little want a lot. And those that get a lot want it all."

Raymond sat back in thought, scratching his chin. There were times when he wished that he still smoked, and this was one of them. "How much did Nathan put in his slush fund?" he asked bluntly.

Robert leaned forward confidentially. "I hear tell that it's a hundred thousand dollars."

Raymond whistled in surprise. "What in hell does Nathan need with a hundred thousand dollars?"

"He travels quite a bit."

"He's got a healthy travel allowance from the church."

"Nathan doesn't always travel for the church."

Raymond's eyes narrowed and his brow wrinkled in a quizzical expression. "What are you saying?" he asked.

"I hear tell he's grown tired of that little wife of his."

Raymond shook his head, a look of protest in his eyes. "I can't believe Nathan is having an affair," he scoffed. "It wouldn't make sense."

"Wouldn't it?" Robert drained his glass, then licked away

the last flakes of ice that clung to its side. "He's good-looking, dynamic, in the prime of life. He's a stud if I've ever seen one. If a man's not getting everything he wants at home, believe me, he'll get it somewhere else."

"But Nathan is a preacher."

"Preachers are human, too."

So they were. But, so often, congregations didn't realize that. They didn't allow their ministers to make mistakes. They couldn't forgive them their mistakes. They didn't want humans in the pulpit. They wanted gods. Thus far Nathan Locke had given them everything they wanted.

Raymond Lynch searched his own soul. He was as bad as the rest of them. He wanted his "God loves" and "Jesus saves" dished up every Sunday by a man who was spotless and without sin. He suddenly broke out in a cold, nauseous sweat and began to feel queasy. *Let him who is without sin cast the first stone,* Raymond told himself. In his mind, he again looked into the begging, the pitiful, the dying eyes of Jimmy Gerald Washington, and he felt the cold, wet rope as it began to tighten around his own throat.

God might be able to forgive.

Man couldn't.

Raymond Lynch couldn't. Raymond Lynch wasn't even for sure that God had forgiven him.

He never asked anyone else about the slush fund, and he never heard anyone mention it. Perhaps it had just been a warped figment of Robert Jensen's imagination. He knew Robert didn't like preachers. He knew Robert, in particular, didn't like Nathan Locke, probably because his wife went running to the pastor's study every time there was an argu-

ment in their home, and Robert argued with Helen almost
every day. Raymond Lynch didn't believe that Nathan Locke
would steal from the church, and he didn't believe his minister had another woman stashed away somewhere. There were
some things that he simply refused to believe. Yet, there
was a nagging doubt gnawing at the back of his mind, and
it would not go away and he cursed Robert Jensen for putting
it there.

Raymond Lynch glanced around the parlor. No one was
saying a word. Everyone was simply waiting for Nathan Locke
to tell them what to vote on and how to vote. Birdie Castleberry sat at his right hand, smiling at no one in particular,
her reading glasses perched on the end of her nose. Her
red dress was the only bright spot in the room, and Birdie
wore a black sweater even in summertime. Her blood was
thin, she said. Air conditioning chilled her right through to
the bone.

Tom Beecher had pushed his chair back against the wall,
out of the way, as though he were simply an outside observer
who had no business even being there. His eyes were bored,
his face haggard. His mind never slept at all. Tom's gray
slacks were baggy, and his wrinkled green tie hung loose
around his neck. His black shoes needed a good shine, and
he was wearing white socks. Tom Beecher definitely knew
how to play the role of a redneck country lawyer. Perhaps,
Raymond sometimes thought, he wasn't playing a role at all.

Alice Setzer's smile was crooked. She always looked as if
she knew something no one else knew or even suspected.
And probably she did. Her black dress was obviously new,
and she fingered the double strand of pearls around her neck,

making sure everyone noticed them. Alice Setzer had never quite accepted the fact that she was no longer the first lady of Vicksburg. Howard Daniels was leaning heavily on the table, representing the board of trustees, ready to give his report, eager to do whatever Nathan Locke wanted him to do. His brow was sweating profusely, and he kept nervously licking his dry lips. Howard Daniels was a working man with thick, beefy shoulders, and his stained white shirt never seemed to fit him quite right. His collar was frayed and the top button was missing. He and Alice Setzer, Raymond decided, were the session's odd couple. She looked Presbyterian. Howard should be out in a brush arbor revival somewhere, clapping his hands, swatting at gnats, and bringing in the sheaves.

Charles Page had built the foundation for Basilwood Presbyterian. He was the patriarch of the church. His sweat, his prayers, his dedication, and mostly his money had made it all possible. There was a time when Charles Page had been a firebrand, a mover and a shaker throughout the northwestern corner of Mississippi. Raymond had even heard tales that Charles rode out front of the Klu Klux Klan back in the days when bombings were commonplace and summer nights smelled of kerosene and burning crosses. But now he was simply a dried up little old man who came to church because there was no place else he wanted to go. He always wore a suit and a tie, neatly pressed, never had an unkind word for anyone, never trusted anybody, and had been on the session since that Sunday morning when the church first opened its doors. It was Charles Page who had personally hand-picked Nathan Locke to lead and direct the spiritual future of Basilwood Presbyterian. Nathan was like a son.

John Heatherly seldom had anything important to offer. He owned his own public relations firm and was a professional politician. He always wore tailored suits, a broad smile, and, Raymond suspected, probably had calluses from shaking hands all over Mississippi. John was always laughing, always talking. After listening to him for a couple of minutes, it was said, you had heard everything that John knew and some of it twice. For John, any session meeting that lasted past eight o'clock was too long. He usually excused himself early. Susan almost always had a party for him to attend even if she had to give one herself.

Wade Ferguson was missing. But then, Wade Ferguson was never around. He was in Natchez that night, Nathan had explained, putting together a hundred dollar a plate dinner for the League of Good Government. Wade had no conscience. One week he helped the Democrats raise money. The next week, he was working with Republicans to fill their dwindling bank account. Then he would sit back and watch them both use the money he had collected to tear each other's heads off. He didn't care. Wade Ferguson simply took his twenty percent off the top and hardly ever voted for any of them.

Only one other chair was empty: Max Gordon wasn't there.

It was strange, Raymond thought. He knew Max Gordon was dead. He had read the obituary in the newspaper. He had attended the man's funeral. He had listened to glowing eulogies, heard women weeping and seen grown men cry. But until now, until this very moment, it hadn't really dawned on him that Max Gordon was actually gone, that Max would not be coming back. His chair would always be empty.

Raymond Lynch felt a sudden chill and shivered.

Nathan Locke's strident voice brought Raymond Lynch
back to the business at hand. He was talking about the new
communication center, the ability and opportunity to link
up with a satellite orbiting the earth so that the whole nation
could hear his message every Sunday morning. He might
even call it God's Link of Love. His words would be heard
by millions from coast to coast, and Basilwood Presbyterian
even had the chance to become as well-known as Robert
Schuller's Crystal Cathedral out in California. Radio could
obviously make it possible. Television could make it happen.

The chill in Raymond Lynch's veins heated slowly, and
began to boil. The minister's ego was getting in his way.
"Who's gonna pay for it?" he asked, interrupting Locke in
midsentence.

Birdie looked aghast.

"Why, we are, Raymond."

"How?"

The slits in Tom Beecher's eyes widened.

Nathan Locke settled back in his chair. He was wearing a
blue open-collar shirt beneath his navy ultrasuede sport coat,
and it revealed a tiny gold chain, holding the golden cross
tightly against his throat. He casually crossed his legs and
quietly studied the schoolteacher's eyes. He could learn a
lot by looking deep into a man's eyes, and he didn't like
what he saw.

"As you know," Locke began softly, diplomatically, "Max
was quite generous to the church when he drew up his will."

"Exactly how much money did he leave for us to build
the communications center?"

"Two point six million. I believe that figure has been published in several places." Nathan Locke reached for the crystal pitcher and poured himself a glass of water, his gaze never leaving Raymond Lynch's face.

Raymond nodded. "I've seen the figure," he said as he adjusted his glasses. "But I don't think Max Gordon knew a damn thing about the communications center."

Alice gasped and hoped it was audible enough for the minister to hear and appreciate her contempt.

Locke wasn't listening. His voice grew cold. "It bears his name."

"Max didn't mention it when he left the money."

"What's your point, Raymond?" Locke snapped.

Raymond shifted his position in the chair. It was hard, and uncomfortable and he could feel the sharp edge of every splinter. His stomach was churning again, and he wondered why he was even having this confrontation with Nathan Locke. It wouldn't do any good. He was simply wasting his time and his breath. What he should do, Raymond knew, was apologize, shut up, and let the preacher go ahead and build his electronic empire. He sighed heavily. Sometimes he hated himself, and this was one of those times.

"I don't think Max Gordon left two point six million dollars to establish a communications center," Raymond said emphatically. "He left it to the church."

"What's the difference," Alice wanted to know.

"There is no difference," Birdie said testily.

"There are better ways to spend the money," Raymond said calmly.

"Just how would you choose to spend it, son?" Tom Beecher asked, inching his chair closer to the table. Nathan Locke

started to speak, but Tom reached out, patted his arm, and
stopped him. The old defense lawyer nodded to Raymond
and waited for an answer.

"This church is too self-serving," Raymond began.

"That's what it's here for," Tom Beecher interrupted, "to
serve its members. Hell, son, that's what all churches try to
do. Some are successful. Some aren't worth a boot full of
goddam spit. You're lucky, son. You go to a church that does
as good a job as the best of 'em and a better job than most.
And I'm havin' a real difficult time tryin' to understand just
why in God's name you've got a burr stickin' up under your
saddle."

"There are others out there who need our help, too." Raymond knew his voice was shaking, and that angered him.

"You talkin' about the blacks, son?"

"And the poor."

Tom Beecher nodded, and his smile was one of genuine
compassion. "I couldn't agree with you more," he said.
There's black people and brown people and poor people and,
hell, even a few rich people out there who need what this
church has got to offer them. But the trouble is, Raymond,
this church is sittin' here on this piece of ground, and they're
all scattered from one side of this great country to the other.
They sure as hell can't come here. But when we get the
communications center in place, we can sure as hell go to
them."

Nathan Locke shrugged. "Raymond," he said softly, "I believe you and I are both fighting for the same thing."

"Bullshit."

Nathan Locke's smile fell from his face. Birdie scowled.

Alice looked shocked. Howard's face reddened. Charles Page opened one eye and wondered what the noise was all about. John seemed confused and uneasy. He didn't like controversy. And Tom Beecher sadly shook his head.

A foreboding silence gripped the room. No one had ever questioned Nathan Locke before. It was heresy.

Raymond sought to control the anger and the confusion that seethed within him. He turned to the minister and said, "Nathan, I'll admit that you're the best preacher I've ever heard. But those people out there in the real world don't need your sermons on Sunday morning. Fancy words won't do them any good when they're hungry, and those people are hungry. They don't have enough to eat. Their children are nothing but skin and bones, and they cry all the time. They don't have any place to sleep at night."

"Let 'em get a job," Howard barked.

"There are no jobs."

"They're just too damn lazy to work."

Raymond slammed his fist on the table. "They're people who need help—our help," he said, the pitch of his voice rising. "With the money Max left us, Basilwood Presbyterian could build the most exciting, most dynamic outreach program in America. Nathan, you can preach to these people for the rest of your life. But they're not gonna believe you when you say God loves them if we don't show them a little love."

Nathan Locke's eyes darkened. Raymond Lynch was making him nervous. Raymond Lynch was a problem he had not foreseen. Tom Beecher had once called him a pain in the ass. Tom Beecher had been right.

"So you want us to feed the hungry," Locke said, folding his hands piously beneath his chin.

Raymond nodded.

"And clothe them."

"Whenever necessary."

"And house them."

"Too many live on the streets. They have no place else to go."

"And care for them when they're sick."

"That's what the Bible says we're supposed to do."

Nathan Locke's face was twisted with disbelief. How could anybody be so stubborn and so naive, he wondered. "And what does God want us to do when the people are still hungry and naked and sick and out on the streets and all of our money is gone?" he asked impatiently.

"It might take every dime we had," Raymond argued, "but we could bring hope and change lives."

"Those people won't change," Birdie snapped.

"They don't want to change," Alice interjected, her smile laced with sarcasm. "They're used to getting everything they need without paying for it, and now that's the only way they know how to live."

"All we ever do is give 'em a bunch of fish to eat," Howard said flatly. "With radio and television, Nathan can teach 'em how to fish. That's what they need. And, by god, that's what they're gonna get."

Raymond Lynch knew the skirmish was over.

The battle had been lost.

As Tom Beecher would so colorfully say, all he had been doing was simply pissing into the wind.

And he had gotten pissed on.

Again.

He was beaten, perhaps. But Raymond Lynch wasn't through. Nathan Locke had defied, or at least ignored, Presbyterian procedure, and he would be held accountable for what he had done. Now. Tonight. Raymond knew that the session did not share his concerns for the welfare of mankind, but surely its members, because of their vows, had to respect and uphold the Book of Order. Presbyterians spent more time bragging about the Book of Order than they did the Bible anyway. To them, it was gospel. It was law. It was order. Men dared not tamper with what it said.

"Who authorized for the two point six million dollars to be spent on the communications center?" Raymond asked.

Howard shrugged his beefy shoulders.

Alice looked at Birdie.

Birdie looked at Tom.

Tom frowned. At last he knew what point Raymond had been trying to make.

"I did," Nathan Locke said.

"You can't."

"A pastor can do whatever he wants," Birdie said defiantly. "He runs the church."

"The session runs the church."

"So?"

Raymond Lynch clenched his jaws. "So Nathan Locke violated the Book of Order."

Howard Daniels was on his feet, jabbing his big fist in Raymond's face. "Are you accusing my pastor of breaking the law?" he bellowed.

Raymond stood and looked him squarely in the eye. "I am. And he did. He's been playing loose and easy with the church's money. But he can't spend a nickel on anything unless the session tells him he can."

"At least he's spendin' it on something worthwhile," Birdie said loudly. The scowl had deepened in her face.

"Nathan Locke just wants to be an electronic superstar," Raymond spit out sharply.

Tom Beecher thumbed through his Book of Order, quickly scanning one page, then another, before looking up, the corners of his mouth hooked into a half smile. "If good old-fashioned Presbyterian policy is all that's troublin' you, son, then we can just eliminate that problem right now," he said. "We'll just let the session vote to spend that money any way it sees fit, and, frankly, I'm afraid I'll have to vote for the communications center and Nathan's link of love."

Birdie applauded. Alice beamed. Howard Daniel and John Heatherly nodded in agreement. Charles Page grinned. He liked to see young upstarts knocked to their knees.

Raymond gambled. "Is the session ready to vote on the money Nathan's hiding in his slush fund?" he asked.

"His what?" Howard looked at Raymond with the same affection he would have for a snake.

"His slush fund." Raymond knew he was on thin ice. He no longer cared. "You know, Howard, the money Nathan uses when he doesn't want the rest of us to know what he's doing."

"I don't know what the hell you're talkin' about," Howard replied testily. "And I don't think you do either."

John shrugged. He was obviously in the dark. Charles coughed, an irritated cough, and lost his grin. Birdie, for a change, was speechless. Raymond could almost smell the hatred on Alice's breath. He had smelled it before.

Tom's expression was as impassive as ever.

A wry smile crossed Nathan Locke's face. Let Raymond Lynch try to martyr him. It would only strengthen his bonds with the rest of his congregation. Maybe putting the yankee bleeding heart liberal on the session had been a mistake. Maybe not. Steel grew stronger when it was forged with fire. So would he. Let Raymond Lynch rant and rave like a lone, senseless voice crying in the wilderness. Let him criticize. Let him condemn. The good people of Basilwood Presbyterian might hear him, but they wouldn't stand for what he was saying. Nathan Locke was their minister, their pastor, their spiritual leader. They wouldn't let him be slandered. All he had to do was give them a chance to defend him.

A touch of anguish deadened Locke's eyes. His voice was broken with humility.

He rose, slowly and painfully.

And he waited until every eye was drawn like a magnet to his face.

"All I wanted to do," he said quietly, "was build our church to greatness. If that is wrong, then I am guilty. All I wanted to do was bring our Lord's good news message of love and hope and faith to as many people in this land as I could possibly reach. If that is wrong, then I am guilty. If what I have done is so bad, if what I have done has broken the

sacred laws of our church, then, my friends, I have no choice
but to resign as your pastor."

Birdie thought she was going to cry. Alice did.

Raymond Lynch bristled. "I move that we accept Nathan
Locke's resignation," he said. His voice quavered.

Every eye looked upon him as though he were a madman.

10

By midnight, the telephones were ringing throughout Vicksburg.

The question was always the same:

"Can you believe . . . ?"

The answer never varied.

"No, I can't."

H

ELEN Jensen had not been able to sleep at all. The call came during the middle of the ten o'clock news, and it shattered her.

"There's a group in church out to get Nathan," Birdie Castleberry said. It was almost a growl.

"What do you mean?"

"Raymond Lynch attacked him at session tonight." She paused, giving her words plenty of time to soak in. "He made innuendoes and accusations that you wouldn't believe in a million years."

Helen felt her blood run cold. "What did he say?"

"He as much as called Nathan a liar and a thief."

"Why?"

"Like I said, there's some people in our church out to get him."

"Who?" The question exploded from Helen's throat.

167

For a moment, there was no response, only the muffled sound of Birdie's exasperated breathing. Finally she said, "All I know is that Raymond Lynch is their voice on the session."

"But Raymond only has one vote," Helen reasoned. "He can't do anything with just one vote. Surely no one else on the session agrees with him."

"Raymond has a loud voice." Birdie said grimly. "He doesn't belong here. He was only sent here to cause trouble, and he's damn good at causing trouble. Raymond can make life miserable for all of us. He can make life a living hell for Nathan."

A living hell.

The words tumbled through Helen's mind as she stared into the darkness of her bedroom. Her sheet was wet with sweat and clinging to her body. Sleep had forsaken her.

A living hell.

She heard the slow, rhythmic breathing of Robert as he lay beside her. He whistled through his nose when he was tired, shrill and grating, and the noise was driving her crazy. It always drove her crazy. And Helen felt the limp pressure of her husband's fleshy hand on her stomach. She pushed it away and turned her back, as he had turned his back on her so many times.

Nathan Locke wouldn't reject her.

But she couldn't have Nathan Locke.

Helen Jensen knew what a living hell was all about.

She could still taste the garlic on her lips where Robert had kissed her goodnight. With clammy fingers, he had fondled her breasts halfheartedly for a few minutes, but when she didn't bother to immediately reach into his shorts, he lost interest and went to sleep without a word. The bastard hadn't really wanted to make love anyway, she told herself. He just felt guilty. It had been so long, and she felt so neglected, and Helen sometimes prayed that Robert would simply go to work some morning and never come home again.

He couldn't quench the fire inside of her.

He had tried, but it burned too hot, and Robert just wasn't man enough to be the man she wanted him to be.

Nathan was.

Poor Nathan.

Why would Raymond attack him? Why would anyone want to run her pastor—their pastor—out of the church he had built? Birdie had even said that Nathan tried to resign. Jesus, she prayed, that was ridiculous. Nathan couldn't resign. He couldn't just walk away and leave her. She needed him too badly. Nathan Locke was her strength. He could make her lie down beside still waters, only he could restoreth her soul. He was the rod, the staff she leaned on. He was her comfort.

Helen closed her eyes tightly.

She could see his face, so clear, so close, and in her imagination Nathan was smiling at her. He was always smiling. She could feel the tips of his fingers upon her skin, hot like a poker, holding her, smothering her, massaging her, deeper now, and faster, so deep, so fast, and every fiber within her was stretched taut, and her nerve ends were on fire, and she was crying, then she was laughing, first to herself, then aloud.

Her moan was low and guttural.

Robert awoke with a start.

"What's the matter?" he asked sleepily.

"Nothing."

"Are you all right?"

"I'm fine."

"Are you sure?"

"Yes, dammit, I'm sure."

"Well, you don't have to be so goddam grouchy about it." Robert yawned, turned onto his back, and, within minutes, was whistling through his nose again.

Helen shuddered without quite knowing why. She wiped a tear from her cheek and stared wide-eyed into the darkness.

Damn Robert, she thought.

Damn that noise he was making in his sleep.

She eased out of bed and walked quickly across the bedroom floor, down the hall, and into the den. For a time, Helen curled up on a velveteen sofa beside the window and looked out at the night. It was so black, so peaceful, its shadows broken only by the fluttering light of a street corner gaslight. The wind hung lifeless in the trees, the avenue was empty. All Helen could see was Raymond Lynch's '79 Pontiac parked against the curb.

Damn Raymond Lynch, too, she said to herself.

She reached for the telephone on the end table and dialed his number.

It rang.

Once.

Then twice.

"Hello." The voice was slurred. Raymond Lynch was either asleep or he had been drinking.

Helen glanced out the window.

Raymond's side of the duplex was still dark.

"Hello."

It suddenly dawned on Helen that she had absolutely nothing to say to the Yankee schoolteacher who had come to
Vicksburg to ruin her life and wreck the career of the only
man she loved.

"Who is this?" The voice was not as befuddled now.

Her breathing was all he could hear.

Her stomach was a cauldron, boiling with anger. Helen
felt a loathing for Raymond Lynch that she had never felt
for any other man.

He had no right to attack Nathan Locke.

He had no right to steal her happiness.

"Go to hell," she snarled and hung up.

Tom Beecher's stomach was bothering him. He had been
up until long past midnight, sipping bourbon and chasing it
with Maalox. He didn't mind controversy. In fact, Tom
Beecher thrived on it. He loved to take off his coat, roll up
his wrinkled sleeves, take a briefcase full of facts, and go to
war in a courtroom or anywhere else. He was a gamesman,
a deadly adversary who went straight for the jugular. He
didn't care whether the kill was clean or messy, whether it
was quick or agonizingly slow.

He could, his opponents swore, take the facts and beat
the hell out of you. Or Tom Beecher could go before the
jury without any facts at all and still win, using nothing but
sheer guts and guile.

He knew how to reach inside somebody's mind, take their
emotions in that big, meaty hand of his, and squeeze.

Squeeze hard.

Squeeze and refuse to let go.

Squeeze until he got the verdict he wanted.

Even as a young man, Tom Beecher had built himself quite a reputation. He only knew one way to argue a case. As he once admitted to a collegue: "I go into that courtroom like a prizefighter goes into the ring. You know, most men aren't born to be counterpunchers. So I hit 'em hard, and I hit 'em early, and I hit 'em with everything I got. It doesn't take long until that damn prosecuter is so worried about dodgin' what I'm throwin' at him, he forgets to hit back." Tom had laughed. "When a man's in trouble, he wants an attorney who'll fight for him and fight like hell. That's me."

So it was.

Tom Beecher could save a man from death row. Or he could put him there. It seldom made him any difference.

Few had ever forgotten the morning that Arthur McGee was found lying in a cotton field, crumpled across two rows of freshly-plowed dirt, and shot nine times at close range, in the face. Arthur was a family man, a quiet man who ran his own little grocery store between Vicksburg and Raymondville. He trusted people. When times were hard and dollars scarce, he let them buy on credit to keep their children fed. He gave every man a chance. Arthur had never turned a hungry man away, and now he was dead, a kindly face with kindly eyes blown away by a drunkard's gun.

Eddie Williams, twenty-two years old, an unemployed pool hustler, had been arrested while sleeping off his liquor. The .38 caliber pistol used to gun a man down was found in the muds and weeds of a bayou that ran behind his house. Eddie Williams only had one chance for freedom.

And Tom Beecher waited all morning for the telephone to ring. It would be Judge T. L. Johnson on the other end, he knew, appointing him to defend Eddie Williams.

The phone call never came.

Shortly after the clock on the courthouse wall struck twelve, the door to his office opened, and four well-dressed, solemn-eyed businessmen walked in. Without a word, they placed four thousand, five hundred dollars on his desk. The saddened residents of Warren County had guessed that Tom Beecher would be the logical choice to defend Williams. They knew of the young attorney's reputation, and they cried for justice. There was no way they could stomach Tom Beecher's emotional tricks and hard-punching antics in the courtroom. And there was only one way to stop him.

Together, going door to door, the four men had raised the money. Now it had been given to Tom Beecher.

"Why?" he asked.

"You could probably keep Eddie Williams off death row," the grim-faced banker told him. "You might just be able to send him there. The district attorney is getting old. He's lost his edge. He doesn't want to lose the case against Eddie. So we're here to hire you as a special prosecutor."

"What does the D.A. say about this?" Tom wanted to know.

"He gave us the first five hundred dollars."

Tom Beecher picked up the bills, slowly counted them, then pitched them into his bottom drawer. The banker nodded. The men left. Vicksburg slept better that night. It hadn't been able to sleep at all since Arthur McGee had fallen crumpled and quite dead upon those two rows of newly-plowed earth, leaving his blood to stain the cotton.

The courtroom was jammed every day of the trial, and

Tom Beecher felt a little uneasy sitting at a table where he
had never sat before. He glanced over at the long, lean,
slumped shoulders of Eddie Williams. His brown hair was
too long and had been slicked back with a couple of dabs of
Wildroot Cream Oil. His mother had testified, "Buck is too
chicken-hearted to be brutal enough to kill a man in cold
blood. As a child, he never liked to hurt anything."

Tom Beecher raised an eyebrow.

Buck. Did she call him Buck?

During the afternoon break, he put in a call to Asa Harper
who ran the pool hall and who had taught Eddie Williams
to make a pretty good living shooting eight ball.

"The boy's daddy was always called Buck," Asa said, "and
when Eddie was no more than knee high to a grasshopper,
his daddy got to callin' him Buckshot."

Buckshot.

Tom Beecher grinned.

Buckshot Williams.

It was the only name those twelve good men and women
on the jury ever heard Tom Beecher use when he talked
about the accused, and he talked about him long, emotionally,
and often. On the fourth day, Tom stood to face them one
last time, his face glistening with sweat, his suit rumpled,
his voice like thunder. He stood there, slowly twirling the
.38 caliber murder weapon around his finger, and his words
were as solemn as judgment day:

> "Buckshot Williams,
> with a heart of hate,
> sealed his fate
> with a thirty-eight."

He crumpled to his knees, jerking and quivering, reliving those final moments as each shot, each of nine shots, had slammed into the dying body of Arthur McGee.

And Tom Beecher, in a low, raspy voice, had these final words for a wide-eyed, red-eyed jury:

> "Can we sit idly by?
> Don't break the faith with us who die,
> or we won't sleep,
> you and I."

The jury did not break the faith. Forty-five minutes later, those twelve good men and women, still wide-eyed and red-eyed, returned to the courtroom and said that Eddie Buckshot Williams must die.

Tom Beecher, it was whispered in the far corners of courthouse corridors, was never really concerned whether any of his clients were guilty or innocent. To him, it was all a sport. Someone had to win. Someone had to lose. As he had said time and again, "In a trial the best team always wins." Tom Beecher seldom lost.

"Do you ever have trouble sleeping at night?" Nathan Locke had once asked him.

"Why do you ask?"

"Not everybody you defend is innocent."

"I can generally prove they are."

"But let's just suppose you got somebody off scot-free," Locke proposed, "and then later you found out that person was guilty. How would you feel then?"

Tom Beecher pulled his worn fedora down over his eyes and flashed a wry grin. "The fee I charge 'em is punishment enough," he drawled. And maybe it was.

No, the old attorney wasn't afraid of a good fight. Anytime.
Anywhere. But it troubled him that a conflict had suddenly
reared its ugly head, and he had not even seen it coming.
He never went into battle unprepared, and he was unprepared as hell when Raymond Lynch, right out of the blue,
went on the offensive against Nathan Locke.

For awhile, Tom Beecher feared that somehow, in some
way, Raymond had learned about the handwritten will of
Max Gordon that he himself had destroyed. That frightened
him. And he hadn't been frightened in a long time. Tom
didn't mind bending a few rules and twisting a few facts,
but he was just too damned old to get caught breaking any
laws. His pride would be trampled on. His dignity would
suffer. And his pride and dignity were about all that Tom
Beecher had left important to him. He wouldn't live long
enough to spend his money.

About three o'clock, he finally convinced himself that no
one, especially not Raymond, knew of Max Gordon's illicit
entanglements with Martha Landers. Max had only been an
aging man, afraid to grow old, trying one final time to hold
on to his youth. Martha had given him something to be proud
of. But then, hookers were good at that. She had wrapped
those long, spindly legs around him, given him a few nights
of pleasure, and Max had given her just about everything
he owned. And poor Martha didn't even know it.

Neither did Raymond.

Tom Beecher had made sure of it.

The Mississippi River left behind no traces.

Or did it?

The doses of bourbon had gotten smaller as the night wore
on. He drank the Maalox straight from the bottle.

Birdie Castleberry and Alice Setzer were waiting on him when Tom Beecher walked an hour late into his office. Neither looked to be in a particularly good mood. He couldn't blame them. He had faced better days himself.

"Mornin', ladies," he said wearily.

"What are you going to do about Raymond?" Birdie asked.

Tom grinned crookedly and opened the blinds, blinking as the flood of sunlight poured into the room. That's one thing he could say in favor of Birdie Castleberry. She might be loud and obnoxious sometimes, flaunting her third-generation money, exercising the power it gave her. But Birdie didn't waste a lot of anybody's time out beating around the bushes. She always got straight to the point. She knew what she wanted, and generally she got it, or she kept browbeating people until she did.

Spoiled bitch, Tom Beecher said to himself. Aloud, he said, "I'm not for sure if I—or anyone else—needs to do a damn thing about Raymond Lynch. Not right now anyway."

The room darkened noticeabley as a cloud shrouded the sun. Birdie's eyes blazed angrily, matching the scowl on her face.

"Somebody needs to shut him up."

Tom shrugged, and his shoulders were sagging. "Something stirred up Raymond. I don't have any idea in hell what it was. But I'm bettin' he's like one of them danged old Civil War cannons we got sittin' on every street corner around here. He had one shot. He fired it. Now he's through."

"What if you're wrong?" Alice asked, looking at him across the top of her reading glasses. The color had drained from her pinched face. She was nervously playing with the gold chain around her neck. Her legs were crossed, and Tom, out of habit, glanced up under her skirt and wished he hadn't.

"What if Raymond keeps going around telling those lies about Nathan?"

"Who's gonna believe them?"

"Somebody might."

"Nobody's that crazy."

"Raymond believes them."

"He's just shooting in the dark."

"If you shoot long enough," Alice said caustically, "you might hit something." She paused. "Even in the dark."

Tom Beecher nodded and sighed. Alice should know, he thought. When it came to lies and gossip, she just might be the biggest distributor in Mississippi. And he also knew what all good defense lawyers had always known: if a lie is told often enough, it starts to sound like the truth. At least it did to juries. At least the lies did when he told them.

"What do you want me to do?" he asked.

"Stop him," Alice snapped.

"Just how do you propose I do something like that?"

Birdie leaned back in her antique chair, and a strange, cherubic smile flashed without humor across her face. It was sweet, too sweet, almost demonic, and Tom was forced to look away. The smile sickened him.

"I bet Wendell Anderson would know what you could do about Raymond," Birdie purred, and her words cut Tom Beecher to the quick. "Why don't you dig up Wendell and ask him?"

Tom's eyes were suddenly clouded. He was sweating as though stricken with a fever, and his round face became ashen, the color of death.

He had lived so long condemned by his own conscience, a man guilty without a trial. For twenty-two years, he had carried the weight of his secret in silence, lying awake at night, waiting, wondering, afraid that someday somebody would learn of the deed he had done.

But no one knew.

Tom Beecher had been sure of it.

No one had ever known.

For a moment, he thought his heart would stop. His chest felt as though it had been caught in a vacuum, and the breath of life itself was being slowly squeezed out of his lungs. His pulse raced wildly, out of control, and Tom could feel it pumping hard against his throat. He tried to lift a hand in protest, but his arm was lifeless, paralyzed. The room grew dark, then faint, and he could hear his heart pounding against his chest, the sound of a sledgehammer on raw meat.

Jesus, he prayed.

Birdie Castleberry knew.

All of these years she had known.

How in God's name had she found out?

All Tom Beecher could see was the smile on her face, taunting him, tormenting him. He stared at it in silence until Birdie and Alice walked out of his office without bothering to close the door behind them.

Helen Jensen had been frightened, then appalled. Now she was angry.

Nathan Locke was a good man, a decent man. He had helped allay her fears during those troubled, insecure months when she thought Robert was going to divorce her. He had hammered a little common sense back into her head the night she threatened to walk out on Robert. He had even persuaded Jeremy to abandon his nights on the wild side. Jeremy hadn't come home again, but at least he was off the streets.

Robert and Jeremy still didn't see eye to eye. They squabbled, and they fought, and sometimes she thought that they probably even hated each other. But then, Helen knew she didn't really understand her son or what caused his sullen, defiant moods either.

Nathan Locke did. Jeremy could talk to Nathan.

Slowly she was seeing the boy's life begin to change. Jeremy had gotten his hair cut and styled. He had thrown his ragged jeans away. He wanted his clothes cleaned and pressed. He even polished his shoes and kept the dirt dug out from beneath his fingernails. Helen hadn't smelled the stench of cheap booze on his breath for days. Jeremy's eyes were clear, and he swore to her that he had given up pot. He hadn't smoked, he said, since that night the preacher had whipped Moon and physically dragged him off the streets.

Nathan Locke was a man he could respect. Nathan Locke had made a difference.

Now somebody was out to crucify him.

Wearing a red, backless sundress, Helen stormed into the church and marched toward Nathan Locke's study, her footsteps sending apologetic echoes throughout the sanctuary. Somewhere a telephone was ringing, and she could hear the far-away whine of a lawnmower just beyond the stained glass windows.

Helen found the minister alone, seated on the edge of

his desk, his back to the doorway. He was holding a cup of coffee in one hand, the telephone receiver in the other. His hair seemed unusually dark in the dim light, and Helen's eyes were massaging his broad shoulders as she sat down.

"Thank you," she heard Locke say softly. "I appreciate your concern."

A pause.

Then, "There's no reason to worry, Mrs. Bauman. I know everything will be all right."

A pause.

And finally, "Yes, ma'am, God will find a way."

He gently replaced the receiver on the hook and turned to face the puffy, waxen face of Helen Jenson. Her jaws were set firmly. She was obviously wearing too much makeup, particularly too much mascara to hide the redness in her eyes. It wasn't working. Helen looked very much like she might break out and start crying again at any moment.

"You can't resign!" she said. It was almost a shout.

Locke shrugged. "I may have to."

"You can't let a little weasel like Raymond Lynch run you out of your own church."

"It's not my church."

"Then who in hell does it belong to?"

"God." Nathan Locke straightened his yellow and blue striped tie and walked around the desk. "God owns it," he said solemnly. "God runs it. I'm just the caretaker."

"That's not true," Helen argued, her voice cracking.

"Raymond thinks I'm guilty of doing some pretty terrible things," Locke told her, carefully watching Helen's eyes. He saw the tears even before they came.

"Raymond was lying."

"Lies are a lot like poison." Nathan uneasily shifted his feet. "They can eat away at what people think about each other. They can kill a man's career. They can destroy a church."

Helen was on her feet. "I won't let that happen."

"It may be too late."

"You can't leave," Helen pleaded.

"I'll do whatever is best for the church."

"We'll fight." Helen's eyes were irrational.

"People only get hurt when there's fighting within a church," Locke reasoned.

"I don't want you to leave." She grabbed his arm and squeezed it tightly. "I love you too much."

A look of surprise crept into Nathan Locke's eyes.

"I mean, we all love you," Helen corrected herself, stumbling over her own words. Her face was flushed, and she abruptly turned away.

Locke wrapped his arm around her, and Helen felt herself being pressed against him, her head leaning against his shoulder. She caught her breath and looked up as he kissed her lightly on the cheek.

"Thank you for caring," Locke whispered.

She waited for him to let go.

He didn't.

"Thank you for being here when I need you," he said, and Helen could feel the warmth of his smile against her face. Her hands were trembling, and the pressure of Nathan Locke's fingertips digging into the flesh of her back was almost more than she could stand.

She wanted him now.

More than ever.

She would give herself to him, openly, willingly, with love, without shame.

For a day.

For a night.

For an hour.

Forever.

No one would ever know.

Why didn't Nathan ask? Didn't he know? All he had to do was ask.

He released her and stepped away.

Helen Jensen waited.

All he had to do was ask.

"Thank you for coming," Locke said, his voice low and compassionate. "Any time you ever want to see me, day or night, I'll be here for you.

Day.

or *night*.

"I'll call." Helen's voice was barely audible.

"That's never necessary."

Nathan Locke wanted her, too. There was no doubt in Helen's mind. She could see it in his eyes, hear it in his voice. He would be there for her anytime she needed him. Day—or night. The ache began to burn again inside her, and it was almost unbearable. Tears blurred her eyes. His kiss still lay wet against her cheek, and she touched his face with the hot palm of her hand.

Day.

Or night.

Nathan Locke would be there.

Nathan Locke had promised.

Helen Jensen suddenly turned, walked in a stupor from his study and back out into the empty sanctuary of the church.

Wade Ferguson found Raymond Lynch wandering alone through the forsaken streets of Rodney. It had once been a wealthy river town with merchants down on the docks trading a thousand bales of cotton a year for fine whiskey, Havana cigars, fancy laces, and fine linen. In those days, there had been two banks, two widely read newspapers, five doctors, and a red brick schoolhouse. Rodney even boasted the first opera house in Mississippi. And only four miles away, Presbyterians had founded their Oakland College.

But in the summer of 1864, a great white sandbar had risen out of the currents of the mighty Mississippi, causing the river, Rodney's sole lifeline, to alter its course. The riverbed dried up, and so did Rodney.

Raymond Lynch looked around him and sadly shook his head. The city had borne the brunt of a raging fire, and time had taken a deadly toll. It was crumbling at his feet, and the vines had already smothered the brick walls of old abandoned buildings. Rodney was virtually a ghost town, decaying with age and neglect.

Raymond glanced up as Wade Ferguson's Lincoln Continental eased to a stop beside the dirt road that wound its way into town. He leaned against the rusting pumps of a deserted filling station and watched as Mississippi's Number One political fund raiser got out of the car, a perpetual smile plastered on his face.

Wade waved.

He looked out of place.

Raymond nodded. "Times must be getting hard," he yelled.

"How's that?"

"It looks a little strange you driving all the way out here to raise money from people in a town that don't have either money or people."

Wade laughed. "Shoot, boy," he said, "You're the only one I've been lookin' for. They told me down at the historical society that I just might be able to catch up with you out here." He was taking his tan coat off, and his matching tie hung loosely around an open-collared white shirt.

Raymond felt his muscles tighten defensively. He didn't know why, but Wade Ferguson frightened him. Wade was not an imposing man, barely standing five–foot-eight, and he was at least forty pounds overweight from eating too many tough steaks at too many of his own hundred-dollar-a-plate banquets. His skin was pinkish, and his English Leather cologne was too strong even out in the open on a windy day. It was no secret that Wade Ferguson had powerful connections in powerful places, legal and otherwise, and he wasn't afraid to use them. He was a man with loyalties to no one but himself.

Raymond frowned as he squinted into the sun. Wade Ferguson had certainly gone to a lot of trouble tracking him down in the middle of a godforsaken ghost town.

Why?

His mouth was dry and tasted like cottonseed. Raymond spit into the dust. The juices in his belly curdled. There was no reason to lie to himself.

He knew why.

Raymond Lynch had raised hell with the preacher.

Wade Ferguson had come to put him in his place. His shoulders stiffened.

"How much do you know about Rodney?" Wade asked.

"Not a lot."

"Back when cotton was king, this was a bodaciously rich little community," Wade told him. "Why old Andrew Jackson, Henry Clay, and Zachary Taylor used to walk along this same old street where we're standin' now. Everybody around here thought Taylor wasn't nothing' more than a cantankerous old codger, and that's about all he was. But, hell, he got himself elected twelfth president of the United States, so I guess he did something right."

"I guess he had a good fund raiser," Raymond said, a sly smile on his face.

"Not good enough, boy," Wade said loudly, "He needed somebody like me. Hell, if I'd a been raisin' money for him, old Zack Taylor could've been the tenth president."

"I don't think you came all the way out here to discuss Zachary Taylor's presidential campaign," Raymond said abruptly, turning to walk away.

Wade Ferguson ran his short, stubby fingers through a head of thinning, brown hair and followed, shuffling his way through the soft, chalky dust that caked onto his black patent leather shoes.

"No, I didn't," he admitted. Then his grin broadened. "I hear tell you nailed old Nathan's ass last night."

His words hit Raymond with the sudden impact of a rifle shot. The schoolteacher stopped dead in his tracks.

"I asked a few pointed questions," Raymond said. "They seemed to upset a few people."

"I bet they did." Wade's laughter rolled down the empty street. "I can just see old Birdie now. I bet she was sittin' there squirmin' like somebody had shoved a corkscrew up her ass." He laughed again, louder this time. "Damn amighty! I wish I'd been there to see it."

The frown deepened on Raymond's brow. "I'm not sure I understand," he said.

"Nathan's been rapin' that church for a long time," Wade answered. "He was a pretty good old boy when he came here, but he got too much power, and power'll corrupt anybody." He paused, then added, "Even preachers."

"Why hasn't somebody tried to stop him before now?"

"They're scared of him, boy."

"How about you, Wade?"

Wade Ferguson rolled his eyes. "I've watched Nathan Locke for a long time now," he said. "I know what he's done and who he's done it to, and why he did it. I know the women he's fucked, and the men he's screwed. Of course, I know that about a lot of people."

Raymond Lynch shook his head in disgust. "Somehow, I always looked upon preachers as holy men." His laugh was full of irony.

"Some of 'em are." Wade slung his coat over his shoulder. His sweat was beginning to show in scattered streaks across his crinkled white shirt. "And some of 'em are like Nathan Locke. He can't keep his hands off of what belongs to somebody else."

"Money?"

"And women."

"Why, dammit!" The bad taste lingered in Raymond's mouth, and he could feel disappointment, then anger surging through his veins. "Why does he have to be like that."

"Nathan's a glamour boy." Wade threw his head back and let a warm Mississippi breeze dry the sweat on his face. "Some preachers want a church. He wants an empire. He's got big plans, and he's not gonna let anybody stand in his way. He wants to be on top, and bein' on top—takes money. When he needs it, he simply takes it."

"Who lets him?"

"Who stops him?"

Raymond's shoulders slumped, and the sun reflected sharply off his glasses. The whole world became a sudden blur. He frowned and turned his back to the river.

"It looks to me like he's taking an awful big risk if he's got as many women on the line as you tell me he has," Raymond said, thrusting his hands into his pockets.

"Not really." Wade's grin was one of envy. "Nathan's a manipulator. He's big, good-lookin', a ladies' man, and he takes advantage of it. Nathan controls the women, and they control their husbands. He tells them what to do, and they tell their husbands what to do. And Nathan Locke does whatever he damn well pleases."

"He's a sonovabitch," Raymond spit out.

"He's a fuckin' genius."

"Who's he fucking now?"

"He's spendin' a lot of time with Robert Jensen's wife."

Raymond's frown deepened as the splintered shade of a sweetgum tree slashed across his face. "Helen doesn't seem like Nathan's type," he said.

"If Nathan can use her," Wade replied, "she's his type."

"Why don't you blow the whistle on him?" Raymond asked,

nervously kicking the dry delta dirt with the toe of his boot.

"Frankly speakin', I don't have the guts for it." Wade Ferguson's laughter turned sour. "There are some big-monied boys around Vicksburg, and I've been doin' business with 'em for a long time now. Nathan Locke's got 'em in his hip pocket. If I make him mad, I make them mad, and I can't afford to lose 'em. It's that simple."

"You're a damn coward," Raymond blurted out.

Wade nodded. "I couldn't have said it better myself," he replied.

"So where does that leave me?"

"There's a lot of folks in that church who believe the same way you do, Raymond." Wade stepped across a patch of dry, rustling weeds and leaned against a spiked wrought-iron fence. "They're just waitin' for a leader." He grinned. "Presbyterians like a good fight. They just need somebody to show 'em how and a good cause to fight for."

He nodded toward the old abandoned red brick church just behind the fence, still stately in the glow of the afternoon sun. "Presbyterians sure had themselves a good fight there," Wade Ferguson continued. "It was back during the war between the states. The crew of a Union ship had been invited by a Northern sympathizer to attend Sunday morning services there.

"Right after they all got through singin', a Confederate scout marched down the aisle and told the preacher, 'I'm sorry to interrupt your sermon, parson, but I just wanted to inform your visitors that the church is surrounded and they're my prisoners.'"

Wade grinned. "Those Yankee Presbyterians tried to fight

their way out of the trap, and seven of 'em did make it back
to the ship. They trained their guns on the little church and
started poundin' the hell out of the town with cannon fire."

Wade shook his head. "They probably would have leveled
Rodney, but those old Southern boys sent word that they
would hang all seventeen prisoners unless the ship ceased
firin'.

"The cannons stopped, and the war at Rodney was over."
Wade Ferguson shrugged and began walking back down the
street. "It was over in a hurry," he yelled back over his
shoulder. "But it was a helluva good fight while it lasted."

Raymond Lynch's skin suddenly felt dry and clammy.
"Who's Nathan Locke gonna hang if I don't stop firing at
him?" he called to Wade.

"Nathan Locke's gonna hang you regardless of what you
do." Wade pitched his coat into the backseat of the Lincoln
and tried to kick the dust off his shoes.

Raymond sighed, glanced back over his shoulder and saw
a cannonball, tainted with rust, still embedded in the aging
brickwork over a front window of the church. He figured
the next one fired by Nathan Locke would be embedded
up his ass.

11

Wade Ferguson stopped at a pay telephone alongside the road out of Port Gibson, gave the operator his credit card number, and waited for Birdie Castleberry to answer.

"I ran into Raymond Lynch today," he began.

"Did he mention Nathan?"

"That's all he wanted to talk about."

"Raymond's like an old dog with a bone," Birdie bit her words off sharply. "He's got his teeth sunk in deep, and he won't let go of it."

Wade scratched his chin and waited for the noise of a passing truck to fade away.

"He's spreadin' the rumor now that Nathan's shackin' up with some woman in the church."

Birdie's gasped. "Did he say who it was?" she asked.

"Helen Jensen."

The line crackled.

"Helen Jensen?" Birdie laughed laconically.

"That's what he said."

"Raymond couldn't have been serious."

"Raymond was as serious as lip cancer."

"Just wait until Nathan hears this," Birdie said.

By the time Wade Ferguson got back to his car, Nathan Locke had heard. By the time he drove past Vicksburg's city limit sign, Helen Jensen knew as well.

TOM Beecher watched the sun rise through the windshield of his Buick Riviera, parked back among the ancient pines that shielded him from the street. His back hurt, and his legs were cramped from sitting too long in one place. A dull ache gnawed into the pit of his stomach, and Tom was still belching onions from the greasy cheeseburger he had eaten the night before. His eyes were dull, he needed a shave, and at the moment he didn't really give a damn.

An early morning mist rose from the muddy crest of the Yazoo River and coiled through the trees, turning the sky a blushing pink as the night regretfully loosened a sweaty grip on Vicksburg. Tom Beecher had the windows rolled down, and an uneasy wind ruffled through his hair. He rubbed his eyes with the backs of his hands, wished for a fresh cigar, and had never felt more alone in his entire life.

Tom Beecher had come during the night to see Wendell

Anderson, and the strength was sapped from every fiber of his body. He had forgotten Wendell. No, that wasn't true. He had tried many times to erase any thoughts of Wendell from his mind, but the jaded memory of the man's half-crazed face had kept staring at him, mocking him, rebuking him day and night for more than two decades. Wendell Anderson was a nightmare from which he could neither awaken nor escape.

Tom Beecher shuddered.

A breath of cold air touched his cheek.

As cold as tempered steel.

As cold as the tempered steel in Wendell Anderson's hunting knife.

Wendell was a killer, or so the prosecutor had argued. He had, according to those who took the oath and testified, picked up seventeen-year-old Bertha Borders shortly after ten o'clock on an unusually warm September night as the black girl hitchhiked her way home from the Greyhound bus station. Wendell had been drinking too much. But then, Wendell was always drinking too much, and Bertha had long, lean legs, a thin waist, and high, haughty cheekbones that somehow made her seem foreign and exotic, especially in the moonlight. Wendell was laughing when he stopped his car. That's what a witness said. Bertha was laughing when she got in. The laughter stopped.

A coon hunter found her body thirteen days later, lying in a ditch on the southern edge of the Delta National Forest, about a dozen miles out of Redwood. Bertha's clothes had been torn off of her, wadded up, and her panties stuffed into her mouth. Her hands and feet were tied together with barbed wire. A coroner said that she had been raped probably more than once. And her throat was cut. It had taken Bertha, he surmised, at least three hours to die. Vicksburg would have been in shock if Bertha had not been black. Her death occupied three paragraphs on the back page of the morning newspaper, wedged in between the public notices and a three-column ad for lightweight McCullough chainsaws.

Wendell Anderson was a short, squat man with thick, wide shoulders and black curly hair who worked in a Yazoo City cotton gin. He was a better-than-average stud poker player, spent almost every weekend hunting squirrels down along the Big Black riverbottom thickets, and would arm wrestle, he bragged, any hairy-legged sonovabitch tough enough or drunk enough to lay a five-dollar bet on the back table of the Crazy Baby Bar. R. C. Quaid, a beefy ex-pro lineman who once played third string offensive tackle for the Detroit Lions, was the only man who ever beat him.

"I thought you was the king," R. C. had taunted.

Wendell gritted his teeth.

"You ain't no king." R. C.'s laugh was ugly. He lay both of his broad, scarred hands on the table and looked down at them proudly. "Now those," he said, "are the hands of the king."

Wendell never flinched. With a single fluid motion, he slipped his hunting knife from its slick-leather scabbard, twirled it once in the air, grabbed the handle, and jammed the blade into the tabletop.

R. C. Quaid screamed in an agony he had never experienced on a football field.

His blood splattered across Wendell's face.

R. C.'s eyes rolled back in their sockets.

Wendell licked the blood off his lips.

R. C. fainted dead away, leaving the third finger of his left hand lying on the table, severed neatly just above the championship ring he had bought in a pawnshop for right at two hundred dollars and some few cents.

Wendell reached into his hip pocket, pulled out his last five dollars and dropped them, one at a time, beside R. C. Quaid's quivering body. He hated to lose, but nobody could say Wendell Anderson had ever welshed on a bet.

He lived in a shotgun renthouse alongside the railroad tracks just north of Vicksburg with the only girl he had ever loved, and Wendell Anderson was envied by every red-blooded male in Warren County. His wife was tall, statuesque, and raven-haired. Her skin was creamy and without blemish, and if it hadn't been for the faded secondhand dress she wore, Vickie could have easily passed for a high-dollar fashion model. She certainly had the looks for it.

The year Vickie finished the tenth grade, she watched her mother waste away and die of tuberculosis. Her daddy was a railroad man, and he caught a freight headed north one morning and never came back again. Wendell Anderson stopped by the old homeplace late one afternoon and found Vickie crying in the shower, her tears blending with the water that streamed down upon her bare breasts. She was, he swore, the most beautiful girl he had ever seen, naked or clothed. Three days later, he drove down to the Crazy Baby Bar, won two arm wrestling matches and paid a justice of the peace ten dollars to pronounce them man and wife.

"She's a helluva woman," Charlie, the bartender, said when Wendell brought her in to the bar to meet his friends.

Vickie smiled sweetly.

"She ain't yet, but she's gonna be," Wendell retorted. He ordered cheap bourbon for everyone he knew.

"She's a mite young," Alfred, the truck driver, said, mumbling his words behind a toothless grin.

"She'll grow up." Wendell laughed heartily.

Alfred nodded and put a fatherly arm around Vickie's tiny waist as he reached for his glass of bourbon and Coke.

Wendell cut his laughter short.

Alfred squeezed her.

Wendell frowned.

Alfred's hand dropped down and rested upon the girl's well-rounded buttocks. He lifted his drink to toast her. He hadn't quite gotten the glass to his lips when Wendell hit him across the bridge of his crooked nose with a half-filled Rebel Yell bottle. It took two hours and thirty-six stitches to close up the gash on the old man's face. In the Crazy Baby Bar, no one but Wendell Anderson ever touched Vickie's soft and sacred body again.

Tom Beecher first saw Vickie Anderson about sunrise on an Easter Sunday morning. He had come down to the police station to take a statement from an out-of-state, unemployed short order cook who had been caught inside the Old Southern Tea Room about three o'clock, long after the last customer was supposed to have been gone.

Without bothering to introduce himself, Tom sat down in the cell, pulled a yellow legal pad from his briefcase, and looked around the thin, middle-aged, nondescript man who squatted on the concrete floor beside him.

"Name," he said.

"Edgar Fifer."

"Address."

Edgar shrugged. "I'm just passin' through," he answered.

"What in hell were you doin' down at the Southern Tea Room in the dead of night?" Tom Beecher yawned.

Edgar stared at him, rubbing a two-day growth of graying whiskers on his face. "Who the hell are you?" he asked cautiously. "I ain't got no business talkin' to you."

"I'm your goddam attorney," Tom snapped. He didn't like being jostled out of bed by the telephone before daylight. "You did want an attorney, didn't you?"

"Not particularly." Edgar spit on the cell floor.

"You got one anyway." Tom shoved his fedora back on his head. "The court appointed me. Now, tell me what the hell you were doin' in the Southern Tea Room while the rest of this goddam city was asleep."

"I was lookin' for a job."

"Bullshit."

Edgar shrugged his bent shoulders. "So I was hungry."

Tom glanced down at the man's elbow. It was wrapped in a white towel, soaked thoroughly with blood. "What happened to you?" he asked.

"I didn't come out when the police told me to, so they sent that damn German shepherd in to get me." The prisoner paused, slapped his empty pockets, and asked, "You got any cigarettes on you?"

Tom Beecher handed him a crumpled pack. Edgar lit a filter tip, laid his head back against the bare wall, and inhaled slowly, holding the smoke for as long as he could in his throat. He blew it all out at once and continued, "The dog found me hidin' behind a stack of crates. That snarlin' sonofabitch grabbed me, jerked me out, and damn near chewed my fuckin' arm off."

Tom Beecher sighed. God, he hated these court appointed cases. He didn't need them. He could refuse them any-time he wanted. But for some masochastic reason that even the young and infamous Tom Beecher didn't under-stand, he kept accepting whatever cases the judge gave him, always threatening to quit, never quite getting around to doing it. That morning when the telephone jarred him awake he had almost quit. And he had neither sympathy nor remorse for the thin, leathery-faced man who sat beside him. He and society would both be a lot better off, he told himself, if some irate cop had been trigger-happy, blown Edgar Fifer's head off, and buried him in a pauper's grave.

Tom coughed. He didn't think he would ever get used to a jail cell. The air around him was stifling, and the stench of human waste was virtually unbearable. He looked hard at Edgar. The short-order cook had his eyes closed, and he was blowing ragged smoke rings toward a mustard yellow ceiling.

"If you'd a been smart, you would have just come on out when the police told you to," the attorney said. He yawned. His voice was dry and listless.

Edgar nodded. "Yeah," he answered, "but they didn't ex-plain it to me like that damn dog did."

Tom Beecher sighed again. He placed his legal pad back in his briefcase, stood, coughed one last time, and nodded for the jailer to unlock the cell door. Edgar Fifer, he knew, was one of those odd fixtures within the judicial system who would always be more trouble than he was worth. Tom didn't particularly want to defend the derelict. And the district attorney certainly did not want to waste his time prosecuting,him. So ultimately, Edgar Fifer would wind up back out on the streets, drifting from place to place, a petty thief who would keep on being a petty thief until somebody—a friend, an enemy, or the law—finally laid him to rest in a grave without flowers.

Tom Beecher had just heard the sharp metallic sound of the cell door locking behind him when he saw Vickie Anderson walk into the lobby of the Vicksburg police station. The sudden sight of her stunned him, and he whistled low under his breath.

"Now that is what you call yourself a real woman," the old jailer said, rubbing his bald head. "I get a hard-on just talking to her over the telephone."

Tom Beecher couldn't answer. He simply stared.

Vickie's jeans were old and faded, but they clung tightly to her legs and buttocks as though they were part of her skin. Her blouse was white, virginal white, and the top button had been torn off or bitten off. Tom could see the rising bulge of her breasts as Vickie breathed, though they were partially hidden by a blue bandana that had been tied around her neck. Her black hair fell loosely around her shoulders, and it bounced lightly when she walked. Her earrings were silver and turquoise, big and round, the kind gypsies wore. And her red flats were scuffed and faded from walking too many miles down some dusty delta backroad. Her smile was tired and somewhat apologetic.

"Who is she?" Tom Beecher asked finally. His voice was hoarse. He coughed to clear his throat.

"Vickie Anderson."

"You sound like you know her pretty well."

"Not as well as I'd like to," The jailer folded his arms and laughed lustily. "She comes in here a lot."

"Why?"

"Her old man spends a lot of his time in jail."

"What's his problem?"

"Drinks a lot. Gambles a lot. Fights a lot. You name it. If somebody is out there raisin' hell, you can just bet that Wendell Anderson is involved in it or on his way." The jailer shook his head. "Wendell Anderson is a mean sonofabitch."

"What's he in for now?"

"A danged old Chevy had him blocked in down at the Crazy Baby Bar last Saturday night. He couldn't get out, and it made him mad, so he moved the car himself."

"There's nothing wrong with that."

"Wendell Anderson moved it piece by piece, usin' a fuckin' crowbar."

Tom Beecher removed his fedora and buttoned the front of his double-breasted coat. He was a much younger man then, broad shouldered and slim waisted, and age had not yet robbed him of his thick, brown hair. He smiled broadly and easily, and his eyes were free of the cynicism that would shackle him in later years.

"What's she here for?" the attorney asked. "To pay his bail?"

"If she can afford it."

"How high is it?"

"How high do you want it to be?"

Tom Beecher reached into his pocket, pulled out a twenty dollar bill, and pressed it into the palm of the jailer's hand. "High enough."

He stood beside the doorway, listening as Vickie Anderson said, "I want to get Wendell out. I was told his bond was a hundred dollars."

The jailer thumbed casually through the papers on his desk, looked up finally, and told her, "There must be some mistake, Mrs. Anderson. Right here, it says bail has been set at two hundred dollars."

She frowned. "But I only got a hundred dollars."

"Maybe you misunderstood."

"But I only got a hundred dollars." Vickie's face turned pink, then crimson, as she glanced desperately from the wad of dirty bills in her hand to her empty purse. She looked flustered, and there was a faint tremor in her voice. "Wendell will kill me if I don't get him out."

The jailer shrugged. He had heard it all before.

Tom Beecher touched her arm. "Maybe I can help you," he said.

So he did.

The attorney sat at a back table in the Old Tea Room all morning, listening attentively as Vickie Anderson spilled out her tale of woe. Yes, she was married to Wendell Anderson. No, she didn't love him. Yes, she had gotten married much too young. No, there had been no one else to take care of her. Yes, Wendell had beaten her. Yes, he stayed drunk most of the time. Yes, she was scared of him. No, she didn't have anywhere else to go.

"I'll help you," Tom Beecher had whispered softly.

"How?"

"I'm an attorney."

"Does that mean you'll represent Wendell?"

Tom nodded.

"I can't afford an attorney."

"You can afford me."

Vickie looked nervously away. Her hands were shaking badly now, and her eyes were wide with fright. "That means Wendell will be comin' back home, don't it?" She flinched, and there was anxiety in her voice.

Tom shook his head.

Bewilderment replaced the fear in Vickie's eyes.

"That means," he said slowly, carefully, "that you won't ever have to worry about Wendell Anderson hurting you again."

He took her hand in his and squeezed it.

"I don't want to go home no more," Vickie said.

"You don't have to."

Tom Beecher awoke that night and turned to face the woman who had soothed the raging beast inside of him. She was sprawled amidst the wet, tangled sheets, her skin stark and bloodless in the glare of the moonlight. Her hair fell untamed upon the pillow, and a shadow dimmed her face. Her breath warmed his shoulder, and Tom saw a deep, purple bruise left by teeth marks on the inside of Vickie's right thigh.

Damn, he thought. *Did Wendell do that? Or did I?*

He lay his hand on the bruise and gently began to stroke
it until Vickie awakened, smiled a sleepy smile, and willingly
came into his arms again. He was a gentle man. Wendell
had always treated her like a bitch in heat. She was Wendell's
private whore. With Tom, she could be a lady, his lady,
every night, all night, and she wondered how many nights
it would take before he tired of her body and realized that
she had no place in his social world. By morning, Tom
Beecher was unabashedly and unashamedly in love with another man's wife.

The sun was late in the sky by the time Tom rolled out
of bed, threw a red velvet robe around his sagging shoulders,
and staggered in a daze toward the kitchen. His apartment
was filled with the smell of eggs, and bacon frying in its
own grease. He could hear Vickie, and she was humming
along with the radio, some damn rock and roll song he had
never heard before. He stopped when he reached the doorway and saw her. All she had on was his wrinkled shirt,
and Tom couldn't take his eyes off those long, tanned legs
that had been wrapped around him for most of the night.

He kissed Vickie on the back of her neck before she was
aware that he had come into the room. She giggled, and
the fear, the bewilderment had vanished from her eyes.

Tom held her tightly until the bacon had burned and the
eggs were stuck to the bottom of the skillet.

Breakfast was ruined.

He didn't give a damn.

He wasn't hungry anyway.

Tom unbuttoned the shirt, slipped it from around her
shoulders, and dropped it beside his red velvet robe.

In his downtown office, Tom Beecher's telephone rang most of the day, and there was no one in to answer it.

That night, while Vickie slept, he thumbed through the newspaper, and his eyes were drawn to a small, three-paragraph story virtually buried on the back page. The body of a young black girl had been found lying in a ditch near Redwood. She had been brutally raped. Her throat was cut.

Tom leaned back in the overstuffed chair and closed his eyes, contemplating what he had read, and a strange series of thoughts began to unravel in his mind.

Wendell Anderson liked young girls, maybe even black ones. Wendell Anderson lived near Redwood. Wendell Anderson had been known to abuse women, even his own wife. Wendell Anderson carried a hunting knife.

It all made sense. Maybe Tom was just tired. Maybe he was crazy. But it all made sense to him.

Tom Beecher got up and walked to his bed, sitting down next to Vickie's sleeping body, being careful not to awaken her. She looked so young as the moonlight played recklessly upon her face. She was so beautiful. Her life had been so hard, and Tom Beecher knew that he could change all of that. He did not want to lose her, and there was only one way to keep her. Wendell Anderson must be put away where he could never reach either of them.

Tom thought for a moment. Then he smiled.

Two days later, Wendell Anderson was charged with the murder of Bertha Borders, and nobody in the courthouse cared whether he lived or died or even if he was innocent.

Oliver Baker owed Tom Beecher a favor. "Yes, suh," Oliver would tell the court. "I seen Bertha get in Mistuh Anderson's

car, and that's the last time me or anybody else evuh saw
her walkin' and breathin' and alive. Yes, suh, he was drinkin',
and she was laughin', and they was carryin' on somethin'
awful. Yes, suh, he come down to nigger town a lot when
he was lookin' for somethin' he couldn't get at home."

And Slick Alexander, Tom Beecher knew, would say anything for a hundred dollars and a cheap bottle of wine. "That's
the man," Slick said to the judge, jabbing a crooked finger
straight at Wendell Anderson's hostile face. "That's the man
I saw drivin' away with Bertha. I begged her not to go, but
she wouldn't pay me no mind, and now she's dead. That's a
mean man, your honor. I seen him cut R. C. Quaid's finger
off one night just because he lost a arm wrestlin' match. I
do believe, your honor, that that's the meanest damn man I
ever saw."

It took the jury an hour and fifteen minutes—including
lunch—to convict Wendell Anderson of second degree murder. It was the only murder trial Tom Beecher ever lost,
and he watched with a placid face while his client was dragged
away in chains, screaming like a mad man, his eyes wild,
spitting and cursing with every breath he took. "I'll get you,
you sonofabitch," Wendell yelled. "I'm comin' back, and I'm
gonna cut your fuckin' head clean off," were the last words
Tom Beecher ever heard Wendell Anderson say.

On the day her divorce became final, Vickie Anderson,
was wed in a simple ceremony to the honorable Tom Beecher,
attorney-at-law. She was, the matrons of society said, a lovely
bride. Yes, Tom Beecher was indeed a fortunate man to find
such a stunning wife. Yes, she would be quite an asset to
his budding political aspirations. No, they didn't believe that
Tom had ever looked happier in his life.

None of them had ever heard of Wendell Anderson. Oh, they might have read his name in the one-column, five paragraph story on page twelve that mentioned his murder conviction. But his name didn't mean anything to them. And no one was aware that Wendell Anderson had been the man to steal Vickie's virginity back when she was sixteen years old and struggling to survive, barefoot and abandoned, on the wrong side of Vicksburg.

No one knew the truth.

Tom Beecher had been sure of it.

For most of thirty-two years, the secret had been his and his alone. The old jailer was long dead. Oliver and Slick had just sort of drifted away. They were the kind to be gone for months before anybody missed them or realized they had left town.

Tom Beecher shivered. He couldn't forget the demonic gleam that had shone ominously from somewhere deep within Birdie Castleberry's eyes.

She knew the truth.

He should have known. Birdie Castleberry made it her business to know the truth about everybody, no matter how sordid or incriminating it might be.

The truth was a powerful weapon. In a courtroom, it was the greatest defense of all. In the wrong hands, it could be devastating. Men would kill to keep certain truths veiled behind a curtain of secrecy.

Tom Beecher was one of them.

Birdie Castleberry, he decided, must know that, too. He was vulnerable, and she would exploit that weakness to her advantage every chance she got. For her, there was no statute of limitations.

As long as Tom Beecher lived, he would be a puppet on a string manipulated solely by her whims and wishes, and he would never be able to escape the hold she had on him.

What she wanted, he would do. He had no choice.

What she wanted was for someone to stop Raymond Lynch.

"How?" he had asked.

"Go dig up Wendell Anderson," she had replied in a voice as disturbing as an indictment.

So Tom Beecher had come to be with Wendell Anderson one last time, and he sat there during the night, parked back among the ancient pines, the dull ache gnawing into the pit of his stomach. He had been forced to face reality, to look again at an ignoble past that had not stayed buried.

He would stop Raymond Lynch.

Somehow.

Some way.

But Tom Beecher knew that neither he nor Vickie would ever have peace of mind again, not with the knowledge that Birdie Castleberry would forever be standing in the near shadows, always looking over their shoulders with the beady eyes of a hungry vulture.

As he started his Riviera to leave, the mist began to lift slowly from the ground, and Tom could see the first rays of a morning sunlight touching a small granite tombstone that set crookedly in the eastern corner of the cemetery. There were no other graves around it. Wendell Anderson had been an outcast in life. In death it was no different for him.

Two weeks before his parole from prison, Wendell Anderson had been found hanged in his cell, the thick strip of a dirty sheet tied around his neck.

Suicide was the official verdict.

It just didn't make sense, argued some of the guards who had known him best. In two weeks, Wendell Anderson would have been a free man. Why in hell would he want to kill himself?

One report said, in medical terms, that Wendell was a dead man long before the hanging even took place. There was no evidence of strangulation. His neck had been broken. At the inquest, however, neither the report nor its existence was ever mentioned at all. Only one copy had been made, and Tom Beecher paid handsomely to have it destroyed, a thousand dollars more, in fact, than it had cost him to keep Wendell Anderson from ever coming back home.

Or did Birdie have a copy as well?

He didn't doubt it at all, and the sweat lay cold and clammy against his face.

Promptly at nine o'clock, Tom Beecher walked into the small, cluttered office of Lou Holland, a private detective who had been on the old attorney's payroll for years. Looks could definitely be deceiving. Lou's hair was gray, his face gaunt and wrinkled, his black polyester suit worn slick in places. He never put on any kind of a tie, smoked too much, and the double layer of gold chains he wore always looked as though they belonged on somebody else's neck. Lou was soft-spoken and deadly efficient. He had neither morals nor scruples, and he knew when to keep his mouth shut, all of which made him an ideal private detective.

He glanced down at the eight by ten color photograph that Tom Beecher placed on the desk top in front of him.

"Who's the guy?" he asked.

"His name is Raymond Lynch."

"What does he do?"

"He's a schoolteacher."

"Where does he live?"

"Here."

"What's the address?"

Tom Beecher tossed one of Raymond's soiled business cards down beside the photograph.

"Where'd he come from?"

"Somewhere in Massachusetts."

"Why? They got schools in Massachusetts."

"I don't know." Tom shrugged. "Maybe he liked the climate."

"Bullshit."

Lou Holland studied the photograph closely, then asked, "Is he married?"

"No."

"Has he ever been married?"

"I don't know."

"Does he date anybody?"

"Not that I know of."

"Is he queer?"

Tom shrugged again.

"What do you want me to do, Tom?"

"Learn everything you can about him. Everybody's got a little dirt in his past. I want to know what Raymond Lynch has got to hide."

Lou nodded. "When do you need it?"

"Before the week's out."

"It'll cost you."

Tom reached for his checkbook. "It always does," he said.

12

Helen Jensen was seated on a stool beside her vanity mirror when she saw Robert come striding into the bedroom, wearing nothing but his jockey shorts. His belly was bloated, his chest barren.of any hair, and the pimples on his spindly legs were streaked red where he had been scratching them. He should at least have the decency to wear pajamas, Helen thought to herself, and she turned away from him.

"I'm tired of fighting the battle for Nathan Locke alone," she began.

"Why should you even be fighting for him in the first place?" Robert laid a sweaty palm on her shoulder.

"He's a good man."

"He's a money-hungry son of a bitch."

Helen whirled around, her eyes flashing. "He's certainly done more for Jeremy than you ever have," she snapped.

Her words were like a slap across the face.

"So what do you want me to do?" Robert asked loudly.

"Raymond's your friend. Talk some sense into his head. Shut him up." Her voice quavered. "I don't care if you have to run the bastard out of town on a rail."

Robert grinned and ran his hands inside Helen's robe, pressing them against the soft skin of her buttocks. "What are you gonna give me if I do?" There was a gleam in his eyes.

Helen hesitated, then realized she would do anything for Nathan Locke. She kissed Robert and almost gagged.

RAYMOND Lynch eased his old Pontiac alongside the curb, killed the engine, and sat for awhile in the solace of the darkness, listening as a half-hearted summer rain tap danced against the top of his car. The sky grumbled back in the west, and an occasional flash of lightning danced above the trees that lined the driveway leading to Bill and Marcy Freeman's new and fashionable brick home. Raymond wasn't really that well acquainted with the couple. He did know that they were in their mid-thirties and had been transferred to Vicksburg from Memphis. Marcy sang in the choir on Sunday mornings, and Bill taught church school, but that was about all.

Now they wanted to see him.

He wondered why.

And he dreaded to find out why.

Raymond knew he was becoming paranoid, and he didn't

213

like the feeling. To him, it seemed as though every eye was always on him, accusing him, condemning him, disapproving every word he spoke against Nathan Locke. He had suddenly found himself to be a man without friends. Even those who knew him best and those, Raymond thought, who liked him best had begun to treat him like a leper.

"It's not that I don't like you anymore," Robert Jensen had told him a few nights ago when he refused a beer. "It's just that I'm better off not being seen with you."

Friends had become strangers.

Raymond Lynch didn't trust strangers.

His phone was never silent anymore. It rang at all hours of the night. Some of the voices he recognized. Birdie's cackle, Alice's sarcasm, Helen's anger were all unforgettable. Howard Daniels cursed him. Charles Page had threatened to get him fired, and the old man probably had enough money and power to do anything he wanted to do to anyone who crossed him.

They might ignore what he was trying to tell them about Nathan Locke.

They would probably even beat him.

But Raymond Lynch would be damned if he ran again.

Still, he wasn't taking any chances. Without really thinking about it, he had even found himself beginning to sit with his back to the wall, and he seldom went out anymore. He was afraid to go alone. There was no one else willing to go with him, and he couldn't blame them.

Then came Marcy's telephone call about five o'clock that afternoon. It was short and cryptic.

"Bill and I would like to talk to you," she had said in a strained voice.

"What about?" He had tried, probably without succeeding, to sound calm and unperturbed.

"We're troubled about some things."

"Aren't we all."

"Can you be at our house about eight tonight?" The strain was becoming more pronounced in Marcy's voice.

"Sure." Raymond paused, then added, "Why not?"

She had hung up without saying goodbye.

Raymond glanced at his watch. It was eight–fifteen. He was already late. Maybe he shouldn't even go in at all. He certainly wasn't in the mood for another confrontation with a pair of Nathan Locke's vigilantes.

The rain slackened.

What the hell, he decided.

Raymond slipped out of the car, bowed his back against the wind, and ran quickly up the rock and concrete sidewalk to the Freeman's front door. It opened before he ever got a chance to ring the bell.

"I'm glad you could come," Marcy said. "We were afraid you wouldn't."

She took him by the arm and ushered him into the den.

It was crowded. Raymond guessed there might be as many as thirty couples, maybe even more, sitting there, standing around a pool table, all, no doubt, waiting for him, probably waiting to convict him. In one quick visual sweep, it was difficult to tell. He could put a name to a few of the faces, but most of them were only vaguely familiar. He had crossed

their paths at least once, perhaps even twice, in the holy
sanctuary of the Basilwood Presbyterian Church. The laughter, the talking died away as soon as he walked into the
room, and he could feel those eyes smothering him in a curious and uncomfortable sort of way.

Bill Freeman shook his hand. "Can I get you a drink?"
he asked.

"Please. Bourbon."

"How would you like it?"

Raymond's gaze again swept across the odd assortment of
faces that kept staring at him.

But were they accusing?

Condemning?

Raymond smiled. "I'd like it straight," he said and turned
so that his back would be pressed against the natural pine
paneled wall.

Bill Freeman poured from a Wild Turkey bottle. "I guess
you know everybody here," he said.

"I recognize most of the faces," Raymond answered.

"There's been a lot of talk that Nathan's gotten caught
with his hand in the till."

Raymond took the glass from Bill's outstretched hand.
"That's my opinion," he said.

"Can you prove it?"

"No."

A worried frown worked its way into Bill Freeman's brow.
"I understand that you asked for Nathan's resignation at session the other night."

Raymond shrugged. He saw others beginning to gather

in closer around him. "Nathan threatened to resign, that's all," he answered. The Wild Turkey burned his tongue.

"Then I guess you had him backed up against the wall," Bill Freeman saluted Raymond with his glass of whiskey. "You must have been hitting old Nathan pretty close to home."

"Why do you ask?"

Raymond Lynch heard a familiar ring of laughter coming from the doorway, and he saw Wade Ferguson pushing his way to the front of the crowd. "That's an old politician's trick," he bellowed. "Get'em cornered, and they cry on your shoulder and pull at your heartstrings and threaten to resign. They put the blame for their misfortune on your shoulders, send you off on a guilt trip, make you feel lower than a snake's belly in a wagon rut. The next thing you know you're on your knees, begging 'em not to resign." Wade's laugh was louder now. "And you know what, Raymond? It works damn near every time." He slapped Bill Freeman on the back, wiped the rain from his face, and said, "Now let me have some of that sippin' whiskey, and let's get down to business."

As Bill tossed a few ice cubes into Wade's glass, he told Raymond, "That's not the first time Nathan Locke has ever threatened to resign."

"And it won't be the last," Wade interjected.

"It might be," Marcy Freeman said softly. "But that's up to you, Raymond."

He raised an eyebrow in surprise.

"There's never been anybody with enough nerve to stand up and face Nathan Locke eyeball to eyeball before," Bill

said, placing an arm around his wife for support. "He's a
helluva good preacher. He's built a helluva strong church.
He deserves credit for that, and I'll be the first to give it to
him. But now he's more interested in power than he is in
the needs of his congregation." Bill's shoulders slumped as
though the weight of the world were laying heavy on them.

"I'm not quite sure I understand," Raymond said, his eyes
clouded with confusion.

"A man like Nathan Locke doesn't change overnight," Bill
replied. "For him, it's been a long time coming. A lot of us
saw it happening, but we didn't do a damn thing to stop it.
I had a chance to stand up to Nathan when I was on session.
But at the end of a gut-wrenching argument one night, he
threatened to resign, and like Wade says, I went home and
felt like a cold, cruel, heartless sonovabitch. The next morning
I was in his office, apologizing, and begging him to forgive
me. Ever since then, I've just sat back, kept my mouth shut,
and wished to God I hadn't been such a coward."

There were tears in Bill Freeman's eyes.

The room was so quiet, all Raymond could hear was the
uneven sound of his own breathing.

Even Wade Ferguson looked subdued.

"I told you that you weren't in this alone," he said softly
to Raymond. "Every group has its silent majority, and the
people you see around you tonight are just a small part of
those at Basilwood Presbyterian who feel the same way you
do." Wade winked.

Raymond Lynch felt the tension drain from his body. For
so long he had felt so alone. Maybe he hadn't been alone

after all. The room blurred momentarily, and he knew a tear had dampened his own eyes.

He slowly shifted his gaze from face to face and saw concern—or was it fear?—in them all. Raymond realized his hand was trembling, and he hurriedly set the glass on the counter beside him. He forced a smile. "I'm in a little bit of a shock," he said finally. "A lot of people told me I was crazy for taking on Nathan, and I was beginning to think they were right. Maybe they were wrong after all." Raymond sighed and folded his arms. "What do you people want me to do?"

"Keep the pressure on," Bill answered. "You're the only voice we have on the session now. You're the only member there Nathan Locke doesn't have in his hip pocket."

"I don't know what good that will do," Raymond said caustically. For some reason, the bourbon had begun to taste bitter.

"Keep hammerin' away, boy," Wade retorted. "Keep old Nathan's feet to the fire. If he's guilty, he may panic. When a man panics, he starts makin' mistakes, and those mistakes can hang him."

Raymond felt a ripple of apprehension surge through him. "I didn't have a whole lot of ammunition to start with," he conceded, "and I've pretty well used what I had." He nodded for Bill to add fresh bourbon to his glass, then continued, "I've heard rumors that Nathan has a slush fund, and that's illegal as hell, but I don't have any proof. I know for certain that Nathan violated the Presbyterian Book of Order when he and he alone decided to spend Max Gordon's millions on a radio and television center. Only the session can make those kinds of financial decisions, but, hell, the session will back Nathan on anything he wants to do, legal or illegal, either before the fact or after it. They may be good people, but they think it's heresy to oppose the preacher."

Bill nodded. He understood. He had been there. And by his own admission, he had wilted under the strain.

"If you want more ammunition, we'll give it to you," Marcy Freeman said softly, brushing her thick red hair away from her face. She motioned for Raymond to take a seat on the den sofa and told him, "I personally don't know if Nathan has broken any laws or violated any books of order, but I do feel that he has reached the point where he cares a lot more about our financial statements than he does about our soul."

"He wants power," Greg Kaufman snapped bitterly.

"And recognition," Jana Smith added.

"Basilwood's not big enough for him anymore," Kenneth Elmore said tersely. "Hell, Nathan Locke hasn't moved to shake my hand in two years, and has never darkened the doorway of my house. He's too busy hobnobbin' with the rich folks, dreamin' about gettin' his face on television so everybody can send him money and tell him how wonderful he is."

"Television's a great way to reach a lot of people," Raymond said, remembering Nathan's impassioned argument before the session.

Kenneth's face darkened furiously. "Hell," he spit out, "Nathan's got enough people to reach in his own backyard, and he's doin' a piss poor job of takin' care of them."

Kenneth's wife was squeezing his arm, trying to calm him,

but he kept ignoring her. He was wound up now, and the veins were protruding from his neck. "Nathan said he wanted to resign. Well, that's fine with me. I think the son of a bitch ought to take his damn TV show and go somewhere else with it."

Several heads nodded in agreement.

Raymond Lynch sensed that raw emotions were beginning to boil, rising to a fevered pitch. Fears, concerns, grievances, anger had been bottled up so long, and now they were spilling out into the open. And for most, it was painful.

Greg's father had died two years ago. He had asked Nathan to come and talk to him. He waited, he said. Nathan Locke never came.

Marcy talked of her surgery. She lay for weeks in a hospital bed, and there had been no visit, no phone call, not even a card from her minister.

"The bastard's too busy prayin' for himself to pray for anybody else," Kenneth roared.

"I don't want him in my house if I've got any troubles," Harold Hogan said bluntly, rolling up his sleeves. "I don't trust him. As far as I'm concerned, Nathan Locke ain't got no business prayin' for me. God ain't got time to listen to men like Nathan Locke."

"If I die anytime soon," Greg blurted out, "just make sure you find somebody else to preach my funeral. Old Nathan probably wouldn't do it anyway unless it was on TV."

"I want a pastor who's a friend," Jana said. "I'm not sure Nathan even knows my name."

"He doesn't care about your name," Kenneth snapped, "unless it's signed on the bottom of a check."

"Did you ever know Horace and Dolores Hampton?" Bill
Freeman asked.

Raymond didn't.

It didn't matter.

"Horace was a charter member of Basilwood Presbyterian,"
Bill continued. "In nineteen eighty-three, he was relieved
of his position on the board of trustees and asked to find
another church."

"Why?" Raymond asked.

"He lost his job."

"Is that all?"

"That was enough." Bill sighed sadly. "Nathan likes members who can pay their own way."

"Did Nathan ask Horace to leave?" Raymond asked.

"He didn't have to. Tom Beecher did it for him."

"Tom Beecher does all of Nathan's dirty work," Kenneth
added. "That way, Nathan keeps his hands clean."

Raymond shook his head in amazement. It all sounded so
incredible. "I thought Tom Beecher was just a harmless, old
over-the-hill lawyer who liked to hear himself talk and always
slept through church on Sunday."

Kenneth Elmore's laugh was filled with disgust. "Tom
Beecher is a sly old sonovabitch," he said. "Nathan tells Tom
what he wants to do, and Tom makes sure he gets away
with it."

"Don't underestimate him," Bill warned.

"He's dangerous." Greg stared at the ice slowly melting
in his glass.

Wade Ferguson crossed the room and fumbled for a moment with the Wild Turkey bottle. "A few years ago," he
said, "we had a new member who had just moved down

from some big city back east, Baltimore, I think it was."
Wade paused to fill one jigger, then two, with the bourbon.
"Paul was president of a manufacturing company that had
come to town, and as near as I can remember, he had been
a ruling Presbyterian elder for at least ten years, maybe more.
He was loud, arrogant as hell, and he didn't like the way
our session members were chosen."

"Paul told me they were handpicked by Nathan Locke,
and Presbyterians, at least honest Presbyterians, just didn't
allow that to happen. It gave a preacher too much control.
It gave him too much power. He could then rule a church
like a dictator, and the session would simply rubber stamp
whatever he wanted done. Well, Paul, bein' the type of person he was, kept on raisin' hell every chance he got, and
finally old Tom quietly and politely asked him to shut up
about it." Wade raised the glass to his lips, and his hands
were shaking. The bourbon spilled on the front of his shirt,
but he appeared not to notice. Maybe he just didn't care.

"Did Paul drop the matter?" Raymond asked.

"He was too stubborn for that."

"What happened?"

"Two weeks later, he was fired." Wade Ferguson's face
was beaded with sweat. "A month later, his wife left him
and filed for divorce." He drained the glass with one long
swallow. "Before the year was out, Nathan Locke had
preached his funeral."

"What killed him?"

"His car hit a concrete viaduct about three o'clock one
morning. The police said he had been drinking, and he went
to sleep at the wheel."

"You don't sound like you believe them."

"In fifty-seven years, Paul had never taken one single drop of hard liquor. The first time he tried whiskey, it made him sick. It made him sick to even think about drinking."

"You must have known him pretty well."

Wade Ferguson turned away, his shoulders sagging. "Paul was my older brother," he said. His words were nothing but a whisper, but they sounded like thunder in the hushed room.

He poured himself another drink to steady his nerves.

"Paul had everything," Wade continued. "Nathan Locke took it away from him."

"Can you prove it?" Raymond felt silent fear rising up within him.

"Can you ever prove anything against Nathan Locke?" Wade asked rhetorically. "Hell, no." He provided his own answer, and the anger in his eyes had turned to self pity.

"We gotta stop Nathan," Bill said.

"We gotta stop him now." Kenneth rubbed the palms of his hands nervously together.

Greg placed a firm hand on Raymond's shoulder. "You're the one hope we have," he said.

Raymond Lynch walked away and stared out the glass patio door, watching the rain as it cascaded off the roof and dug a narrow trench in the flower beds. The daffodils had been beaten flat.

"I can't do it alone," he said quietly.

Raymond waited for someone to answer.

No one did.

"In the Presbyterian Church," he said, "you can't get rid of a pastor without a congregational vote. If it comes to that, you'll have to stand up in that sanctuary before God, friend, and enemy alike, stare Nathan Locke dead square in the eyes, and vote against him. That's a tough thing to do." He paused to let reality sink in, then asked, "Can you do it?"

"You have our support," Marcy Freeman said.

"And our votes." Kenneth's voice was sharp and decisive.

Raymond nodded wearily. He knew they might not be enough.

13

For more than an hour Wade Ferguson sat cloaked in the darkness of his own bedroom, staring at the telephone beside him.

Shortly after midnight, he took a deep, tortured breath and dialed Birdie Castleberry.

"Who is this?" she snapped, as caustic as always.

"Wade Ferguson."

"What the hell do you want at this hour?"

"I've just come from a little get-together over at Bill and Marcy Freeman's house," he said. "Nathan just may have a lot more trouble than he thought."

"What do you mean?"

"There's a mob comin' after him now, and they're demandin' his resignation. Raymond's got 'em stirred up pretty good."

"How many?"

"Probably a hundred or more."

Wade could hear Birdie muttering under her breath as she hung up the phone. A wave of nausea swept over him. He hated Nathan Locke. God, how he hated him. But Wade had always been a master at hedging his bets. Both sides in the controversy needed him, he decided. Both sides were depending on him. He would come out a winner regardless of who won the conflict. That was the only way Wade Ferguson knew how to play.

NATHAN Locke had reached the coffee shop early. He had been awake since Birdie Castleberry's disturbing phone call jarred him out of a deep and troubled sleep sometime around five-thirty, and he was in a disgruntled mood. Locke kept telling himself that there was no reason to concern himself with Raymond Lynch. In stark reality, Raymond was no more of a threat than a gnat buzzing around his head on a late summer day, but even gnats could be annoying, and Nathan Locke had grown decidedly tired of being verbally assasinated by the carpetbagger history teacher from Massachusetts.

He had too many plans, too many dreams.

Raymond Lynch was trying to screw them up.

Damn Raymond Lynch.

It hadn't been so bad when there was only one, lone, pitiful voice rising up in opposition against him. But now, if the information Birdie had gotten from Wade was correct, Raymond had taken a fistful of rumors he couldn't prove and was handing them out to anyone who would listen to him. And apparently, there were a lot of people listening, more than even he had anticipated. Locke grinned sardonically to himself. There was no real reason to worry about that. One good sermon would take the wind out of all of the bastards.

He could shame them.

He could damn them.

He could scare the hell out of them.

Locke's contemptuous grin broadened, and a touch of cynicism edged into his eyes. They burned as brightly as tongues of flame.

Or he could efficiently and meticulously discredit Raymond Lynch, drape him in ridicule and scorn, hang him out for all to see, and leave him to strangle slowly on his own lies.

Locke ordered eggs, sunny side up, and black coffee, and he felt better already, better, in fact, than he had in days. He was on his second cup by the time Jeremy Jensen walked into the dining room to join him.

The boy had definitely changed. His rebellious scowl was gone, and the deep-seated rage that once dwelt within him had faded from his eyes. He was clean-shaven, had a quick smile, and there was a vigor in the way he walked.

"Good morning, Jeremy," Locke said, glancing at his watch. "You're right on time."

"I've been up for hours already."

"Good for you." Locke nodded toward the empty chair beside him. "Have you eaten yet?"

"I'm not hungry."

Locke chuckled. "You nervous?"

Jeremy's voice cracked slightly. "I just don't want to keep Mister Daniels waiting, that's all."

"I don't blame you." The minister took the paper napkin from his lap, tossed it on top of his plate, and scooted his chair away from the table. He rose and stretched, and he felt a twinge of pain work its way like a splinter between his shoulder blades. Probably stress, Locke thought. He hadn't slept well for a week, and last night he had tossed and turned until Birdie's phone call rousted him out of bed. Nancy had even said she heard him cry out during the night, and that was not like Nathan Locke at all. He knew he needed to get away for awhile. He was tired of people smothering him, never giving him a moment's rest or a day he could call his own.

He wrapped a fatherly arm around Jeremy, and together they walked out into the bright, blinding sunshine of an ideal July morning. A gentle wind pushed out of the south, and the day felt fresh, scrubbed clean by the evening rain. The leaves on the trees glistened, puddles had collected in a haphazard fashion alongside the cracked sidewalk, and the storm clouds from the night before had fled the sky.

Nathan Locke turned his black Cadillac toward downtown Vicksburg, driving slower than usual long the slippery brick streets. He quietly studied Jeremy's thin, handsome face and decided that the lanky young man definitely had his mother's features, particularly her ivory complexion and green eyes. He had always been partial to green eyes. Helen Jensen could be a striking woman when she wanted to be. But try as he might, Locke had never been able to picture her sleeping with Robert. But then, he couldn't imagine any woman taking off her clothes for Robert Jensen. A lot of people who didn't belong together were sure doing their best to stay together, and he and Nancy, Locke confessed to himself, were just as guilty as any of them.

He finally broke the silence. "Have you thought any more about going back home?" Locke asked Jeremy.

The boy's smile quivered, but he didn't lose it. "I've thought about it," he said.

"And what have you decided?"

"I'm scared to go back."

"Your mother misses you."

"Mom doesn't hassle me." Suddenly the smile was gone. "My dad doesn't want me back home."

"Has he ever told you that?"

"No, sir." Jeremy fidgeted in his seat. "He doesn't have to tell me. I can see it on his face. All I have to do is walk into a room, and he gets mad and starts screaming at me. Then Mom interferes, and he starts screaming at her, too." Jeremy stared out the window, watching a squirrel as it darted out of the traffic and disappeared back among the oaks that encircled the Duff Green Mansion. "Some day, I'm afraid he's gonna hit her," the boy said finally.

"Your daddy wouldn't do that." Locke tried to ease his fears.

"If he does," Jeremy said, his voice flat and without emotion, "I'm gonna kill him."

Nathan Locke sighed deliberately to show his aggravation, and pulled his car into a narrow parking space beside Howard Daniels's commercial printing company. He was glad to be there.

"Here we are," he said, calm and relaxed, hoping to soothe the tension that suddenly held Jeremy in its grasp.

The boy nodded, and his face brightened. Once more, the violent rage within him began to diminish, but Locke knew that it would always be there, boiling like molten lava just below the surface, and neither of them ever knew when it was about to erupt. Jeremy was trying hard to control his emotions, but too many pills, too many needles, too much cheap liquor had left his nerves ragged and shattered. Locke had seen war affect men the same way.

Howard Daniels was waiting on them in his office. He may have been the president and sole owner of the printing company, but he certainly didn't give the appearance of being an executive. Howard wore khaki pants that were streaked with a variety of colored inks, primarily black, and his white shirt was old and yellowed. His office was just as unkempt, and he sat on the edge of a secondhand wooden desk cluttered with estimates and invoices.

He rose to shake Locke's hand, cautiously studying the slender young man who stood beside him.

"Howard, I'd like for you to meet Jeremy Jensen," Locke said.

The printer nodded.

Jeremy nervously licked his dry lips.

"You're Helen's boy, aren't you?" Howard asked.

"Yes, sir."

"I haven't seen you around with your mama since you were just a kid," the printer said.

Jeremy looked flustered.

"I'll be honest with you," Locke said to Howard. "Life hasn't been real easy for Jeremy lately. It's not easy for any teenager these days. But Jeremy's working hard to turn his life around. All he needs is a chance, Howard, and I'm hoping you can give him one."

"He ought to thank God he's got a friend like you goin' to bat for him."

"He needs all the friends he can get." Nathan Locke's broad, infectious smile exuded confidence in himself and in those around him. "Like I told you by phone," he continued, "Jeremy is looking for work, and frankly, Howard, I personally believe he'll do a great job for you."

Howard Daniels folded his thick, muscular arms and grinned. Whatever Nathan Locke wanted was fine with him. His minister's word was gospel.

He turned to Jeremy. "Ever worked in a print shop before?" he asked.

"No, sir. But I can learn."

"It's demanding work, and I can be a tough sonofabitch to get along with sometimes."

"I can handle it."

"We don't always quit at five o'clock," Howard said matter-of-factly. "If there's a big job on the press, we stay with it until it's finished, even if that's midnight."

"I don't mind. I don't have a lot to do in the evenings anyway."

Howard Daniels reached out, took Jeremy's right hand and looked at it closely for a moment. It was white and soft, free of any calluses that he always associated with hard work. He frowned. Howard Daniels was the kind of man who found it difficult to trust anybody who didn't have at least one raw blister and the promise of another on his hands.

"Printing's a dirty job," he said.

Jeremy nodded as though he understood.

"And the pay's not much."

"It doesn't take much for me to get by."

Howard rubbed his chin, picked up the work orders from his desk, and stared at them briefly. Finally he looked back at Jeremy and said, "I'll start you out cleaning the presses for three dollars and fifty-five cents an hour."

A smile flickered across Jeremy's face. "That sounds like as good a place as any to start."

"You're damn right it is," Howard thundered, his voice booming throughout the shop. "I started out cleaning presses when I was fifteen years old, and now I own the whole damn company."

He laughed loudly, and Jeremy laughed with him.

Nathan Locke rocked back on his heels and felt as though the weight of the world had been lifted from his shoulders. Jeremy Jensen had wallowed on the bottom for awhile, but he had certainly climbed out of the pits in a hurry. All he had needed was for somebody to grab him by the shoulders and jerk him to his feet. Dear, sweet Helen had been so worried about him. She should be proud of her son now. It would always be a struggle, and he might stumble once or twice along the way, but Jeremy was going to make it all right now. Nathan Locke was sure of it.

14

Raymond Lynch was ready to celebrate. He was no longer alone in his battle against the preacher, and it was a good feeling. He sat at a back corner table in the Beechwood Lounge and barely raised an eyebrow when Robert Jensen eased into a chair across from him. He wasn't worried. Helen opposed him, but Helen's husband had always been a friend.

However, there was irritation etched deep in Robert's pudgy face. "Why don't you cut out this one-man crusade against Nathan Locke," he said.

"Locke's violating the Book of Order."

"Who gives a shit?"

"I do."

"Then hell, Raymond, why don't you just find another church where you and the pastor get along, and quit stirring up trouble here."

Raymond frowned. "Why should you care?" he asked. "You don't spend much time in church anyway."

Robert sighed in a disgruntled sort of way. "You've pissed my wife off," he answered. "And she's makin' life miserable as hell for me."

Raymond shrugged. "Maybe that's because you don't have a dick long enough to shut her up."

Robert hit him before he ever saw the blow coming, and Raymond tumbled to the floor, his mouth salty with the taste of his own blood.

NATHAN Locke did not like the look that clouded Tom Beecher's face. The venerable old attorney had been waiting for him all morning, standing in a darkened corner of the church study as though he were trying to conceal himself in the shadows. Tom had not even bothered to turn on the desk lamp, and the color had drained from his wrinkled face. At first glance, Locke had not been able to discern whether his old friend and ally was angry or frightened or both.

"What's the matter?" he asked, closing the door behind him and walking briskly toward his desk to hide the sudden uneasiness he felt. "You look like death warmed over."

"Where the hell you been?" Tom snarled.

"Out doing God's work." Locke laughed.

"Cut the bullshit," Tom snapped. "You got a problem."

"I'm used to them by now." The minister switched on his antique lamp, sat down in his high-backed, black leather chair, and turned slowly around toward his attorney.

Tom Beecher rested his gnarled hands on the desk, leaned forward until he was only inches away from Nathan Locke, and acrimoniously bit off each word, then spit it out in the preacher's face. "You've got a helluva lot bigger problem than you thought you had," he said.

Locke tried to appear unconcerned. "I know about the meeting at Bill and Marcy's house," he said. "It doesn't bother me."

"To hell with Bill and Marcy."

Locke feigned indifference. "And I know Raymond's out doing what he can to drum up a little opposition against me," he said, "but it won't do him any good. He's just pissing in the wind, Tom. You and I both know that."

"Fuck Raymond Lynch."

Nathan Locke nervously shifted his position in the chair and wondered why the room had suddenly gotten so warm. He loosened his silk tie and realized that his collar was soaked with sweat. He was even beginning to feel the heat from Tom Beecher's penetrating stare.

"What's the matter?" he asked again, less arrogant this time. The lamp reflected harshly off the attorney's grim face and had cast a hard shadow against the wall.

"I got a phone call this morning that disturbs me a great deal," Tom said, and there was an unfamiliar, disconcerting tremor in his voice.

"Who was it from?"

"Martha Landers."

Nathan Locke jerked his head up. He felt as though someone had kicked him savagely in the gut. He caught his breath, then lost it. He tried to mask his emotions but knew he had failed miserably. His face became drawn and twisted with the same anguish that was churning unmercifully in the pit of his stomach.

He opened his mouth to speak, but nothing came out.

"Martha Landers wants her money," Tom said tersely.

Locke's shoulders slumped, and the sweat lay cold, almost icy, against the back of his neck.

"How did she find out?" he asked weakly.

"Max Gordon left her a copy of his goddam will."

"Why in hell would he do that?"

"She apparently had given him something he hadn't had in a long time, and he was trying to repay her."

"Sex?"

"Love."

Nathan Locke was ashen-faced, disgusted, sick.

"A man will do damn near anything for love," Tom Beecher said, his voice softening.

Locke stood up and took a deep breath. The shock was beginning to wear off now.

"Whores don't fall in love," he said sharply.

"Martha Landers did."

"Is that what she says?"

Tom Beecher nodded gravely. "That's what she believes. Eunice Gordon may have been the wife. Martha Landers is convinced that she is the widow."

"Not in the eyes of God, she isn't," Locke snapped.

"God doesn't make judgement on wills," Tom reminded him. "The courts do. We've got one will that gives Basilwood Presbyterian Church two point six million dollars. Martha has another one that gives most of the money to her. Our will, my friend, is out of date as hell."

Nathan Locke weighed the facts in his mind, and he didn't

like what they told him. "If we took it to court, then," he said slowly, "you are still convinced that a whore like Martha Landers could beat the church." It sounded ridiculous.

"If she were my client, she would sure as hell win."

Locke's right hand closed to a fist, and he slammed it against the desk top.

"Max Gordon was a stupid son of a bitch," he growled.

"Any man who kills himself is a stupid son of a bitch."

A puzzled frown darkened Nathan Locke's granite face. The past month, it seemed, had simply been one disgusting day after another, and he wondered if they would ever stop.

"What do we do now?" he asked.

"We don't have any choice."

Locke pointed toward Tom Beecher. "You're calling the shots," he said coldly.

"We might as well pay Martha Landers a visit," Tom replied as he straightened his gray fedora and ambled toward the door. Nathan Locke followed him on unsteady legs, the distinct and nauseous odor of fear lingering in his nostrils.

The two men drove in silence, each lost in his own random thoughts, to the small, ramshackle motel that was set just off the highway and back in a small thicket of pines. It had no name. It needed none. Those who wanted to go there knew how to find it, and they could rent room by the day, by the night, or by the hour. Many a young Mississippi boy had taken a new, hard-earned twenty dollar bill and discovered his first taste of love behind its closed doors. The seasoned hookers never stayed long enough to grow old, and their rooms were seldom vacant for more than a week before new girls moved in. Martha Landers had taken up residence there three days after Max Gordon's funeral.

Dudley Elrod ran a quiet place, a clean place, and the law seldom bothered him, except, of course, during election time. Tom Beecher had even closed the motel down during one of his reelection bids for attorney general. "Well, I didn't exactly close it down," he confided to his friends, "I just rented the whole damn place for a month, locked its doors, and let the girls take a vacation. Hell, they needed the rest, and I needed their votes." He carried the no-name motel, twenty-two to nothing, and was later quite favorably impressed with how much better the girls looked wearing a tan.

Nathan Locke pulled his black Cadillac into the gravel driveway and quickly surveyed the parking lot. It was empty. During the early afternoon heat of a summer day, it was almost always empty. But by midnight, there would be a truck parked in front of every door, with a new vehicle coming in to take its place every thirty minutes or so.

Locke stopped beside the office. There was no light on. Dudley was probably somewhere in the back, catching up on his sleep or watching a soap opera on television.

"What room is she in?"

"Number eighteen's what she said."

Nathan Locke braced himself. "Let's go," he said.

The motel had been built just before the advent of World War II, back when it was more appropriately known as a tourist court, and wives always insisted on checking the rooms before checking in. Wives didn't come there much anymore, not unless they were looking for part-time work. Sometime during the early nineteen fifties, Dudley had added green asbestos shingles, and most of them were chipped pretty badly now. The outside window facings hadn't been painted in years, and the screens were rusted and torn. The motel was so quiet, Locke wasn't for sure anybody was home any-where in the whole place.

He paused before a door with the number eighteen on it, glanced furtively at Tom Beecher, took a deep breath, and knocked sharply.

He waited.

The only sound he heard was the rustling of a restless southern wind in the pines.

The preacher knocked again, harder this time.

The door opened slightly, and he saw a pair of timid eyes staring at him from out of the darkness of the room.

"What do you want?" asked a voice that matched the eyes.

Tom Beecher stepped forward, removed his fedora, and bowed slightly. "Martha," he said softly, "is that you?"

"Yes."

The timid eyes were squinting into the sun.

"I'm Tom Beecher, and I know you must remember my good friend and pastor, Nathan Locke."

Silence.

Locke was aware of an odd odor, sweet, sickeningly so, coming out of the room behind her. He almost gagged and turned his face toward the wind.

"I hope we're not disturbing you," Tom continued.

"No." The voice was that of a child, hesitant, somewhat puzzled and confused.

The doorway was still just a crack.

Martha Landers was still nothing more than a pair of timid eyes, darting apprehensively from out of the darkness.

"I'm the attorney handling Max Gordon's estate," Tom said patiently. "You and I talked earlier today."

There was a squeal of recognition, and Martha Landers came out of the room.

The smell was stronger now. And *sweeter.*

"You brought the money, then," she said innocently, and her eyes lost their timidity. "You brought me Max's money. He'll be so glad to know that you did."

Martha Landers was barefoot and dressed only in a soiled slip. The hem was frayed, and the nylon strap over her right shoulder had broken. Martha had tied it back together. Her brown hair was oily and in tangled disarray. It apparently had neither been washed nor combed for weeks, probably, Locke thought, not since Max Gordon's death. Her face was emaciated and devoid of makeup, yet her smile was suddenly bright and sincere. Her fingernails were broken, her hands and knees were skinned, and there were traces of dried blood on her bare, unshaven legs.

Tom Beecher smiled in a patronizing sort of way, took Martha's hand in his, and gently patted it. "I don't have the money just yet," he carefully explained. "You know how slow banks can be and how much red tape you have to go through to get anything done. First, I'm afraid I need to check Max's will and make sure it's legal."

"Oh, it's legal," Martha said matter-of-factly.

"I'm sure it is."

"Max wrote it himself."

"That's what I understand."

"I watched him write it." She smiled sweetly, leaned against the door, and closed her eyes. "We were there in bed one night . . ." Martha's voice trailed off, and her eyes hardened. "You did know Max was in love with me."

Tom nodded.

Her smile returned. "We were there in bed one night, and Max said I was the most wonderful girl he had ever known." Her words were coming rapid fire now, and she was beginning to tremble. "He said he loved me. He said he loved me over and over again, and he said he would never leave me no matter what happened, that he would always take care of me, and he wrote out his will, and he put my name in it, and he didn't put his wife's name in it, and he said there would be enough money there to last me for the rest of my life, and I would never have to go hungry or sleep with another man besides him again, and I swore I wouldn't, but I don't have the money, and I'm hungry, and I can't get Max to love me anymore."

Martha Landers jerked as though she had been hit with a volt of electricity, then another one. Her head pitched forward, and her slender shoulders convulsed violently. Her eyes were wide and disbelieving as though they had seen the other side of death itself.

Then the smile was back on her face.

A gentle smile.

Pure.

And chaste.

"Max will always love me," she whispered.

"Can I see the will now." Tom Beecher's voice had grown firm, and it jarred Martha Landers back to reality.

"If you need to."

"I do."

"Then please come in," she said sweetly.

Martha turned and disappeared from the bright sunlight that had bathed her face.

Tom Beecher and Nathan Locke followed her into the room. The shades were closed, and the curtains had been drawn. The darkness was overwhelming, and it took a few minutes for their eyes to adjust to the dimly-lit chamber. Clothes, caked with dried mud, had been thrown on the floor. Chicken bones had been gnawed clean and were lying in a pile on the dinette table, surrounded by food that had grown stale and soured. The spicy odor slapped them coldly in the face, a fragrance sweet and stifling, the stench of burning incense, crushed jasmine, and rotting magnolia blossoms, hanging heavy and oppressive around them, smothering the senses, and for a frightening moment, Nathan Locke thought he was going to pass out. His eyes watered. He couldn't breath, and he found himself gasping for air.

"I don't have the will," he heard Martha say. Her voice sounded so thin, so far away.

He coughed and felt his own vomit burn his throat.

"Where is it?" Tom asked huskily.

"Max has it."

They turned and watched in horror as Martha Landers, her mouth still twisted in that curious and innocent smile, sat down on the edge of her bed, leaned over and gently kissed the gray, decaying lips of Max Gordon.

"Jesus Christ," Tom groaned.

Nathan Locke's knees buckled, and he backed up against the wall for support. The room spun, and he pressed both hands against his eyes to hide the hideous sight before him.

Max Gordon's head was turned on the pillow, facing him, and there was a mocking grin on his blackened face. Raw flesh had peeled away from his cheekbones, and his eye sockets were hollow, haunting, wide with the sudden shock he must have felt when he heard the blast of the shotgun and realized for one frozen instant that it was too late to undo the deed he had done. Had it seemed like an eternity? Was there any pain at all or only sudden silence and darkness? It was the last sound Max Gordon would ever hear, and now he lay in death, as he had so many times in life, upon the stained and rumpled sheets of Martha Landers's bed. In his hands, clasped together in prayer the way the undertaker had placed them, he held the last remaining copy of his handwritten will.

As Locke fought to clear his head, he saw Tom Beecher reach down and remove the folded paper.

"Thank you," the old attorney said.

Martha's smile had turned sad.

And Locke felt a surge of sympathy—or was it pity?—for her. She was so young. Or had she ever really been young? She had known so many men in her time, but only one had ever treated her kindly. She undoubtedly had heard a lot of them say that they loved her. But only one had meant it. Poor Max. He had been trapped by his wealth and his reputation. Martha could not escape her poverty and her shame. They needed each other. They probably even deserved each other. But she had ruined his life. And now he had ruined hers. Both had been madly in love.

Finally both had simply gone mad.

Locke could almost imagine Martha Landers down on her knees, hidden by the darkness of night, digging down to

Max Gordon's casket, forcing it open, pulling his body out
of the grave, and dragging it across the cemetery to her car.
It must have taken her hours, probably until almost sunup.
All that had been left for her to do was simply fill in the
loose dirt, rearrange the canopy of flowers, and drive back
to the motel. Since then, she had talked to him, fussed over
him, tried to feed him, and slept with Max Gordon every
night. Martha Landers refused to give up the man she loved.

Tom Beecher slowly and methodically read through the
handwritten will until he was satisfied that all four pages
were there. He neatly folded the sheets again and slipped
them into the breastpocket of his crumpled coat.

"What happens now?" Martha asked, fidgeting with the
buttons on Max's shirt, slowly unfastening them.

Tom started to speak, but he had nothing to say. He placed
a gentle hand on Martha's bare shoulder and squeezed it to
comfort her.

"There won't be any money, will there?" There was the
hint of a tear in her voice.

"No, ma'am. There won't be."

Martha's chin quivered, but she held her head high.

"Men have always lied to me," she said.

Tom brushed a shock of unruly hair away from her face.

"Max lied, too, didn't he?" Martha looked up, and a single
teardrop slipped down her cheek.

Max sighed. "I think Max loved you very much," he said.

"No, he doesn't." Frustration replaced the sadness in her
eyes. "I try every night, just like I always did, but Max won't
make love to me anymore."

Tom nodded at Locke, and both men walked out the door,
leaving Martha Landers lying in Max Gordon's arms, her

sobbing face pressed tightly against the ragged, rotting flesh of his shattered and fragmented skull.

Nathan Locke almost made it across the parking lot before he fell to his knees and threw up, his body jerking as though he had been hit by a volt of electricity. His head pitched forward, and his broad shoulders convulsed violently. His eyes were wide and disbelieving as though they, too, had seen the other side of death itself.

Or maybe he had just seen hell.

And Nathan Locke didn't believe in hell.

Tom Beecher ignored him. He tore the copy of the will into tiny shreds, tossed them into the air, and let the restless southern wind scatter them through the pines.

15

Eunice Gordon was hosting an afternoon tea in the flower garden of her home when the phone call came from the Warren County Sheriff's Department.

The past few weeks had been hard on her. Losing Max had been a shock, and then Eunice began hearing terrible rumors about her husband. She did not believe them. She refused to believe them and could not understand why anyone would want to defame or disgrace the good, reputable name of Max Gordon.

She simply blamed the gossip on jealousy.

People hated people who had money, and she and Max had always had a lot of money.

For a time, Eunice had been in seclusion, preferring to be alone, not even talking to her closest friends. But that, she finally told herself, was a foolish thing to do. She needed her friends, especially now.

They were all sitting around her now, gingerly sipping their tea, smiling, laughing, and being extremely careful not to mention the name of Max Gordon.

It was Susan Heatherley who brought the ringing telephone to Eunice.

"Hello." There was a definite lilt to her voice.

It was the last word she said.

A moment later, Eunice had dropped the phone and fainted dead away, her teacup falling and breaking on the stone patio at her feet.

TO some who heard Nathan Locke that Sunday morning, his sermon seemed to be disjointed, full of loose ends that were never quite tied together. He spoke for less than fifteen minutes, talking first about the serpent that had slithered through the Garden of Eden, tempting, then deceiving Eve, and finally describing the troubled, tortured mind of a disciple named Judas Iscariot the night he slipped through the Garden of Gethsemane to betray his Lord and Savior.

Locke gazed out at the congregation, and a faint smile played at the corners of his mouth. He could see traces of confusion and bewilderment in the eyes that stared back at him. There was a hush throughout the sanctuary. No one coughed. Not even a baby was crying.

Nathan Locke almost laughed.

He had them now.

He had them all.

253

He had them right where he wanted them.

Everyone he wanted to be in church that day had come. His eyes sought out the dissenters, and he could see them shifting uncomfortably in their seats. His oblique message apparently had not been lost on them. He hadn't expected it to be. Their guilty faces were shining with sweat, and they glistened in the sunlight that came pouring in through the seven stained glass windows that lined the eastern wall of the church. Locke had purposely changed the thermostat on the air conditioner that morning, raising the temperature several dramatic degrees in the sanctuary. There were some people he wanted to see sweat.

Bill Freeman was holding Marcy's hand, and their eyes were wavering slightly. Greg Kaufman and his wife were no longer able to look at him. Greg had always been loud, but then most weak men are, Locke told himself. He thought for a moment that Jana Smith might break out in tears. Only Kenneth Elmore had his head up, his arms folded in defiance. They were the vocal ones. They were the ones he knew he had to break. The rest were merely sheep who would fall into line and obey the strongest voice. They might disagree with him from time to time, but they would never openly defy him. Ultimately, they would simply follow wherever Nathan Locke chose to lead them.

He didn't have to look for Raymond Lynch.

He knew where Raymond would be sitting, there in his usual place on the back row pew.

Nathan Locke couldn't help himself. He smiled at Raymond Lynch.

The snake.

The betrayer.

With calm hands, he closed his Bible and pushed his hand-written notes aside. Locke moved from behind the lecturn and stepped down across the altar to the sanctuary floor.

The smile had not left his face.

"I stand before you today," he said, "in the midst of the most troubled and disappointing time I have ever had the misfortune to experience within a church."

His voice was soft and compassionate, but every word echoed forcefully throughout the congregation.

"For more than a decade," Locke continued, "I have laughed with you and cried with you, prayed with you and worked with you to build a church that we could all be proud of."

A few began to nod their heads in agreement.

"It's God's church." His deep voice grew louder. "It's our church. We are God's people, the ones He chose to carry on His great mission of love."

More heads were nodding now.

"We are a strong church when we all stand together," Locke reminded them, "when we all pull together, when we are all pulling together in the same direction. That's not just what I want us to do. That's what God has commanded us to do."

He paused and waited for the echo of his words to die away. The silence was chilling.

"But now, I'm sad to say, there is unrest in our church. There is friction in our church. There are those who say that Nathan Locke should no longer be your pastor."

He heard a disgruntled "No," then other voiced complaints

scattered here and there throughout the congregation, and Locke raised his hands to quiet them.

"There are those who say that Nathan Locke is not fit to be your pastor."

"Don't listen to them, pastor," someone yelled.

"There are those who say that Nathan Locke is greedy and selfish, that he no longer cares about you, that he no longer loves you, that he's never there to be with you or comfort you when you need a helping hand."

A woman began to cry.

"They don't know what they're talkin' about," Howard Daniels blurted out.

Locke heard a flurry of whispers rise up around him, and he waited until they quieted down to speak again.

"Our church—my church, your church, God's church—has a definite mission: to reach out and touch as many people as we can across this great land of ours, to carry God's holy word to as many ears as will hear it."

He slowly began walking down the center aisle, and every eye was fastened to him, trapped in the reflection of his gold cross. "God has made it possible for us to do that," he said. "But that has made some of you here this morning unhappy, even bitter. So you have attacked Nathan Locke."

He paused, his eyes pointedly searching out each one who had criticized him, and his face grew stern and angry.

"You haven't attacked Nathan Locke," he thundered. "You have attacked this church."

A pause.

"You are polarizing this church."

A pause.

"You are destroying this church."

A pause.

Nathan Locke could almost feel the sudden wave of alarm and anxiety as it swept like a hot wind across the congregation. He saw his allies exchanging worried glances, then they, too, began to seek out the dissenters with dread and suspicion burning deep in their eyes.

"So many worked so hard to build this church," he said in a hoarse whisper. "All it takes to destroy this work of ours is one pathetic and disturbed soul."

Nathan Locke stopped beside Raymond Lynch.

Raymond could feel the blood in his veins run cold. Every eye, he knew, was on him, and he would have run if he hadn't known that so many were supporting him, depending on him to lead the fight against Nathan Locke. He took a deep breath, clenched his jaw, and looked up at the minister. Locke had not even acknowledged that he existed.

"There is," he said simply, "a snake amongst us, just as surely as Satan sent a snake to destroy the truth and the beauty that was the Garden of Eden.

"He is deceiving you.

"He is lying to you.

"He attacks me.

"He only wants to destroy you.

"He is a man to be feared.

"He is a man to be pitied."

Raymond Lynch felt every muscle tense in his body. His face was crimson. Until that moment, he had never really hated anyone.

He hated Nathan Locke.

"We have an elder amongst us," Locke continued, "who vowed to do everything within his power to uphold the peace and the unity of this church.

"He lied to you then.

"He is lying to you still.

"He has confused the issues. He has spread rumors and instigated gossip solely to benefit his own personal gains. He has betrayed the sacred confidences of your church.

"He has hurt me, to be sure.

"But more importantly, he has hurt you.

"He has turned his back on you.

"He has turned his back on God."

Locke's voice rattled the windows behind him. He had not yet looked down into the face of Raymond Lynch. But now he laid a firm hand on the man's shoulder, and Raymond could feel the heat generating from the preacher's fingertips.

He shuddered, and he found it difficult to breathe.

The sanctuary was suffocating.

"A snake has crept among us," Locke said, softer now.

"He's here to poison us.

"He's our Judas Iscariot.

"He is here to betray us all.

"I've known of his kind before. During my years of professional study and investigations into human behavior, I have many times witnessed the rise—and the fall—of men like Elder Lynch."

Raymond jerked as if he had been shot.

"He's not a leader, but he wants to lead.

"He's weak, yet he thirsts for power.

"He wants to control you.

"He wants to rule you.

"Or he will ruin you.

"In psychiatric terms, he is suffering from what is commonly known as megalomania."

Nathan Locke bowed his head and prayed his closing prayer. No one listened.

Every eye was fastened on Raymond Lynch.

Elder Lynch.

An out-of-towner.

A yankee.

And, God forbid, a *megalomaniac*, whatever that was.

Raymond pushed his way through a stunned crowd at the back of the church. His eyes found Marcy Freeman. "You have our support," Marcy had promised him. Embarrassed, she looked quickly away, held onto Bill's arm, and together they hurried out the door. Bill Freeman had been a coward once before. He would always be a coward. Raymond turned in quiet desperation toward Kenneth Elmore. His had been the angriest voice of all that stormy night. "You sure as hell have our votes," Kenneth had told him. Now Kenneth dropped his head and turned away. Jana Smith had tears in her eyes when she stopped to throw her arms around Nathan Locke's neck and hug him tightly. Greg Kaufman refused to shake Raymond's hand. And Wade Ferguson walked briskly past him without even bothering to speak.

Damn them, Raymond thought.

Damn them all.

He was their last hope, they had said. He was their only hope to rid the church of the villain who stood in its pulpit.

Nathan Locke must go. That's what they had said. We'll

stand behind you. That's what they had vowed. Now it was time to stand up and be counted, and where the hell were they all?

Raymond Lynch was standing alone.

It surprised him, though he knew it shouldn't have.

It made him angry, and he wanted to hit something or somebody. Fuck 'em, he told himself. Fuck 'em all. If they wanted Nathan Locke that badly, they deserved the bastard.

Helen Jensen was suddenly in his face. "You won't run my pastor out of my church," she yelled. "I won't let you." A scowl had twisted her face until it looked more animal than human, and again the smell of hatred began to smother him.

"Excuse me," he said, trying to push his way past her.

The grin on Tom Beecher's face was one of contempt. He stood in Raymond Lynch's path and would not move.

He laughed. It was an evil laugh.

"This church doesn't need the likes of you," Howard Daniels snarled.

Raymond ignored him.

"We were a happy little church until you came here and tried to ruin it all for us," Charles Page accused.

"Go to hell," Raymond whispered under his breath.

Susan Heatherley grabbed him, her painted fingernails sinking into his arm, waited until she was sure that Nathan Locke was watching her, then spit in Raymond Lynch's face.

16

Raymond Lynch felt like throwing his telephone across the room.

He had called the Freemans. All he wanted was an explanation of some kind. Marcy refused to talk to him. Bill, she said, wasn't home.

Marcy, he suspected, was lying.

There was no answer at Kenneth Elmore's place.

Wade Ferguson had hung up on him.

Raymond stared at himself in the mirror. He was a grown man now, and it had been a long time since he saw a grown man cry.

The phone rang. He answered it.

"This is John Madison," the voice said. "I direct the choir at Basilwood Presbyterian."

"I know who you are."

"I've had all of Nathan Locke I can stand," John explained. "I'm willing to help you if you need me."

"How can you help?" The fire had gone out of Raymond.

"Have you heard about his slush fund?"

"I've heard rumors about one."

"I've got a photostatic copy of the secret bank records, complete with records of his deposits and his withdrawals, and they all have Nathan Locke's signature on them."

The fire was rekindled within Raymond Lynch. He wasn't crying anymore.

NANCY Locke's plane had landed in Nashville late. The summer rains slowed her down, and she had missed her first flight out of Jackson. The fog had delayed her second one for more than an hour, and it was almost ten–thirty by the time her taxicab pulled in front of the downtown Sheraton Hotel. She paid her fare, tipped the driver a dollar and hoped it was enough, then picked up her overnight bag and walked slowly, wearily, toward the lobby.

"Need some help, ma'am?" a bell captain asked.

"No, thank you."

He held the door open and Nancy Locke stepped inside. She wandered if Nathan were already asleep.

He had been under so much strain lately that the distance between them had widened more than ever. She knew that she had never lived up to his expectations, not physically, sexually, nor emotionally. She had been a disappointment to him time and again, and it sometimes surprised her that Nathan had not divorced her years ago. She had been jealous and suspicious and never the kind of wife a preacher needed. So often he had accused her of being dispassionate and frigid, and maybe he was right. Nancy detested the world of reality. She had tried to hide from it. It was so frightening, so unfair.

Until recently, Nathan Locke had always been a tower of strength in her sight. Nothing bothered him. Nothing could penetrate that cold steely exterior of his. His broad back was able to shoulder the burdens of whatever troubled anyone in his church, and he never flinched, no matter how heavy they became. He was wise and able to solve every problem he faced except the one he encountered at home.

She was his problem. Her drinking was his problem. Their marriage had obviously fallen apart, and it all was her fault. She would no longer deny it to either herself or Nathan.

Until now, it had never dawned on Nancy that her husband might really need her to lean on when times got rough. God knows he was too proud to ever admit it.

But during the past few weeks, she had seen a frightening change begin to take place in her husband. His nerves were becoming unraveled. He was on edge, always about to explode, and Nathan had lost weight. He was never hungry, and he spent more and more of his time alone, a recluse locked in his own study, and she often heard him cry out during the night.

Nathan didn't sleep much anymore. Maybe he was afraid to go to sleep. And she didn't know why. He would not tell her about the mental anguish that tortured him, the nightmares that were wrecking his life.

For the first time since she had known him, Nathan Locke desperately needed someone to support him, to believe in him, to love him.

Nathan Locke needed her, and the thought thrilled her. Nancy felt more alive than she had in years. Until now, she had never been a real part of his life.

She had simply gone her way. He had gone his, usually to the Sheraton in Nashville. More than once Nancy had found a receipt from the Sheraton while she was rummaging through his suit pockets, always for a single room.

She had doubted him.

But he had always been alone.

She would never again leave him to face a crisis alone. It was a promise she had made on the airplane somewhere over Tennessee, and it was as sacred to her as her wedding vows.

Nancy Locke had poured her last bottle of gin down the commode without any remorse.

She didn't need it anymore.

There was no longer any doubt in her mind.

Then she packed an overnight bag and called to make flight reservations to Nashville.

Nathan had fled there the way he always did when he needed to get away for a few days of rest to clear a troubled mind. The members of his congregation were always squabbling about something, and they never left him alone, never gave him any peace. They were like piranahs, devouring him piece by piece, day after day, night after night, until he was forced to find a place of refuge, a place of escape.

He always came to Nashville.

He always came alone.

"Why?" she would question.

"I have to deal with some matters for Presbytery," he always answered.

Maybe he did.

She didn't know.

All she knew was that Nathan Locke needed her, and she had come to be with him, to support him, talk with him, hold his hand, and maybe he would hold her all night.

It had been so long.

She quivered with anticipation.

Nancy walked shyly to the registration desk. "I need a key for Nathan Locke's room," she told the late-night clerk.

He was busy trying to reconcile his statements for the day. "Who are you?" he asked.

"I'm Nathan's wife."

He arched an eyebrow as if to say, "Sure, lady."

Nancy dug into her purse, pulled out her driver's license, and showed it to him.

The clerk handed her a key to room 364 without a word.

She smiled her gratitude and walked away. He probably didn't really care if she were Nathan's wife or not, she told herself. He probably thought she was nothing more than a wanton woman on her way to satisfy an out-of-town man's carnal lusts for the night.

Nancy laughed to herself.

Maybe he was right.

On the third floor, she paused long enough in front of the hallway mirror to straighten her hair in case the wind and dampness had mussed it up. Nancy added fresh lipstick and wet her neck with a touch of expensive perfume.

She smiled at herself. The dark circles were gone from her eyes. It was the youngest she had looked in years.

She hoped Nathan would notice. He would be so surprised.

Nancy hoped he would be pleased to see her.

She put the key into the lock and gently twisted it, quietly pushing the door open.

As Nancy walked inside the room, her eyes widened in an unfathomable horror. She abruptly dropped her bag and tried to scream but couldn't.

Nathan Locke lay naked on the bed, breathing heavily, rutting like an animal, entangled in the arms of his lover.

The scream finally came just before she hit the floor.

17

*Birdie Castleberry was sitting on Alice's front porch, waiting
for her when she returned home.*

"Did you hear about Nancy Locke?" she asked.

*"No, what's wrong with her?" Alice didn't sound too con-
cerned.*

*"She went with Nathan to Nashville and collapsed in their
motel room."*

"Is she all right?"

*Birdie sadly shook her head. "I doubt if she'll ever be all
right again."*

"Why?"

*"Nathan had to put her in a mental institution this morning.
She was, I hear, in a catatonic state, and nobody knows if
she'll ever be in her right mind again."*

Alice gasped. "What happened to her?"

*"Too much stress, I guess." Birdie shivered. "You know
she had a nervous breakdown once before, and God only
knows how much strain she and Nathan have been under
lately. I don't see how either one of them has stood it this
long."*

She paused, then added:

"I hope to hell Raymond Lynch is satisfied now."

*Alice sadly shook her head. "He certainly ruined a sweet
little woman," she said.*

*"Yeah," Birdie spit out, "and just when Nathan needed
her most."*

R AYMOND Lynch waited alone on the dark end of the
church parking lot, back where a cluster of live oaks blotted
out any reflection from the flickering streetlight. Time was
running out on him.

He checked his watch.

In four minutes the specially called Saturday night meeting
of session would be beginning, and he knew he would have
to walk in and face the ridicule, the scorn of Nathan Locke
again. He dreaded the thought. Raymond's stomach had been
hurting all day, as though acid and hot grease were churning
through his entrails, and he blamed it on nerves.

He saw the headlights of a car swing down a back alley
that ran alongside the church, and Raymond strained to see
if it might be John Madison's light gray BMW.

The car passed.

It was packed with teenagers. Their faces were obscured,

271

but the sound of their drunken laughter spilled out into the night, and a thrown Stroh's beer bottle struck the pavement and shattered at his feet. Raymond ignored it.

He checked his watch again. Seven–twenty-eight.

John Madison was late. He had telephoned shortly after noon, interrupting Raymond's bologna sandwich lunch, and his deep, melodious voice was low and urgent.

"I understand that Nathan has called a special session meeting tonight," he said.

"Yeah. I've just gotten my notice."

"Do you know what it's about?"

"I have no idea."

"Maybe Nathan's going to give you a chance to repent." John snickered. His meager attempt at humor fell flat.

"I don't think Nathan Locke gives a damn about me anymore. He beat me Sunday morning, and he knows it. Those sons of bitches who were calling for his scalp are safely back in the fold now, and I'm dangling out here on the end of a limb all by myself."

"Nathan won't be satisfied until he saws it off and sees you bust your ass on the ground."

Raymond sighed and took a swig of cold beer. "You're probably right," he admitted.

"Well, you can quit worrying, and the Reverend Nathan Locke can start worrying." John Madison was in dead earnest.

"You've got the bank records then?"

"Not all of them. It hasn't been easy, Raymond, sneaking around, keeping an eye on Nathan's office, waiting until his secretary runs off to the potty, rummaging through his files, praying she won't get back and find me there." He paused, then added, "I don't have a lot of experience breaking the law, you know. If Nathan catches me in there, we can just kiss those bank records goodbye."

"I appreciate what you're doing, John."

The choir director laughed spitefully. "I just wish I could be there to see Nathan's face when you pull those records out and shove 'em up the session's collective ass." "When can I get them?"

"I should have the only two I'm missing by tonight."

"By seven–thirty?"

"I'll meet you back behind the church parking lot."

"What if you don't make it on time."

Hell, if I'm running late, I'll just bring them on in to the session room. Maybe I'll get to see that bastard squirm after all."

"Nathan won't like that."

"To hell with Nathan Locke."

"He'll fire you."

There was a long pause at the other end of the telephone, then Raymond heard John Madison say bitterly, "I just don't really give a damn anymore."

Raymond Lynch glanced nervously down the street as a cloud reached out to cover the moon. The street was empty and ominously cloaked in total darkness. He couldn't wait any longer. John Madison was definitely late. He sighed, and it was the sound of defeat.

Maybe John wasn't even coming.

Raymond turned, kicked the broken glass aside, and walked briskly across the parking lot and into the church.

Only one room was lit.

He took a deep breath, opened the door, went in, and took his place in the last empty chair beside the conference table. The frustration in Raymond's eyes betrayed the broad cocky grin that he forced onto his face.

Nathan Locke was standing at the far end of the table, talking in hushed tones with Morris Adams.

Morris Adams.

Raymond frowned.

What in hell was the head man at Presbytery doing here tonight, he wondered.

Locke turned, and Raymond caught his eyes.

Locke smiled.

Cold.

And piercing.

The smile slowly twisted into a sneer.

And Raymond felt himself jolted by a sudden chill.

He looked back at the door and folded his arms defiantly, tightening his fists, hoping that no one could see his hands shaking. He felt feverish and knew that the back of his blue denim shirt was already soaked with sweat.

Where was John Madison?

God, please let John get here in time, he prayed. He doubted that God heard.

Nathan Locke had probably gotten to Him first.

Raymond's gaze swept quickly around the table. Not a soul was missing. Not a soul was looking his way.

Raymond Lynch was a pariah.

As far as the rest of them were concerned, Raymond Lynch just simply didn't exist anymore.

The truth of the matter struck him as funny, and he almost laughed out loud.

Hell, he thought, they were right.

It should have been him to resign, not Nathan Locke. He should have had enough sense to get out of town before they threw him out of town.

Where the hell was John Madison anyway?

John was the last realistic hope he had.

Those illegal and secret bank records, he told himself, were the only things left he could use to nail Nathan Locke's crooked and conniving hide to the wall.

"Let us pray," the preacher said.

All heads were bowed.

All eyes were closed.

"Our Heavenly Father," Locke began reverently, "thank you for this time of peace in our midst. Thank you for the renewed spirit of reconciliation and cooperation that has returned to your church. Thank you, Lord, for loosening the chains that had bound us so tightly, for removing the cancer that had been growing so large and so deadly within us. Thank you, Heavenly Father, for casting out the devil that walked amongst your people and sought to destroy the great work that you have willed for us to do. Amen. And amen."

Shit, Raymond thought.

He had been right.

Nathan Locke sure had a way with words, and the preacher had gotten to the Good Lord first.

Raymond Lynch didn't have a chance.

Well, maybe there was once chance left, he told himself.

He looked again at the door and waited for John Madison to appear.

"Before we formally begin our business at hand tonight," Nathan Locke said loudly, "I have one announcement to make. Basilwood Presbyterian Church must begin tomorrow morning an official search to find and hire a new choir director."

He paused and cut his eyes sharply toward Raymond Lynch.

"It is with regret this evening that I present you with John Madison's resignation."

"When is it effective?" Tom Beecher asked, strictly for the record.

"Immediately."

"What reason did he give you for resigning?" Charles Page wanted to know.

"He had none."

"Where's John going now?" It was Raymond, and he hardly recognized his own voice.

"He doesn't know."

The sneer flickered briefly on Nathan Locke's face, and Raymond knew that he was probably the only one there who had caught it. Perhaps he was the only one there suspicious enough to catch it. Locke seated himself and nodded toward Morris Adams. With a wave of his hand, he turned the meeting over to the Executive Presbyter.

Adams stood, straightened the white carnation on his lapel, clasped his hands together, and silently surveyed the members of the session. "As you know," he began, "there has been an unfortunate period of unrest within the congregation of Basilwood Presbyterian. When these sorts of unpleasant things happen, we at Presbytery are often invited to step in and see what we can do to return peace and harmony and unity to the church. So that's why I am here tonight."

His smile was bland but well practiced.

"I personally am not the kind of man who likes to beat around the bushes in these matters," Morris Adams continued. "I'd rather cut through the red tape, cut through all the formalities, cut through all the rumors and gossip and inuendoes, and get straight to the root of the problem. Is that all right with all of you?"

Tom Beecher nodded and seemed to speak for them all.

Morris Adams turned to face Raymond.

"Elder Lynch," he drawled, "I believe that it is you who have brought these unfortunate and unnecessary charges against Reverend Locke, and it is you who have pressed the issue in session, as well as in secret, closed-door rump meetings with various members of the congregation. Am I right, sir?"

Raymond shrugged. He knew he was beaten.

But, hell, he thought, that was no reason to give up. Nathan Locke and his henchmen, every goddam one of them, had already taken his pride, his respect, his esteem, his good name away from him. He had nothing else to lose.

His eyes blazed.

His nostrils flared.

He stood in open defiance, his hands on his hips, and snapped, "Damn straight, I did. And you know why, Mister Morris Adams? I did it because Nathan Locke is as guilty as hell of the violations I have brought to your attention. You can turn your back on the truth. The high and almighty session of this Church can continue to ignore the facts that are as plain as the noses on their faces if they want to. But I'll be damned if I have to kiss Nathan Locke's ass every time he turns around just because he happens to occupy the pulpit on Sunday morning. He's the preacher. So what? He's also a man, and men make mistakes, and, by God, Nathan Locke has made some serious mistakes. And if the Presbyterian hierarchy is not run by a bunch of chickenshit assholes, you will hold him accountable for every goddam one of them."

Birdie Castleberry gasped.

For Howard Daniels, his hatred ran even deeper.

Wade Ferguson's face turned white.

Charles Page shook his head in disbelief.

Tom Beecher clapped his hands together in mock applause. "You don't have a lot of sense, Raymond," he said. "But, by damn, you got yourself a bellyful of guts."

Nathan Locke leaned forward, his elbows resting on the table, his brow furrowed, the muscles jerking involuntarily in his clenched jaws.

If looks could kill, Raymond knew, he was a dead man.

But what the hell, he thought.

So he was a pariah. So he had fought a losing battle against his minister. It didn't make any difference to him. Not anymore. Raymond Lynch knew that he had two more years remaining on the session, and he vowed to himself that those would be the most two miserable years of Nathan Locke's life. The war against Nathan Locke was no longer simply right versus wrong. It was no longer merely an obsession with him. It had now become a personal vendetta. It was his turn to sneer.

"Are you through Elder Lynch?" Morris Adams asked.

"For the time being."

"Thank you, then. You may be seated." Adams paused a

moment to thumb through the notes he had spread out before him on the table. Finally he looked up and continued, "We have heard from Elder Lynch, and now, I believe, there is someone else that members of session might want to hear."

Morris Adams walked slowly and dramatically across the floor and opened the door to an adjoining chamber. Every eye was focused on his every movement.

Raymond Lynch did not recognize the gaunt gray-haired man in the black polyester suit who sauntered into the room. But he had never forgotten the small black woman with the pained face and accusing eyes who slipped in behind him, wearing a yellow flowered jersey dress along with scuffed brown shoes that had been cut out along the toes. God knows, he had tried to forget her. But God wouldn't let him.

His face paled, and Raymond Lynch began to die inside.

"Would you please identify yourself to the session?" Adams asked the man.

"Sure. I'm Lou Holland." He straightened the double layer of gold chains around his neck. "I'm a private detective."

"And why did you ask to come here tonight?"

Holland ground out one cigarette and paused just long enough to light another.

"I happened to run across a lady who I believe your session here needs to know about."

"Why, Mr. Holland."

He grinned, and his teeth were crooked. "Because she knows Mr. Raymond Lynch." His grin grew wider, and the cigarette dangled loosely from the corner of his mouth. "She knows him pretty damn well."

Morris Adams turned his attention to the woman. Her

eyes were downcast, and she kept folding and unfolding the faded white-lace handkerchief in her hands. Adams touched her arm, "Would you care to sit down?" he asked softly.

"No, thank you."

"Could you tell us your name, please?"

"Alma Washington." She held her head a little higher."

"Where is home for you, Mrs. Washington?"

"I lives in Braxton, Massachusetts."

"Do you have any children, Mrs. Washington?"

"Yes, sir." She stopped and corrected herself. "No, sir. I did once, but I don't have no children anymore."

"Could you explain, please?"

"I had a boy, Jimmy Gerald. He was a good boy, too. He was always good to his mama. But he's dead."

Her eyes were filled with tears, and she dabbed at them with her handkerchief.

Morris Adams put a gentle arm around her, and her shaking shoulders crushed the white carnation against his chest. "Could you tell us what happened?"

"Jimmy Gerald never caused nobody no harm. He stayed mostly with his own kind and never laid out none at night. He work hard. He work hard most the time, and he always bring his money home to his mama. That's what we eat on, and that's all that we had to eat on." Her voice faded to a whisper. "But they killed him. They took my boy out, and they killed him. Nobody ever prove that they did, but they did, and I know it."

"Who killed your son, Mrs. Washington?"

Her face hardened, and she whirled around with eyes flashing and pointed straight at Raymond Lynch's face.

"That man right there did," she screamed. "He said he was my boy's friend, but my boy didn't have no friends. He went out to get my Jimmy Gerald for me, and when he come back, my Jimmy Gerald was dead."

Her voice chilled the room.

"They took my Jimmy Gerald out and drown him in that muddy old river just because my boy was black."

Jesus, Raymond prayed as he closed his eyes and tried to drive the nightmare of a dying boy's screams from his mind.

18

Raymond Lynch put the lights of downtown Vicksburg behind him and turned his old Pontiac toward Louisiana.

He did not know where he was going.

He only knew that he had to free himself of the guilt, the shame, the dishonor that was piled up around him like a grave digger's dirt.

Nathan Locke had won.

For now.

Forever.

Nobody could beat him.

Raymond thought how foolish it had even been for him to even try and outfight, even outwit, Nathan Locke. It was absurd. It was ridiculous.

He laughed. He couldn't control himself, and the laughter became louder, wild and frenzied.

The harder he laughed, the faster Raymond Lynch drove.

He was laughing as hard as he could when the Pontiac slammed into the concrete abutment of the Mississippi River bridge.

There was a sudden silence, and the world went black.

Raymond opened his eyes and stared at the moon through a cracked windshield. He felt blood seeping into his eyes, and his left arm was twisted awkwardly beneath him.

He sighed, not knowing whether to be relieved or mad. Damn, he said to himself, I'm still alive.

F OR the last two hours, Helen Jensen had tossed and turned in her bed, unable to sleep, trying, without much success, to tune out the harsh, guttural sounds of Robert's incessant snoring beside her.

Her face was warm, and there was a faint and familiar ache rising up within her.

She touched herself and began to cry.

Robert had come home late that Saturday night, the smell of whiskey sour on his breath. He almost never came home early anymore.

"Business is good," he would say. "I was working late again."

And he seldom came home sober.

"I was out drinkin' with a client," was the only reason he ever gave.

Helen had eaten dinner alone, as usual, taken her bath,

and was curled up on the den sofa, reading a dog-eared back copy of *Cosmopolitan* when Robert finally came staggering into the house.

He dropped his jacket on the floor and tossed his tie toward a red-striped, wing-back chair in the corner. It missed. Robert stood in the doorway, swaying slightly, his legs spread apart, blinking hard to focus his eyes.

Helen looked up.

Robert was staring at her, chewing on a toothpick, and he slowly began to unbutton his shirt.

The stare became a leer.

"Get your fuckin' clothes off," he said.

"You're drunk, Robert."

He swaggered across the room, his blue, transparent eyes sweeping over Helen's body, reached down, and ripped her robe open, tearing the buttons loose, ignoring them as they scattered across the carpet.

"Get your fuckin' clothes off." It was a growl.

She slapped him.

He spit out his toothpick, and a savage grin spread across his face.

"So you want to play rough," Robert said, his words slurring together. "Hell, I'll show you how to play rough."

He hit her once, and Helen's head snapped back.

He hit her again with a closed fist, and she fell limp across the sofa, her face buried in the hand-stitched throw pillows that Helen sometimes slept on while she waited for Robert to come home at night. She was barely aware of his pudgy hands tearing off her gown, leaving red, ugly streaks where the material cut angrily into her flesh.

She felt as though she were floating.

Hanging somewhere in limbo.

A faceless woman, unable to breathe beneath a sweating, writhing weight she could not move.

A faceless man was clawing at her naked body.

Biting her.

Violating her. Invading her.

Hurting her.

Helen grunted in pain.

Robert slapped her again.

And again.

He was in a drunken frenzy.

Slapping her.

And kissing her.

And she gagged on the smell of whiskey.

And onions.

Robert kept pounding her buttocks against the floor, a mad man, pounding faster and faster, harder and harder.

Helen wanted to scream.

She gritted her teeth.

It was all over in a minute or two.

Helen felt the weight removed from her body, and she opened her eyes. Robert was standing above her, breathing heavily, wiping his mouth, grinning like a gladiator, his pants and shorts still wrapped in a wad around his ankles.

Helen groaned.

God, she thought, Robert hadn't even had the decency or taken the time to remove his shoes.

Helen took another bath before she went to bed that night, and she lay there in the darkness, listening to the satisfied snoring of her husband.

The bastard, she thought.

He had been drunk, and he raped her, and there wasn't a damn thing to do but forget about it, and she knew she would never be able to forget about it.

Her face was still raw where he had hit her, and her nipples were sore. For awhile she had even been frightened that he was going to bite them off.

Robert would awaken the next morning, she knew, and never even say he was sorry for what he had done.

He would go on as though nothing had happened.

Probably, he wouldn't even remember.

The bastard, she said again.

She wished to hell she had never let Nathan Locke dissuade her from divorcing Robert. She would be better off if he were dead or at least out of her life for good. Let him breathe his whiskey and onions in some other woman's face.

Nathan Locke.

The very thought of his name calmed her. It soothed the anger inside of her and rekindled the secret passion she had for him.

Nathan Locke.

She pictured his face in her mind and that faint, familiar ache began again to eat away at her. She felt on fire again, and she had never felt that way with Robert.

He had raped her.

Dear God, she prayed, *why couldn't it have been Nathan Locke.*

Strong.

Yet gentle.

Forceful.

Yet caring.

Robert was only her husband.

Nathan Locke was a man who would treat her the way a man was supposed to treat a woman in love.

And she did love him.

From the time Helen first saw him preach, she knew that she would never be completely happy nor fulfilled until she shared a night and a bed with Nathan Locke.

The fire within her grew hotter.

Robert stirred beside her, and Helen watched for a moment as he slept. He wasn't merely sleeping, she finally decided. Robert had been knocked unconscious by the whiskey.

Helen Jensen eased out of bed and wiped away the tears that were like salt in her eyes. She dressed quickly in the darkness, slipped out the front door, and locked the door silently behind her.

The night was heavy with humidity, and the winds were as restless, as warm as she was. It was not yet eleven o'clock but the streets were quiet, especially for a Saturday night. Helen backed her car out into the street and pointed it toward Basilwood.

Maybe she was wrong, she thought.

Maybe she should simply forget Nathan Locke.

But she couldn't.

She had tried.

And it had been an exercise in frustration and futility.

As Helen drove along, she remembered Nathan Locke's whispered words to her in the privacy of his study that day he had hugged her and squeezed her. "Anytime you ever want to see me," he had said. "I'll be here for you."

She wanted to see him.

And he would be there for her. She could feel it, and the ache burned deeper.

Nathan Locke would be waiting.

Day or night, he had said. *Come when you need me.* Now she needed him more than he could ever imagine.

"I'll call," she had told Nathan Locke.

"That's never necessary," he had replied.

It was a promise that kept taunting her.

It was an invitation she had been afraid to accept. After all, he was a preacher, a man of God, and he had a wife. She was a married woman, unhappy, perhaps, miserable, most certainly, but married never-the-less. There were just some risks that she had not been willing to take.

She wasn't afraid anymore.

Helen Jensen turned off her headlights a block away and parked across the street from that Presbyterian manse that was Nathan Locke's home. It was dark.

She straightened the tangles from her hair and put on fresh lipstick, sprinkling perfume along her shoulders and between her breasts. She had done it all so many times, she no longer needed a light or a mirror.

Helen hoped Nathan Locke would find her pretty tonight. She knew he would find her willing, ready to become the woman she had never been before.

After all, she told herself, Nathan was as lonely as she. He had suffered so much. He had borne the brunt of so many lies and rumors that had threatened to destroy both him and his career. For years, he had been forced to watch his wife's mental health gradually and tragically deteriorate before his eyes, and there had been nothing that even he could do for her. He was helpless. Weaker men would have crumbled under the strain, but Nathan Locke had stood tall and unbowed through all of the trials and tribulations that plagued him. Yet in the end, not even his love nor his strength were enough to save the pitiful creature that had been his wife.

Now she was gone, and the house was empty.

Nathan Locke was alone and inside.

Helen smiled to mask her nervousness and ran across the street, hiding her face in the shadows, her long black silk dress flowing gracefully against her legs.

Come anytime, he had said.

Day.

Or night.

And he would be there waiting for her.

The burning ache was like a hot poker now. Helen made her way slowly through the stand of live oak trees, praying that there was no one watching with curious eyes this time of night. Or was it morning already?

Her breath came in short, rapid bursts. Helen paused and glanced around her. The neighborhood was asleep, and she began walking again toward the manse.

A dim glimmer of light caught her eye and left a ragged streak across her face.

Helen stopped dead in her tracks, and for a moment she was afraid to breathe. She pressed her back against a tree and tried to blend into the darkness.

The light was coming from Nathan Locke's bedroom window. Through a narrow opening in the lace curtain, she saw him illuminated in the doorway that led out into the hall.

Naked.

And bronzed.

A god.

Helen felt faint, and the burning ache became almost more than she could bear.

She gingerly stepped forward, mesmerized by the sight of the man before her. He was tall and muscular with bulging arms, a thick and sculptured chest, and a flat stomach. He looked as though he had been chiseled from stone.

Helen pressed her face against the cool window pane, and her eyes dropped below his waist. Her breath left her.

He was beautiful. His whole body had been cleanly shaven, and his skin was glistening with oil.

She watched him saunter to the edge of his bed, his feet crushing the white carnation that had dropped on to the floor, and crawl seductively into the soft, white, and waiting arms of Morris Adams. Locke kissed him on the neck, then on the lips, as their oiled and slippery bodies came together.

Behind them, in the dim light, Helen saw Jeremy sitting wide-eyed on the edge of a chair, naked, slowly masturbating, waiting for his turn to be blessed by the righteous hands of the Reverend Nathan Locke.

19

Sleep was a rare commodity in the Vicksburg suburbs of Basilwood, Mississippi, that Saturday night.

PROMPTLY at two minutes past eleven o'clock on Sunday morning, while the organist was playing Picardy's "Let All Mortal Flesh Keep Silence," Nathan Locke walked triumphantly into the sanctuary, a broad smile radiating from his face.

Raymond Lynch, his eyes downcast, followed close behind him, a thick bandage taped onto his forehead, a cast around his left arm.

The eyes of the congregation swung back and forth between the two men, surprised and somewhat perplexed, watching as they seated themselves together behind the hand-carved wooden pulpit.

As the last notes of the hymn died away, Locke stood and in a loud, strident voice began the morning worship.

"Give thanks to God, for He is good," the ritual began. "His steadfast love endures forever."

"All nations, thank you, O God, for your wonderful works," the congregation read in unison from the morning program. "You satisfy the thirsty, and the hungry you fill."

"Let us worship God," intoned the Reverend Locke.

A strange and expectant hush settled throughout the sanctuary. Only seven days earlier, the members had found themselves engulfed in the most volatile, turbulent Sunday that any of them could ever remember. The memories remained fresh and bitter. The wounds still bled.

Before them were the hunter.

And the prey.

The outsider.

And the preacher.

Together.

The choir sang "Have Thine Own Way," slower than usual, not nearly as smooth and melodious as when John Madison stood there with his big booming voice directing them.

The hymn ended.

And Nathan Locke turned solemnly to Raymond Lynch, motioning for him to step forward.

Raymond took a deep breath and removed a wrinkled piece of notebook paper from his shirt pocket. He slowly unfolded it and placed it on the lectern before him.

His eyes were dull and lifeless.

His voice matched his eyes.

"I stand here this morning," he read, "to apologize to you, the good members of Basilwood Presbyterian Church, and specifically to the Reverend Nathan Locke for the trouble I have caused within this congregation during the past few weeks. I was out of order. I was wrong. And I am indeed sorry."

Raymond Lynch paused to clear his throat.

"The charges I brought against the Reverend Mr. Locke were unfounded and false," he continued, and his voice began to tremble. "I had no right to do so. I had no right to tell the malicious lies that I spread in a selfish attempt to assassinate the character of your minister.

"As a result, I am submitting my resignation from session this morning and announcing that I, Raymond Lynch, will no longer associate myself with Basilwood Presbyterian Church. My leaving, I believe, is necessary for there to once again be peace and harmony within the congregation."

Raymond turned to Locke and read his last line:

"Thank you, sir, for the opportunity to confess my sins and wrongdoing before the church this morning."

The two men ceremoniously shook hands, and every eye followed Raymond Lynch as he walked out of the sanctuary in humiliation and defeat.

Nathan Locke wore the smile of a winner.

He had shouldered adversity well, Morris Adams told him the night before, and he had emerged from the conflict a stronger man. His ties with the church were solid now. His leadership would be unquestioned. His future held no limits.

The church belonged to him.

And so did the members of his congregation.

Nathan Locke reverently bowed his head and led them in the ritual Prayer of Confession. He had written it himself. It said exactly what he wanted it to say, and he knew his people would be listening carefully to the words that he placed so eloquently before them:

"Merciful God, you lead us by the cords of your compassion; we seek your forgiveness through Christ's intercession.

Fill us anew with your Holy Spirit, so that we may faithfully obey your will. When we are vengeful, purge our thoughts of resentment and anger. When we bear false witness, turn us from deceit to trustfulness. Cleanse us of selfish desires, and free us to respond to your holy word. In righteousness, remake us, and through Christ restore us."

Every head was bowed.

Every eye was closed.

No one saw Helen Jensen as she quietly arose from her place on the first pew and reached into her purse. She stood before Nathan Locke, less than five feet away, and pulled Robert's .38 caliber pistol from her purse.

She raised it eye level, clutching the gun with both hands to hold it steady, and aimed it virtually point-blank at Nathan Locke's head.

He didn't see her.

No one saw her.

Nathan Locke was praying, uttering perfect words for a perfect time in his life.

In the name of the Father.

The Son.

And the Holy Ghost.

Helen Jensen slowly squeezed the trigger.

Amen.